Saddle Up
Thoroughbred Horse Stories

KINGFISHER
An imprint of Kingfisher Publications Plc
New Penderel House
283–288 High Holborn
London WC1V 7HZ
www.kingfisherpub.com

First published in paperback by Kingfisher 1994
This edition published by Kingfisher 2007
2 4 6 8 10 9 7 5 3 1

ISBN: 978 0 7534 1527 6

Printed in India
1TR/0207/THOM/MAR/70STORA/C

Saddle Up
Thoroughbred Horse Stories

CHOSEN BY
CHRISTINE PULLEIN-THOMPSON

KINGFISHER

CONTENTS

My Friend Flicka

MARY O'HARA

Ken McLaughlin and his family live on a ranch in Wyoming, where they raise thoroughbred horses.

WHEN KEN OPENED his eyes next morning and looked out, he saw that the house was wrapped in fog. There had been no rain at all since the day a week ago when the wind had torn the "sprinkling system" to pieces and blown all the tattered clouds away. That was the day he had found Flicka. And it had been terribly hot since then. They had hardly been able to stand the sun out on the terrace. They had gone swimming in the pool every day. On the hills, the grass was turning to soft tan.

Now there were clouds and they had closed down. After a severe hot spell there often came a heavy fog, or hail, or even snow.

Standing at the window, Ken could hardly see the pines on the hill opposite. He wondered if his father would go after the yearlings in such a fog as this – they wouldn't be able to see them; but at breakfast McLaughlin said there would be no change of plans. It was just a big cloud that had settled down over the ranch – it would lift and fall – perhaps up on Saddle Back it would be clear.

They mounted and rode out.

The fog lay in the folds of the hills. Here and there a bare summit was in sunshine, then a little farther on came a smother of cottony white that soaked the four riders to the skin and hung rows of moonstones on the whiskers of the horses.

It was hard to keep track of each other. Suddenly Ken was lost – the others had vanished. He reined in Shorty and sat listening. The clouds and mist rolled around him. He felt as if he were alone in the world.

A bluebird, colour of the deep blue wild delphinium that dots the plains, became interested in him, and perched on a bush nearby; and as he started Shorty forward again, the bluebird followed along, hopping from bush to bush.

The boy rode slowly, not knowing in which direction to go. Then, hearing shouts, he touched heels to Shorty and cantered, and suddenly came out of the fog and saw his father and Tim and Ross.

"There they are!" said McLaughlin, pointing down over the curve of the hill. They rode forward and Ken could see the yearlings standing bunched at the bottom, looking up, wondering who was coming. Then a huge coil of fog swirled over them and they were lost to sight again.

McLaughlin told them to circle around, spread out fanwise on the far side of the colts, and then gently bear down on them so they would start towards the ranch. If the colts once got running in this fog, he said, there'd be no chance of catching them.

The plan worked well; the yearlings were not so frisky as usual, and allowed themselves to be driven in the right direction. It was only when they were on the County Road, and near the gate where Howard was watching, that Ken, whose eyes had been scanning the bunch as they appeared and disappeared in the fog, realized that Flicka was missing.

McLaughlin noticed it at the same moment, and as Ken rode towards his father, McLaughlin turned to him and said, "She's not in the bunch."

They sat in silence a few moments while McLaughlin planned the next step. The yearlings, dispirited by the fog, nibbled languidly at the grass by the roadside. McLaughlin looked at the Saddle Back and Ken looked too, the passionate desire in his heart reaching out to pierce the fog and the hillside and see where Flicka had hidden herself away. Had she been with the bunch when they first were found? Had she stolen away through the fog? Or hadn't she been there in the beginning? Had she run away from the ranch entirely, after her bad experience a week ago? Or – and this thought made his heart drop sickeningly – had she perhaps died of the hurts she had received when she broke out of the corral and was lying stark and riddled with ants and crawling things on the breast of one of those hills?

McLaughlin looked grim. "Lone wolf – like her mother," he said. "Never with the gang. I might have known it."

Ken remembered what the Colonel had said about the Lone Wolf type – it wasn't good to be that way.

"Well, we'll drive the yearlings back up," said Rob

finally. "No chance of finding her alone. If they happen to pass anywhere near her she's likely to join them."

They drove the yearlings back. Once over the first hill, the colts got running and soon were out of sight. The fog closed down again so that Ken pulled up, unable to see where he was going, unable to see his father, or Ross or Tim.

He sat listening, astonished that the sound of their hoofs had been wiped out so completely. Again he seemed alone in the world.

The fog lifted in front of him and showed him that he stood at the brink of a sharp drop, almost a precipice, though not very deep. It led down into a semi-circular pocket on the hillside which was fed by a spring; there was a clump of young cottonwoods, and a great bank of clover dotted with small yellow blossoms.

In the midst of the clover stood Flicka, quietly feasting. She had seen him before he saw her and was watching him, her head up, clover sticking out of both sides of her mouth, her jaws going busily.

At the sight of her, Ken was incapable of either thought or action.

Suddenly from behind him in the fog, he heard his father's low voice, "Don't move—"

"How'd she get in there?" said Tim.

"She scrambled down this bank. And she could scramble up again, if we weren't here. I think we've got her," said McLaughlin.

"Other side of that pocket the ground drops twenty feet sheer," said Tim. "She can't go down there."

Flicka had stopped chewing. There were still stalks

of clover sticking out between her jaws, but her head was up and her ears pricked, listening, and there was a tautness and tension in her whole body.

Ken found himself trembling too.

"How're you going to catch her, Dad?" he asked in a low voice.

"I kin snag her from here," said Ross, and in the same breath McLaughlin answered, "Ross can rope her. Might as well rope her here as in the corral. We'll spread out in a semi-circle above this bank. She can't get up past us, and she can't get down."

They took their positions and Ross lifted his rope off the horn of his saddle.

Ahead of them, far down below the pocket, the yearlings were running. A whinny or two drifted up, and the sound of their hoofs, muffled by the fog.

Flicka heard them too. Suddenly she was aware of danger. She leaped out of the clover to the edge of the precipice which fell away down the mountainside towards where the yearlings were running. But it was too steep and too high. She came straight up on her hind legs with a neigh of terror, and whirled back towards the bank down which she had slid to reach the pocket. But on the crest of it, looming uncannily in the fog, were four black figures – she screamed, and ran around the base of the bank.

Ken heard Ross's rope sing. It snaked out just as Flicka dived into the bank of clover. Stumbling she went down and for a moment was lost to view.

"Goldarn—" said Ross, hauling in his rope, while Flicka floundered up and again circled her small prison, hurling herself at every point, only to realize that there was no way out.

She stood over the precipice, poised in despair and frantic longing. There drifted up the sound of the colts running below. Flicka trembled and strained over the brink – a perfect target for Ross, and he whirled his lariat again. It made a vicious whine.

Ken longed for the filly to escape the noose – yet he longed for her capture. Flicka reared up, her delicate forefeet beat the air, then she leaped out; and Ross's rope fell short again as McLaughlin said, "I expected that. She's like all the rest of them."

Flicka went down like a diver. She hit the ground with her legs folded under her, then rolled and bounced the rest of the way. It was exactly like the bronco that had climbed over the side of the truck and rolled down the forty-foot bank; and in silence the four watchers sat in their saddles waiting to see what would happen when she hit bottom – Ken already thinking of the Winchester, and the way the crack of it had echoed back from the hills.

Flicka lit, it seemed, on four steel springs that tossed her up and sent her flying down the mountainside – perfection of speed and power and action. A hot sweat bathed Ken from head to foot, and he began to laugh, half choking.

The wind roared down and swept up the fog, and it went bounding away over the hills, leaving trailing streamers of white in the gullies, and coverlets of cotton around the bushes. Way below, they could see Flicka galloping towards the yearlings. In a moment she joined them, and then there was just a many coloured blur of moving shapes, with a fierce sun blazing down, striking sparks of light off their glossy coats.

"Get going!" shouted McLaughlin. "Get around behind them. They're on the run now, and it's cleared – keep them running, and we may get them all in together, before they stop. Tim, you take the short way back to the gate and help Howard turn them and get them through."

Tim shot off towards the County Road and the other three riders galloped down and around the mountain until they were at the back of the band of yearlings. Shouting and yelling and spurring their mounts, they kept the colts running, circling them around towards the ranch until they had them on the County Road.

Way ahead, Ken could see Tim and Howard at the gate, blocking the road. The yearlings were bearing down on them. Now McLaughlin slowed up, and began to call, "Whoa, whoa—" and the pace decreased. Often enough the yearlings had swept down that road and through the gate and down to the corrals. It was the pathway to oats, and hay, and shelter from winter storms – would they take it now? Flicka was with them – right in the middle – if they went, would she go too?

It was all over almost before Ken could draw a breath. The yearlings turned at the gate, swept through, went down to the corrals on a dead run, and through the gates that Gus had opened.

Flicka was caught again.

Mindful that she had clawed her way out when she was corralled before, McLaughlin determined to keep her in the main corral into which the stable door opened. It had eight-foot walls of aspen poles. The rest of the yearlings must be manoeuvred away from her.

Now that the fog had gone, the sun was scorching, and horses and men alike were soaked with sweat before the chasing was over and, one after the other, the yearlings had been driven into the other corral, and Flicka was alone.

She knew that her solitude meant danger, and that she was singled out for some special disaster. She ran frantically to the high fence through which she could see the other ponies standing, and reared and clawed at the poles; she screamed, whirled, circled the corral first in one direction and then the other. And while McLaughlin and Ross were discussing the advisability of roping her, she suddenly espied the dark hole which was the open upper half of the stable-door, and dived through it. McLaughlin rushed to close it, and she was caught – safely imprisoned in the stable.

The rest of the colts were driven away, and Ken stood outside the stable, listening to the wild hoofs beating, the screams, the crashes. His Flicka within there – close at hand – imprisoned. He was shaking. He felt a desperate desire to quiet her somehow, to tell her. If she only knew how he loved her, that there was nothing to be afraid of, that they were going to be friends—

Ross shook his head with a one-sided grin. "Sure a wild one," he said, coiling his lariat.

"Plumb loco," said Tim briefly.

McLaughlin said, "We'll leave her to think it over. After dinner we'll come up and feed and water her and do a little work with her."

But when they went up after dinner there was no Flicka in the barn. One of the windows above the manger was broken, and the manger was full of pieces of glass.

Staring at it, McLaughlin gave a short laugh. He looked at Ken. "She climbed into the manger – see? Stood on the feed box, beat the glass out with her front hoofs and climbed through."

The window opened into the Six Foot Pasture. Near it was a wagon-load of hay. When they went around the back of the stable to see where she had gone, they found her between the stable and the hay wagon, eating.

At their approach, she leaped away, then headed east across the pasture.

"If she's like her mother," said Rob, "she'll go right through the wire."

"Ay bet she'll go over," said Gus. "She yumps like a deer."

"No horse can jump that," said McLaughlin.

Ken said nothing because he could not speak. It was the most terrible moment of his life. He watched Flicka racing towards the eastern wire.

A few rods from it, she swerved, turned and raced diagonally south.

"It turned her! It turned her!" cried Ken, almost sobbing. It was the first sign of hope for Flicka. "Oh, Dad, she has got sense, she has! She has!"

Flicka turned again as she met the southern boundary of the pasture, again at the northern; she avoided the barn. Without abating anything of her whirlwind speed, following a precise, accurate calculation, and turning each time on a dime, she investigated every possibility. Then, seeing that there was no hope, she raced south towards the range where she had spent her life, gathered herself, and rose to the impossible leap.

Each of the men watching had the impulse to cover his eyes, and Ken gave a howl of despair.

Twenty yards of fence came down with her as she hurled herself through. Caught on the upper strands, she turned a complete somersault, landing on her back, her four legs dragging the wires down on top of her, and tangling herself in them beyond hope of escape.

"Damn the wire!" cursed McLaughlin. "If I could afford decent fences—"

Ken followed the men miserably as they walked to the filly. They stood in a circle watching while she kicked and fought and thrashed until the wire was tightly wound and tangled about her, piercing and tearing her flesh and hide. At last she was unconscious, streams of blood running on her golden coat, and pools of crimson widening on the grass beneath her.

With the wire cutters which Gus always carried in the hip pocket of his overalls, he cut the wire away; and they drew her into the pasture, repaired the fence, placed hay, a box of oats, and a tub of water near her, and called it a day.

"I doubt if she pulls out of it," said McLaughlin briefly. "But it's just as well. If it hadn't been this way it would have been another. A loco horse isn't worth a damn."

Ken lay on the grass behind Flicka. One little brown hand was on her back, smoothing it, pressing softly, caressing. The other hand supported his head. His face hung over her.

His throat felt dry; his lips were like paper.

After a long while he whispered, "I didn't mean to kill you, Flicka—"

Howard came to sit with him, quiet and respectful as is proper in the presence of grief or mourning.

Ken's eyes were on Flicka, watching her slow breathing. He had often seen horses down and unconscious. Badly cut with wire, too – they got well. Flicka could get well.

"Gosh! She's about as bad as Rocket," said Howard cheerfully.

Ken raised his head scowling. "Rocket! That old black hellion!"

"Well, Flicka's her child, isn't she?"

"She's Banner's child too—"

There were many air-tight compartments in Ken's mind. Rocket – now that she had come to a bad end – had conveniently gone into one of them.

After a moment Howard said, "We haven't given our colts their workout today." He pulled up his knees and clasped his hands around them.

Ken said nothing.

"We're supposed to, you know – we gotta," said Howard. "Dad'll be sore at us if we don't."

"I don't want to leave her," said Ken, and his voice was strange and thin.

Howard was sympathetically silent. Then he said, "I could do your two for you, Ken—"

Ken looked up gratefully. "Would you, Howard? Gee – that'd be keen—"

"Sure, I'll do all of 'em, and you can stay here with Flicka."

"Thanks." Ken put his head down on his hand again, and the other hand smoothed and patted the filly's neck.

"Gee, she was pretty," said Howard, sighing.

"What d'ya mean – *was!*" snapped Ken. "You mean, she *is* – she's beautiful."

"I meant, when she was running back there," said Howard hastily.

Ken made no reply. It was true. Flicka floating across the ravines was something quite different from the inert mass lying on the ground, her belly rounded up into a mound, her neck weak and collapsed on the grass, her head stretched out, homely and senseless.

"Just think," said Howard, "you could have had any one of the other yearlings. And I guess by this time, it would have been half tamed down there in the corral – probably tied to the post."

As Ken still kept silent, Howard got slowly to his feet. "Well, I guess I might as well go and do the colts," he said, and walked away. At a little distance he turned. "If Mother goes for the mail, do you want to go along?"

Ken shook his head.

When Howard was out of sight, Ken kneeled up and looked Flicka all over. He had never thought that, as soon as this, he would have been close enough to pat her, to caress her, to hold and examine her. He felt a passion of possession. Sick and half destroyed as she was, she was his own, and his heart was bursting with love of her. He smoothed her all over. He arranged her mane in more orderly fashion; he tried to straighten her head.

"You're mine now, Flicka," he whispered.

He counted her wounds. The two worst were a deep cut above the right rear hock and a long gash in her chest that ran down into the muscle of the foreleg. Besides those, she was snagged with three-cornered tears through which the flesh pushed out, and laced with cuts and scratches with blood drying on them in rows of little black beads.

Ken wondered if the two bad cuts ought to be sewn up. He thought of Doc Hicks, and then remembered what his Dad had said: "You cost me money every time you turn around." No – Gus might do it – Gus was pretty good at sewing up animals. But Dad said best thing of all is usually to let them alone. They heal up. There was Sultan, hit by an automobile out on the highway; it knocked him down and took a big piece of flesh out of his chest and left the flap of skin hanging loose – and it all healed up of itself and you could only tell where the wound had been by the hairs being a different length.

The cut in Flicka's hind leg was awfully deep—

He put his head down against her and whispered again, "Oh, Flicka – I didn't mean to kill you."

After a few moments, "Oh, get well – get well – *get well*—"

And again, "Flicka, don't be so wild. *Be all right, Flicka*—"

Gus came out to him carrying a can of black grease.

"De Boss tole me to put some of dis grease on de filly's cuts, Ken – it helps heal 'em up."

Together they went over her carefully, putting a smear of the grease wherever they could reach a wound.

Gus stood looking down at the boy.

"D'you think she'll get well, Gus?"

"She might, Ken. I seen plenty horses hurt as bad as dot, and dey yust as good as ever."

"Dad said—" But Ken's voice failed him when he remembered that his father had said she might as well die, because she was loco anyway.

The Swede stood a moment, his pale blue eyes, transparent and spiritual, looking kindly down at the boy; then he went on down to the barn.

Every trace of fog and mist had vanished, and the sun was blazing hot. Sweltering, Ken got up to take a drink of water from the bucket left for Flicka. Then, carrying handfuls of water in his small cupped hands, he poured it on her mouth. Flicka did not move, and once again Ken took his place behind her, his hand on her neck, his lips whispering to her.

After a while his head sank in exhaustion to the ground . . .

A roaring gale roused him and he looked up to see racing black clouds forming into a line. Blasts of cold wind struck down at the earth and sucked up leaves, twigs, tumbleweeds, in whorls like small cyclones.

From the black line in the sky, a fine icy mist sheeted down, and suddenly there came an appalling explosion of thunder. The world blazed and shuddered with lightning. High overhead was a noise like the shrieking of trumpets and trombones. The particles of fine icy mist beating down grew larger; they began to dance and bounce on the ground like little peas – like marbles – like ping-pong balls—

They beat upon Ken through his thin shirt and whipped his bare head and face. He kneeled up, leaning over Flicka, protecting her head with his folded arms. The hailstones were like ping-pong balls – like billiard balls – like little hard apples – like bigger apples – and suddenly, here and there, they fell as big as tennis balls, bouncing on the ground, rolling along, splitting on the rocks.

One hit Ken on the side of the face and a thin line of blood slid down his cheek with the water.

Running like a hare, under a pall of darkness, the storm fled eastwards, beating the grass flat upon the hills. Then, in the wake of the darkness and the screaming wind and hail, a clear silver light shone out, and the grass rose up again, every blade shimmering.

Watching Flicka, Ken sat back on his heels and sighed. She had not moved.

A rainbow, like a giant compass, drew a half circle of bright colour around the ranch. And off to one side, there was a vertical blur of fire hanging, left over from the storm.

Ken lay down again close behind Flicka and put his cheek against the soft tangle of her mane.

When evening came, and Nell had called Ken and had taken him by the hand and led him away, Flicka still lay without moving. Gently the darkness folded down over her. She was alone, except for the creatures of the sky – the heavenly bodies that wheeled over her; the two Bears, circling around the North Star; the cluster of little Sisters clinging together as if they held their arms wrapped around each other; the eagle, Aquila, that waited till nearly midnight before his great hidden wings lifted him above the horizon; and right overhead, an eye as bright as a blue diamond beaming down, the beautiful star, Vega.

Less alive than they, and dark under their brilliance, the motionless body of Flicka lay on the blood-stained grass, earth-bound and fatal, every breath she drew a costly victory.

Towards morning, a half moon rode in the zenith.

A single, sharp, yapping bark broke the silence. Another answered, then another and another – tentative, questioning cries that presently became long quavering howls. The sharp pixie faces of a pack of coyotes pointed at the moon, and the howls trembled up through their long, tight-stretched throats and open, pulsating jaws. Each little prairie-wolf was allowed a solo, at first timid and wondering, then gathering force and impudence. Then they joined with each other and at last the troop was in full, yammering chorus, capering and malicious and thumbing noses and filling the air with sounds that raise the hair on human heads and put every animal on the alert.

Flicka came back to consciousness with a deep, shuddering sigh. She lifted her head and rolled over on her belly, drawing her legs under her a little. Resting so, she turned her head and listened. The yammer rose and fell. It was a familiar sound, she had heard it since she was born. The pack was across the stream on the edge of the woods beyond.

All at once, Flicka gathered herself, made a sudden, plunging effort, and gained her feet. It was not good for a filly to be helpless on the ground with a pack of coyotes near by. She stood swaying, her legs splayed out weakly, her head low and dizzy. It was minutes before balance came to her, and while she waited for it her nostrils flared, smelling water. Water! How near was it? Could she get to it?

She saw the tub and presently walked unsteadily over to it, put her lips in and drank. New life and strength poured into her. She paused, lifting her muzzle and mouthed the cold water, freshening her tongue and throat. She drank deeply again, then raised her head higher and stood with her neck turned, listening to the coyotes, until the sounds subsided, hesitated, died away.

She stood over the tub a long time. The pack yammered again, but the sound was like an echo, artless and hollow with distance, a mile away. They had gone across the valley for hunting.

A faint luminousness appeared over the earth and a lemon-coloured light in the east. One by one the stars drew back, and the pale, innocent blue of the early-morning sky closed over them.

By the time Ken reached Flicka in the morning, she had finished the water, eaten some of the oats, and was standing broadside to the level sunlight, gathering in every ultra-violet ray, every infra-red, for the healing and the recreation her battered body needed.

THE WILD HEART

HELEN GRIFFITHS

La Bruja is a wild horse from the South American plains. Famed for her speed, she has been much coveted by El Ciego, an unscrupulous horse-breeder. Now La Bruja has found sanctuary, but not freedom . . .

SPRING WAS COMING to the pampa once again. The summer birds winged across the land once more, shadowing the pampa beneath them, and La Bruja trembled with frustrated eagerness as they flew above the corral where still she was a prisoner, recognizing the season and longing for her freedom.

Angel knew and understood her mood. She had come to accept his friendship at last, permitting herself to be stroked and handled, remembering perhaps her Indian master, but she gave little affection in return. She no longer bared her teeth and flattened her ears at his approach, she no longer shied away, but she never came to him of her own accord, she never sought his friendship, accepting it only because she realized that he meant her no harm.

As a prisoner she was miserable. Her life with Onak had made her restless, but at least with him she could run out her fever for freedom. With Angel, who had never tried to ride her, she had nothing to do but stand in the corral or wander round it time and time again, occasionally brushing noses with the other occupants. She passed the time staring over the fence, watching, listening, and smelling, and when spring came again her listless heart was stirred, forgotten instincts were aroused, and the fast-flying birds called to her with tormenting insistence. *Follow, follow*, was what they cried to her, but she was halted by a stubborn fence.

Angel saw and felt her restlessness. He had studied her closely in his love throughout the months she had been in his keeping and he knew her well. He knew exactly how she tossed her head and pawed the ground, impatient for the feed he brought her; he knew when she was irritable or sleepy or when she had found a sudden interest in something; he knew that she did not love him, that her heart was too wild ever to accept the domination of man, whether kind or cruel, that she was unhappy in her captivity, and many times he wanted to release her, held back only by the knowledge that El Ciego was still waiting for her. He removed the halter from her head, but still he could not give her freedom.

As he came to understand La Bruja, he realized that she was no killer born. True she was wild, true she was savage, but once he had conquered her fear, and let her understand that he would not harm her, he saw that she was quiet and honest. She played him no mean tricks, her vicious eyes became more gentle, and now she rarely flattened her ears. Only fear or cruelty could have driven her to kill the man, and Angel told this to every gaucho who came to the church longing to clear her name, for there were still those who said she should be destroyed for what she had done.

They were surprised to learn that he had tamed her, but they had the word of Father Orlando that it was true, even though she grew anxious and angry when other men came to look at her. After a while some men began to remember that Gregorio had always been impatient with horses, agreeing that perhaps La Bruja had been too much provoked. Angel cleared her name and the fat town barber lost his favourite story.

Angel tried to ignore La Bruja's restless spirit, knowing that he could not let her free even though he longed to make her happy, for in his love he was unselfish and did not wish to keep her against her will. How much he hoped that she would come to return his affection, how often he dreamed that one day he would open the gate of the corral and that she would not venture through it, only to awake and tell himself that she would in reality dash away without a moment's hesitation.

While he gained her trust the winter slowly passed away, and he saw that each day nearer to the spring La Bruja grew more restless, newly searching for a weak spot in the corral, although she had long ago given up any hope of escape.

"Father Orlando, what can I do?" he begged one day. "I want to let her free and yet I know I mustn't."

"Well, Angelito, you can let her free. She will run away and know perhaps ten days of happiness before she's captured once again. Or you can keep her until she's old and has grey whiskers on her muzzle like the others, knowing that she isn't happy but that she's well looked after."

"Ten days of happiness against a lifetime of misery. Which would I choose if it were me?" said Angel. "But if she has the ten days then there will be a lifetime with El Ciego afterwards, from whom we've already saved her, or some other man she hates as much."

"Perhaps, perhaps not," replied the priest. "She's your horse, Angel my son. You must solve the problem, make the choice for her. You know her so well that you should know which she would choose."

Angel said nothing to this. He knew well enough which she would choose, but he could not bear to think of her in another man's possession. He was this much selfish in his love for her. He must have her or she must be free completely. He would not give her to another man.

He sat on the fence and watched her, for the first time in his life facing a seemingly unanswerable problem. He remembered how he had first seen her – a beaten, exhausted creature with bloodshot eyes and choking breath. He remembered how he had always visualized her, galloping with eager legs and wind-blown tail, eyes shining with delight. He saw her now with drooping head and lifeless eyes, and the only thought that gave him gladness was the one in which he saw her free.

Angel saw the payador from a distance, recognizing him by the guitar across his shoulders and the horse he rode, and he hurried to tell Father Orlando of his coming, his troubled heart gladdened by the thought of the old man's company, for he could tell tales of fantasy such as never were found in his religious books and sing songs far more exciting than hymns.

The payador rode a horse which had long been El Ciego's envy. A bronze-coated, black-legged mare she was, and the horse-breeder felt sure that she could foal a palomino colt by Eldorado. Many times had he offered the old man money or horses in exchange for her, but the payador would not part with Thamar, talking of her as if she were a daughter instead of just a horse. When he told El Ciego that the wild La Bruja was her mother, it was because he knew that El Ciego would desire her more and, like many a man, he enjoyed saying no to the horse-breeder.

The payador came to the church for two reasons. One was that he had long neglected his religion and wanted to talk to Father Orlando, and the other reason was that he too had heard of La Bruja's presence there and wished to see the ugly mother of his beautiful Thamar once more.

La Bruja did not know her daughter. Thamar was unsaddled and turned loose in the corral, and La Bruja, in curiosity, examined her and then ignored her, having long forgotten that she had borne colt and filly on the pampa, no longer remembering her grief at their loss. Angel gazed with interest and admiration at the lovely creature, filled with pride to think that she could be the daughter of La Bruja, but his heart grew heavy when he learned from the payador how El Ciego still thought to gain his mare, delight fading from his sun-browned face.

"What's the matter, Ranito?" asked the payador. "Are you afraid that he will steal her?"

"No. I know he won't do that. At least, he would not steal her from me. He would steal her from the pampa, though, where she belongs. Even I don't really own her."

"Tell me about her," the payador urged the serious, sad-eyed boy, as eager to hear stories as to tell them, and Angel gazed into his sympathetic, understanding eyes and knew that here he had a friend.

Gladly he poured out his troubles, unburdening himself as he did so, feeling sure that the payador could help him. He saw how Thamar loved her master, he saw how gently he treated her, how he chided her and spoke to her and called her "friend". For a moment he was even willing to give La Bruja to him, knowing that he would treat mother and daughter alike, but he told the payador, "I want her to be free."

They leaned against the corral fence together, the warm spring sunshine beating down upon them from an azure sky, and Father Orlando joined them, saying nothing but listening to the boy, never realizing until this moment just how much Angel had worried and hoped and feared. The payador said nothing either, only nodding now and again until the boy had finished.

Then he said, "There's only one answer to your problem, Ranito, only one thing to do and you can only do it if you really love La Bruja because it's something very hard."

"I do love her, I do, and I'd do anything for her," Angel vowed. "Tell me what I must do."

"To let her free you must take away that which makes her coveted by other men."

Angel said nothing to this, not understanding. He

frowned and thought and the payador left him to think, knowing that soon he would comprehend. Angel suddenly stared at the old gaucho, disbelief in his innocent, black eyes as he understood.

"You mean, take away her speed? Cripple her?"

The payador nodded, returning Angel's gaze.

"But that's cruel. How could I do it without hurting her? How could she ever trust me again?"

"You cannot do it without hurting her, but once you let her free you won't need her to trust you. Sometimes it's necessary to be cruel in order to be kind, surely you can understand that?"

Angel made no reply, struggling to fit this new idea with all the others he had entertained. Never in his life would he hurt La Bruja, that he knew, and yet the payador was telling him that he must, and hurt her cruelly, if he really wanted to prove his love for her. He knew the despair of being lame, never able to do the things he wanted, and must La Bruja suffer thus and at his hands?

"Is there no other way?" he pleaded at last, looking from one man to the other, seeing the answer in both their eyes.

"The payador is wise," said Father Orlando. "You would do well to listen to him."

"You must do that or keep her for ever. There is no other way," added the payador, and Angel knew he was right.

He sighed and looked at La Bruja, knowing how she strained every nerve in her longing to be free, and he wondered how highly she valued her freedom or whether her love of running was greater. He guessed that the two would be combined and he realized that if he chose he could give her one thing or neither. No matter how much he desired it, he could not give her both.

"Very well," he said at last to the payador. "But you do it, señor, because I cannot. I love her too much to hurt her."

"She won't let me near her, Ranito, you know that. You must do it because she trusts you. Otherwise we will need, ropes and more men to help us, which will only frighten her."

Angel nodded, his face pale and his eyes showing the strain of his heart. He felt sick with fear when the payador handed him his long silver knife, taking it gingerly, looking at it with distaste. He placed it in his own belt at last, thinking that La Bruja might be afraid if she saw it.

"Cut a back tendon," advised the payador. "In the pastern, just above the hoof. One quick stab is all you need but make it a strong one. She won't let you near her a second time."

Angel did not speak. He hopped slowly to the gate of the corral and stood there for several moments, his back to the men, but they could guess by his actions that he was rubbing tears from his face.

With a heavy heart he went up to La Bruja, stroking her gently as often he had done, unable to talk to her for the lump in his throat, hoping she would sense that he loved her, longing for her to understand what he was about to do. For a long time he paused, putting off the moment again and again, trying to make himself realize that once it was done she would never gallop again, that she would be without value to any man.

"Oh, Bruja, Bruja," he said to her at last. "Why wouldn't you come to love me? Why do you love freedom so much? Why is your heart so wild? We could have been great friends, you and I. Instead we shall be two cripples. Be happy on the pampa, ugly cripple. No man will ever want you again."

He leaned against her while he felt in his pocket, suddenly remembering the rosary of black wooden beads he always kept there. He pulled it out and took a piece of La Bruja's long, dark mane in his hands, firmly entwining the rosary among the wiry hairs, the only thing he had that he could give her. La Bruja shook her neck and snorted and then stood still again, sensing Angel's change of mood but not understanding it.

Then Angel took the knife from his belt and felt his way down La Bruja's off hind leg, letting his hand move slowly so that he should not frighten her. It was no easy job, for he was hampered by his crutch, and after a moment he threw the crutch aside and knelt in the dust beside La Bruja, unafraid, not even thinking that she might kick him. He forgot that the payador and Father Orlando were watching him, he forgot everything in that moment except that the deed must be done, and suddenly he filled his heart with courage and stabbed the point of the knife deep into the pastern as the payador had told him.

La Bruja jumped into the air, kicking savagely, squealing with sudden pain, and Angel fell flat on his back as he dodged her hooves, vaguely seeing her dart across the corral and through the open gate, half blinded by dust and tears.

He pulled himself to his knees and watched her, not sure if he had lamed her or not, for she had jumped away quickly enough and seemed to run without impediment. He saw that the dust was damp with blotches of blood and, as he tore his gaze from them to stare again at La Bruja, he saw that she had faltered in her stride, halting to touch her wounded fetlock with her muzzle, unable to put her hoof to the ground.

He had not failed and the tears he had so far stemmed suddenly filled his eyes so that he could not see her limping to freedom. He sobbed as if his heart would break.

Angel never saw La Bruja again. The payador, when he took his leave of the occupants of the little church, rode to the rancho of El Ciego and told him what Angel had done, and often after that, when called upon to sing a song of the pampa, he would sing about La Bruja.

Every now and then a gaucho coming to the church would tell Angel that he had spied La Bruja from a distance and thus the boy learned how she was faring. The spring with its urgent messages passed away, the hot summer too, during which time the thistles grew, flowered, and dropped their seeds; birds nested and hatched their fledgelings; storms refreshed the wilting grass and flowers. Another winter came and went and a year passed by since Angel had kept La Bruja in the corral.

Another gaucho came and said that he had seen the mare with a fine, dark colt and that she wandered along in the wake of a large herd led by a dun-coloured stallion, and then there was no more news of her, for the herd passed from the district and La Bruja was not seen again.

Angel never forgot La Bruja. Even when he became a man and a priest, taking charge of the little church on the pampa when Father Orlando died, he still remembered the wild horse he had befriended and saved, staring at the now empty corral and wondering whether she had found her way to Trapalanda as he believed, for surely in Trapalanda La Bruja deserved to be.

BREED OF GIANTS

JOYCE STRANGER

Peg and her husband Josh breed Shire horses. Josh has just bought another Shire, but has had to borrow money from a neighbour to do so.

PEG'S ANGER DIED when the mare came home. The poor beast's head drooped, she was miserable and bewildered, she could not understand the journey, the strangers about her, nor the unfamiliar field into which she was put. The stallions had been taken to the farthest field, beyond a high hawthorn hedge, out of sight of the mares. The field was divided into large paddocks, and each horse was alone.

The mare was miserable. Whenever Peg came into the yard she yickered to her, looking anxiously over the gate, so that soon Peg was behind with all the chores as she stroked the warm neck, spoke soothingly, and took pony nuts, held in her hand, trying to ensure that the newcomer settled quickly.

Later that day she heard a sudden loud bray. She had forgotten to tie the latch on the gate, and Libby, the donkey, had made her own way into her usual, but now puzzlingly forbidden, field. Anxious that the mare should not be teased, bitten or chased, Peg ran outside, only to see the two animals rubbing noses as if they were long-lost sisters. She kept a wary eye on them, but they roamed together like life-long friends.

By now Sally, the pensioned-off mare, was mourning for the donkey, and when at last the pigs were fed, the chickens cleaned, and the churns scalded, Peg fetched the old grey from the orchard where she had been put for the time being and took her, too, into the big field, leaving the gate open behind them, and holding Sal's headrope, ready to make a hasty retreat if there was trouble.

The new Shire walked towards them cautiously, head outstretched, curious to see the mare. Peg had brought sugar lumps with her, and she held out her hand. The Shire mare nuzzled and blew wetly, took the sugar greedily, looked at old Sally, and huffed. Sally, delighted to see another of her own kind, and also happily crunching sugar, stretched her neck and rubbed her muzzle along the Shire's back. Peg removed the headrope, but remained in the field, watching.

The donkey greeted Sally with fervour. The Shire mare dropped her head and began to feed. Peg felt she could not call her Sensation. It was a ridiculous name.

"I'll call you Polly," she decided, smoothing the sleek mane.

Josh, coming from the stallions' field, saw his wife and grinned to himself. So Peg had come round, after all.

Peg had other ideas.

"Knacker's cheque's come," she said.

"Good. I can pay off some of the feed bills." Josh considered the money.

"You can bank the cheque and the chicken money

and the money I've put by for a new winter coat, and
get straight over to Wellans's and pay for that mare."
Peg's voice faltered a little, and her colour was high.
"We'll not be beholden to anyone, least of all our
neighbours. You ought to be ashamed of yourself, Josh
Johnson."

"But, Peg . . ."

"Get over there right now, or I'll go myself," Peg
said. She looked meaningly at her old bicycle, rattle-
trap, sit-up-and-beg, as old-fashioned as they come, and
almost as old as Ted Wellans. "Get on now, do."

Josh did as he was told. There'd be no peace till he'd
done it. He crashed the gears irritably and the old Land
Rover coughed its way out of the yard, weary with the
abuse heaped on its engine. Only five days before it had
dragged a load from the fields that almost tore it apart
as Josh revved and revved in an effort to get leverage.

Peg went into the house to bake the bread. She was
late, and soon it would be time for milking, which she
could fit in while the dough rose. She whipped up a
sponge cake, made some pastry and put a pie in the
oven, and then, tiring of indoors, walked over to look
at the stallions.

They were peaceful enough. On one side of them,
in the farthest field of all, were the milkers, placid and
cud-chewing. Her handsome Friesians. In the far
corner Maybelle, the bully, stood alone, the other cows
giving her a wide berth. Although they had all been de-
horned, Maybelle could still give little vicious kicks
and butts and make life a misery for the other cattle
when she felt like it.

Don't know how they manage without de-horning, Peg

thought, remembering bruises caused by Maybelle's sudden demonstrations of paddy in the milking parlour. Temperamental as they come, but for all that a fine cow and a good milker, and she had good calves, too.

In the field nearer to the house were the heifers, skittish and frisky. Mostly Friesian, but Josh had bought two Shorthorns at a sale. One of these was missing, and Peg went to look for her, anxious lest she had caught herself in wire, or fallen into the ditch. The other heifers tossed their heads and bolted from her, unused, as the cows were, to people and handling.

There was no sign of the heifer. Puzzled, Peg came out of the field and circled it, looking for a gap. A low moo caught her ear, coming from the wrong direction. Turning her head, she saw one of the stallions, Bruton Cloud, close beside the hedge, amiably submitting to the loving ministrations of a long wet tongue, as the heifer licked him devotedly.

Peg sighed. The heifer would have to go back, and that was not going to be an easy job. Skittish and frisky, she would run all over the fields, trying to escape from the woman she was convinced meant harm to her. Josh could cope. It was time for the pie to come out of the oven, and also milking time.

She left the heifer where she was, and tramped wearily back to the farm, just in time to see the Land Rover rock to a standstill as Josh shot through the yard gate and stamped on the brakes.

"Done it?" Peg asked.

Josh evaded the question.

"What do you think?" he enquired, a caustic bite

behind the words. Peg was always getting at him. He went into the barn to get the feed ready for the horses. It would save time later. The mare needed special rations to breed a strong foal. He did not tell Peg that Ted had refused the money, gambling on a bit of commission when the beast was sold. The money was in the bank and the cheque to Ted torn up. The knowledge that he also had Peg's money added an edge to the guilt that he felt in keeping the facts from her. Ted had promised not to tell.

Women! Josh thought, tedding hay as if it were a personal enemy. *Never know where you are with them. They just don't think straight.*

He ate his supper with his mind on the mare. Dai Evans had thought she was due to foal within the week. She had been pretty near, Dai knew, but old Burrows had not called him in to look at her, taking a pride himself in knowing as much as any vet about horses.

"Think the mare might foal tonight," Josh said abruptly, after walking out to the stable for the fifth time, leaving his supper to congeal on the plate, irritating Peg even further. *Why waste time cooking for the man?* she wondered morosely, toying with her own food, annoyance taking away her appetite.

"Sit down and finish your meal, man," she said, when he stood again. "The mare's all right. It's not her first foal, and she has them easy. Dai told you that."

Josh took his pipe and went into the yard without answering. He stood outside the stable, listening to the mare treading the straw. She was restless, a sure sign. He glanced in at her, and she looked at him sideways, allowing him to fondle her neck, but plainly not interested in him. She had eaten her mash. That was good. He puffed contentedly, watching the swallows skim over the grass, barely six inches from the ground. More rain coming.

Peg clattered the dishes irritably in the sink. She could talk through the kitchen window.

"You moved that heifer back?" she asked.

"Aye. Took her out when I brought the stallions in. Rare old dance she led me, too. Skittish as a goat kid. Full of it."

"You coming in?"

"I'll have coffee here. Mare's coming on. I told you."

"Oh, you!" Peg slammed the window down, made the coffee, and took it outside. Midges were dancing in great clouds under the eaves. They never troubled Josh, but within minutes they drove her indoors again to sit and wonder why she'd married a farmer and tied herself to a life that went on seven days a week, sometimes twenty-four hours a day.

Not had a holiday, not properly, since the boys were little lads and her brother had taken over for a few days. Now their eldest, Jack, and her brother, were both lying in graves in Malaya, and Jim was married and out in Canada with his wife and two little girls, and Dan had gone to Australia to work on a sheep farm. Doing well, both boys, but she wished they'd write more often. She took the bread out of the oven, put it to cool on the wire tray in the pantry, and went upstairs to bed.

As Josh walked into the stable, the mare turned her head to look at him, and then began to pull at a haybag.

His own horses had racks, but the mare was used to a bag, and had looked for it, so he gave her one. She could feed without bending her head. He could not take his eyes off her. Old Burrows had known what he was about, breeding her. She was better than either of his own two mares, and suddenly he thought he would sell one of them and keep Sensation. Polly, indeed! Trust Peg.

He yawned, and went back to the house for a jersey. There was a chill in the air now that the sun had gone down. He looked over the silent fields. The cattle were dreaming, the swallows gone to roost, and in the near-dark the first bats were flittering, swooping, silent, almost shadow-like, on the insects in the air.

A small yowl startled him as Cappy laid a rat at his feet and waited for the swift praise he knew would follow. Cappy was a fine ratter, and Josh valued his services, and made sure the cat knew. Now the black-and-white warrior arched and preened himself, purring loudly. He never ate his catch. Josh took the body and buried it deep in the rose bed.

He walked back to the stable, savouring the night. There was plenty of time yet, he thought, as he glanced inside. He stiffened. The mare's head was down, her eyes intent, looking at something in the straw. He walked in swiftly. The foal lay beside her, wet and only an instant born. She began to lick him placidly, as he lifted his head and stared blindly at Josh, his blue eyes unfocussed.

Peg must see this. At once. Josh ran up the stairs, calling his wife eagerly, so that she, as he shook her wildly, woke, sure that something was wrong, and sat up, wide-eyed and terrified, expecting to hear of disaster.

"The foal's here!"

He was jubilant, eyes excited, hair on end, watching her face anxiously, and when she took in his news and hastily climbed out of the big old double bed he dashed downstairs again, knowing she would be behind him.

Peg could never resist a thing new-born. She dragged on jeans and jersey and hurried downstairs. The foal was already trying to stand. His long legs, the hooves unnaturally big, were crossed. He tried, mystified, to sort himself out while Peg grinned fondly and Josh began to bathe the mare, washing away the discomfort left by the birth. She suffered him quietly, eyes on her son.

When at last the baby was sucking, Peg brought fresh straw, and stood and fondled the mother who gazed mildly back at her, dark eyes proud. The foal was a comfort, making up for strange people and unwelcome surroundings, but she recognized that her new owners meant well and were helping her. She stopped licking the little creature and laid her head against Peg's shoulder, her soft lips gentle.

Peg patted her and praised her and went to make warm gruel. When she brought the pan back she held it, taking pleasure in watching the mare suck greedily, not missing a single drop.

"Spend the night downstairs, watching her," Josh said gruffly. "Can't have anything go wrong now."

Peg nodded. This was routine.

"It's a good job you paid Ted back," she said absently, as the foal turned and flickered his ears at the sound of her voice. He had no fear of people. These, present so soon after his birth, were an instantly accepted part of his new astonishing world, like his mother. He did not even flinch as Peg laid a hand on his grey pelt.

"Just like Polly. He's a beauty!" Peg was enthusiastic.

His sire had been grey, too. He would be another Steadfast King.

"Why is it a good job we paid Ted?" Josh asked, with a sinking heart.

"We can't sell her. You know that. Look at that foal. Think what would happen if we bred her with the Cloud, or even with Sable. Now, that foal would be a sensation. They're both better Shires than Horton Steadfast King. Better than Bruton Majestic. You know that."

"Peg, Peg!" Josh said, exasperated. One minute on him for buying the mare at all, the next black-determined not to part with her.

"We haven't got room." Josh rubbed his hand through his thatched red hair.

"We can manage. Just one mare. Won't make all that difference."

"And the foal?" Josh asked. "We must sell him."

"We'll show him first and get a better price," Peg answered, her eyes dreamy as she surveyed her future champion. "We'll call him . . ." She paused.

"Best name him Bruton Hope," Josh said. "Make our fortune for us yet, maybe."

"You'll keep them?" Peg's voice was eager.

"Go to bed, old girl. The next foal will be called Rare Sensation." He grinned at her, his expression mocking.

"You're an old fool, Josh," Peg smiled at him, her eyes suddenly gentle. "We're both old fools."

She gave a backward look at the foal, now settling to sleep, the mare beside him. Josh had forgotten her, absorbed in a final check on mother and son, and knowing that very soon he would have to face Ted, and this time insist he took the money. He couldn't sell either beast. He couldn't bear the thought of parting with Sensation, who had already shown her gentle nature. And her breeding was superb. He'd have to match her with a grey. He sighed contentedly. She was a wonderful brood mare. It was good to have a grey stallion coming up again among the blacks. He and the Cloud would make a pair.

He settled to dreaming, while Cappy, breathless with anticipation, crouched, eager-eyed, waiting for a mouse to come out of a hole on the other side of the cobbled yard. Marmalade sat in the moonlight and washed, and Tinker, who adored horses, came to see what his master was doing so late at night, and curled up beside the mare in the straw, his eyes, bright with interest, watching the foal.

The cat's ears moved backwards, alert, whenever the little beast snuffled, which was often. The mare did not mind the cat. Old Burrows had had twelve of them, and often two or three kept her company at night, sometimes curling to sleep in the manger, while the kittens played in the straw beneath her feet.

Peg, lying listening to the calling owl, the eerie yelp of the badger going for water in the spilling brook brimful from heavy summer rain that had fallen on the hills, thought of the foal with wonder. She could never be indifferent to the new young animals born on the farm. Each one was a small miracle, and she wished that they need not grow up.

It would be good to watch the new baby find his feet, play in the fields, investigate bracken and heather and buttercup, all parts of the astonishing world that had just been given him.

The thought of the bills nagged at the back of her mind, but for once did not dominate her. Something would turn up. They weren't broke yet, not by a long chalk. It was just the constant juggling that got her down. Not like having a salary paid regularly month by month. And animals needed feeding all the time.

She drifted into a dream which Josh matched, waking. Seeing his new foal carry off every honour there was, at every show in the country. He did not think of fees and the cost of carrying the beasts. Life was suddenly perfect. He went outside to smoke his pipe, and watched dawn lighten the sky, heard the first clear call of a bird, followed by waves of sound that trilled from every coppice and bush, louder and louder, until the world was as wide awake as the cockerel that added his raucous welcome to the dawn.

SILVER BLAZE

SIR ARTHUR CONAN DOYLE

"I AM AFRAID, Watson, that I shall have to go," said Holmes, as we sat down together to our breakfast one morning.

"Go! Where to?"

"To Dartmoor — to King's Pyland."

I was not surprised. Indeed, my only wonder was that he had not already been mixed up in this extraordinary case, which was the one topic of conversation through the length and breadth of England. For a whole day my companion had rambled about the room with his chin upon his chest and his brows knitted, charging and re-charging his pipe with the strongest black tobacco, and absolutely deaf to any of my questions or remarks. Fresh editions of every paper had been sent up by our newsagent only to be glanced over and tossed down into a corner. Yet, silent as he was, I knew perfectly well what it was over which he was brooding. There was but one problem before the public which could challenge his powers of analysis, and that was the singular disappearance of the favourite for the Wessex Cup, and the tragic murder of its trainer. When, therefore, he suddenly announced his intention of setting out for the scene of the drama, it was only what I had both expected and hoped for.

"I should be most happy to go down with you if I should not be in the way," said I.

"My dear Watson, you would confer a great favour upon me by coming. And I think that your time will not be misspent, for there are points about this case which promise to make it an absolutely unique one. We have, I think, just time to catch our train at Paddington, and I will go further into the matter upon our journey. You would oblige me by bringing with you your very excellent field-glass."

And so it happened that an hour or so later I found myself in the corner of a first-class carriage, flying along, *en route* for Exeter, while Sherlock Holmes, with his sharp, eager face framed in his earflapped travelling cap, dipped rapidly into the bundle of fresh papers which he had procured at Paddington. We had left Reading far behind us before he thrust the last of them under the seat, and offered me his cigar case.

"We are going well," said he, looking out of the window, and glancing at his watch. "Our rate at present is fifty-three and a half miles an hour."

"I have not observed the quarter-mile posts," said I.

"Nor have I. But the telegraph posts upon this line are sixty yards apart, and the calculation is a simple one. I presume that you have already looked into this matter of the murder of John Straker and the disappearance of Silver Blaze?"

"I have seen what the *Telegraph* and the *Chronicle* have to say."

"It is one of those cases where the art of the reasoner should be used rather for the sifting of details than for the acquiring of fresh evidence. The tragedy has been so uncommon, so complete, and of such personal importance to so many people that we are suffering from a plethora of surmise, conjecture, and hypothesis. The difficulty is to detach the framework of fact – of absolute, undeniable fact – from the embellishments of theorists and reporters. Then, having established ourselves upon this sound basis, it is our duty to see what inferences may be drawn, and which are the special points upon which the whole mystery turns. On Tuesday evening I received telegrams, both from Colonel Ross, the owner of the horse, and from Inspector Gregory, who is looking after the case, inviting my co-operation."

"Tuesday evening!" I exclaimed. "And this is Thursday morning. Why did you not go down yesterday?"

"Because I made a blunder, my dear Watson – which is, I am afraid, a more common occurrence than anyone would think who only knew me through your memoirs. The fact is that I could not believe it possible that the most remarkable horse in England could long remain concealed, especially in so sparsely inhabited a place as the north of Dartmoor. From hour to hour yesterday I expected to hear that he had been found, and that his abductor was the murderer of John Straker. When, however, another morning had come and I found that, beyond the arrest of young Fitzroy Simpson, nothing had been done, I felt that it was time for me to take action. Yet in some ways I feel that yesterday has not been wasted."

"You have formed a theory then?"

"At least I have a grip of the essential facts of the

case. I shall enumerate them to you, for nothing clears up a case so much as stating it to another person, and I can hardly expect your co-operation if I do not show you the position from which we start."

I lay back against the cushions, puffing at my cigar, while Holmes, leaning forward, with his long thin forefinger checking off the points upon the palm of his left hand, gave me a sketch of the events which had led to our journey.

"Silver Blaze," said he, "is from the Isonomy stock, and holds as brilliant a record as his famous ancestor. He is now in his fifth year, and has brought in turn each of the prizes of the turf to Colonel Ross, his fortunate owner. Up to the time of the catastrophe he was first favourite for the Wessex Cup, the betting being three to one on. He has always, however, been a prime favourite with the racing public, and has never yet disappointed them, so that even at short odds enormous sums of money have been laid upon him. It is obvious, therefore, that there were many people who had the strongest interest in preventing Silver Blaze from being there at the fall of the flag next Tuesday.

"The fact was, of course, appreciated at King's Pyland, where the Colonel's training stable is situated. Every precaution was taken to guard the favourite. The trainer, John Straker, is a retired jockey, who rode in Colonel Ross's colours before he became too heavy for the weighing chair. He has served the Colonel for five years as jockey, and for seven as trainer, and has always shown himself to be a zealous and honest servant. Under him were three lads, for the establishment was a small one, containing only four horses in all. One of these lads sat up each night in the stable, while the others slept in the loft. All three bore excellent characters. John Straker, who is a married man, lived in a small villa about two hundred yards from the stables. He has no children, keeps one maid-servant, and is comfortably off. The country round is very lonely, but about half a mile to the north there is a small cluster of villas which have been built by a Tavistock contractor for the use of invalids and others who may wish to enjoy the pure Dartmoor air. Tavistock itself lies two miles to the west, while across the moor, also about two miles distant, is the larger training establishment of Capleton, which belongs to Lord Backwater, and is managed by Silas Brown. In every other direction the moor is a complete wilderness, inhabited only by a few roaming gipsies. Such was the general situation last Monday night, when the catastrophe occurred.

"On that evening the horses had been exercised and watered as usual, and the stables were locked up at nine o'clock. Two of the lads walked up to the trainer's house, where they had supper in the kitchen, while the third, Ned Hunter, remained on guard. At a few minutes after nine the maid, Edith Baxter, carried down to the stables his supper, which consisted of a dish of curried mutton. She took no liquid, as there was a water-tap in the stables, and it was the rule that the lad on duty should drink nothing else. The maid carried a lantern with her, as it was very dark, and the path ran across the open moor.

"Edith Baxter was within thirty yards of the stables when a man appeared out of the darkness and called to her to stop. As he stepped into the circle of yellow light thrown by the lantern, she saw that he was a person of gentlemanly bearing, dressed in a grey suit of tweed with a cloth cap. He wore gaiters, and carried a heavy stick with a knob to it. She was most impressed, however, by the extreme pallor of his face and by the nervousness of his manner. His age, she thought, would be rather over thirty than under it.

"'Can you tell me where I am?' he asked. 'I had almost made up my mind to sleep on the moor when I saw the light of your lantern.'

"'You are close to the King's Pyland training stables,' she said.

"'Oh, indeed! What a stroke of luck!' he cried. 'I understand that a stable-boy sleeps there alone every night. Perhaps that is his supper which you are carrying to him. Now I am sure that you would not be too proud to earn the price of a new dress, would you?' He took a piece of white paper folded up out of his waistcoat pocket. 'See that the boy has this tonight, and you shall have the prettiest frock that money can buy.'

"She was frightened by the earnestness of his manner, and ran past him to the window through which she was accustomed to hand the meals. It was already open, and Hunter was seated at the small table inside. She had begun to tell him of what had happened, when the stranger came up again.

"'Good evening,' said he, looking through the window, 'I wanted to have a word with you.' The girl has sworn that as he spoke she noticed the corner of the little paper packet protruding from his closed hand.

"'What business have you here?' asked the lad.

"'It's business that may put something into your pocket,' said the other. 'You've two horses in for the Wessex Cup – Silver Blaze and Bayard. Let me have the straight tip, and you won't be a loser. Is it a fact that at the weights Bayard could give the other a hundred yards in five furlongs, and that the stable have put their money on him?'

"'So you're one of those damned touts,' cried the lad. 'I'll show you how we serve them in King's Pyland.' He sprang up and rushed across the stable to unloose the dog. The girl fled away to the house, but as she ran she looked back, and saw that the stranger was leaning through the window. A minute later, however, when Hunter rushed out with the hound he was gone, and though the lad ran all round the buildings he failed to find any trace of him."

"One moment!" I asked. "Did the stable-boy, when he ran out with the dog, leave the door unlocked behind him?"

"Excellent, Watson; excellent!" murmured my companion. "The importance of the point struck me so forcibly, that I sent a special wire to Dartmoor yesterday to clear the matter up. The boy locked the door before he left it. The window, I may add, was not large enough for a man to get through.

"Hunter waited until his fellow grooms had returned, when he sent a message up to the trainer and told him what had occurred. Straker was excited at hearing the account, although he does not seem to have quite realized its true significance. It left him, however, vaguely uneasy, and Mrs Straker, waking at one in the morning, found that he was dressing. In reply to her inquiries, he said that he could not sleep on account of his anxiety about the horses, and that he intended to walk down to the stables to see that all was well. She begged him to remain at home, as she could hear the rain pattering against the windows, but in spite of her entreaties he pulled on his large mackintosh and left the house.

"Mrs Straker awoke at seven in the morning, to find that her husband had not yet returned. She dressed herself hastily, called the maid, and set off for the stables. The door was open; inside, huddled together upon a chair, Hunter was sunk in a state of absolute stupor, the favourite's stall was empty, and there were no signs of his trainer.

"The two lads who slept in the chaff-cutting loft above the harness-room were quickly roused. They had heard nothing during the night, for they are both sound sleepers. Hunter was obviously under the influence of some powerful drug; and, as no sense could be got out of him, he was left to sleep it off while the two lads and the two women ran out in search of the absentees. They still had hopes that the trainer had for some reason taken out the horse for early exercise, but on ascending the knoll near the house, from which all the neighbouring moors were visible, they not only could see no signs of the favourite, but they perceived something which warned them that they were in the presence of a tragedy.

"About a quarter of a mile from the stables, John Straker's overcoat was flapping from a furze bush. Immediately beyond there was a bowl-shaped depression in the moor, and at the bottom of this was found the dead body of the unfortunate trainer. His head had been shattered by a savage blow from some heavy weapon, and he was wounded in the thigh, where there was a long, clean cut, inflicted evidently by some very sharp instrument. It was clear, however, that Straker had defended himself vigorously against his assailants, for in his right hand he held a small knife, which was clotted with blood up to the handle, while in his left he grasped a red and black silk cravat, which was recognized by the maid as having been worn on the preceding evening by the stranger who had visited the stables.

"Hunter, on recovering from his stupor, was also quite positive as to the ownership of the cravat. He was equally certain that the same stranger had, while standing at the window, drugged his curried mutton, and so deprived the stables of their watchman.

"As to the missing horse, there were abundant proofs in the mud which lay at the bottom of the fatal hollow, that he had been there at the time of the struggle. But from that morning he has disappeared; and although a large reward has been offered, and all the gipsies of Dartmoor are on the alert, no news has come of him. Finally an analysis has shown that the remains of his supper, left by the stable lad, contain an appreciable quantity of powdered opium, while the people of the house partook of the same dish on the same night without any ill effect.

"Those are the main facts of the case, stripped of all surmise and stated as baldly as possible. I shall now recapitulate what the police have done in the matter.

"Inspector Gregory, to whom the case has been

committed, is an extremely competent officer. Were he but gifted with imagination he might rise to great heights in his profession. On his arrival he promptly found and arrested the man upon whom suspicion naturally rested. There was little difficulty in finding him, for he was thoroughly well known in the neighbourhood. His name, it appears, was Fitzroy Simpson. He was a man of excellent birth and education, who had squandered a fortune upon the turf, and who lived now by doing a little quiet and genteel bookmaking in the sporting clubs of London. An examination of his betting-book shows that bets to the amount of five thousand pounds had been registered by him against the favourite.

"On being arrested he volunteered the statement that he had come down to Dartmoor in the hope of getting some information about the King's Pyland horses, and also about Desborough, the second favourite, which was in charge of Silas Brown, at the Capleton stables. He did not attempt to deny that he had acted as described upon the evening before, but declared that he had no sinister designs, and had simply wished to obtain first-hand information. When confronted with the cravat he turned very pale, and was utterly unable to account for its presence in the hand of the murdered man. His wet clothing showed that he had been out in the storm of the night before, and his stick, which was weighted with lead, was just such a weapon as might, by repeated blows, have inflicted the terrible injuries to which the trainer had succumbed.

"On the other hand, there was no wound upon his person, while the state of Straker's knife would show that one, at least, of his assailants must bear his mark upon him. There you have it all in a nutshell, Watson, and if you can give me any light I shall be infinitely obliged to you."

I had listened with the greatest interest to the statement which Holmes, with characteristic clearness, had laid before me. Though most of the facts were familiar to me, I had not sufficiently appreciated their relative importance, nor their connection with each other.

"Is it not possible," I suggested, "that the incised wound upon Straker may have been caused by his own knife in the convulsive struggles which follow any brain injury?"

"It is more than possible; it is probable," said Holmes. "In that case, one of the main points in favour of the accused disappears."

"And yet," said I, "even now I fail to understand what the theory of the police can be."

"I am afraid that whatever theory we state has very grave objections to it," returned my companion. "The police imagine, I take it, that this Fitzroy Simpson, having drugged the lad, and having in some way obtained a duplicate key, opened the stable door and took out the horse, with the intention, apparently, of kidnapping him altogether. His bridle is missing, so that Simpson must have put it on. Then, having left the door open behind him, he was leading the horse away over the moor, when he was either met or overtaken by the trainer. A row naturally ensued, Simpson beat out the trainer's brains with his heavy stick without receiving any injury from the small knife which Straker used in self-defence, and then the thief either led the horse on to some secret hiding-place, or else it may have bolted during the struggle, and be now wandering out on the moors. That is the case as it appears to the police, and improbable as it is, all other explanations are more improbable still. However, I shall very quickly test the matter when I am once upon the spot, and until then I really cannot see how we can get much further than our present position."

It was evening before we reached the little town of Tavistock, which lies, like the boss of a shield, in the middle of the huge circle of Dartmoor. Two gentlemen were awaiting us at the station; the one a tall fair man with lion-like hair and beard, and curiously penetrating light blue eyes, the other a small alert person, very neat and dapper, in a frock-coat and gaiters, with trim little side-whiskers and an eyeglass. The latter was Colonel Ross, the well-known sportsman, the other Inspector Gregory, a man who was rapidly making his name in the English detective service.

"I am delighted that you have come down, Mr Holmes," said the Colonel. "The Inspector here has done all that could possibly be suggested; but I wish to leave no stone unturned in trying to avenge poor Straker, and in recovering my horse."

"Have there been any fresh developments?" asked Holmes.

"I am sorry to say that we have made very little progress," said the Inspector. "We have an open carriage outside, and as you would no doubt like to see the place before the light fails, we might talk it over as we drive."

A minute later we were all seated in a comfortable landau and were rattling through the quaint old Devonshire town. Inspector Gregory was full of his case, and poured out a stream of remarks, while Holmes threw in an occasional question or interjection. Colonel Ross leaned back with his arms folded and his hat tilted over his eyes, while I listened with interest to the dialogue of the two detectives. Gregory was formulating his theory, which was almost exactly what Holmes had foretold in the train.

"The net is drawn pretty close round Fitzroy Simpson," he remarked, "and I believe myself that he is our man. At the same time, I recognize that the evidence is purely circumstantial, and that some new development may upset it."

"How about Straker's knife?"

"We have quite come to the conclusion that he wounded himself in his fall."

"My friend Dr Watson made that suggestion to me as we came down. If so, it would tell against this man Simpson."

"Undoubtedly. He has neither a knife nor any sign of a wound. The evidence against him is certainly very strong. He had a great interest in the disappearance of the favourite, he lies under the suspicion of having poisoned the stable-boy, he was undoubtedly out in the storm, he was armed with a heavy stick, and his cravat was found in the dead man's hand. I really think we have enough to go before a jury."

Holmes shook his head. "A clever counsel would tear it all to rags," said he. "Why should he take the horse out of the stable? If he wished to injure it, why could he not do it there? Has a duplicate key been found in his possession? What chemist sold him the powdered opium? Above all, where could he, a stranger to the district, hide a horse, and such a horse as this? What is his own explanation as to the paper which he wished the maid to give to the stable-boy?"

"He says that it was a ten-pound note. One was found in his purse. But your other difficulties are not so formidable as they seem. He is not a stranger to the district. He has twice lodged at Tavistock in the summer. The opium was probably brought from London. The key, having served its purpose, would be hurled away. The horse may lie at the bottom of one of the pits or old mines upon the moor."

"What does he say about the cravat?"

"He acknowledges that it is his, and declares that he had lost it. But a new element has been introduced into the case which may account for his leading the horse from the stable."

Holmes pricked up his ears.

"We have found traces which show that a party of gipsies encamped on Monday night within a mile of the spot where the murder took place. On Tuesday they were gone. Now, presuming that there was some understanding between Simpson and these gipsies, might he not have been leading the horse to them when he was overtaken, and may they not have him now?"

"It is certainly possible."

"The moor is being scoured for these gipsies. I have also examined every stable and outhouse in Tavistock, and for a radius of ten miles."

"There is another training stable quite close, I understand?"

"Yes, and that is a factor which we must certainly not neglect. As Desborough, their horse, was second in the betting, they had an interest in the disappearance of the favourite. Silas Brown, the trainer, is known to have had large bets upon the event, and he was no friend to poor Straker. We have, however, examined the stables, and there is nothing to connect him with the affair."

"And nothing to connect this man Simpson with the interests of the Capleton stable?"

"Nothing at all."

Holmes leaned back in the carriage and the conversation ceased. A few minutes later our driver pulled up at a neat little red-brick villa with overhanging eaves, which stood by the road. Some distance off, across a paddock, lay a long grey-tiled out-building. In every other direction the low curves of the moor, bronze-coloured from the fading ferns, stretched away to the sky-line, broken only by the steeples of Tavistock, and by a cluster of houses away to the westward, which marked the Capleton stables. We all sprang out with the exception of Holmes, who continued to lean back with his eyes fixed upon the sky in front of him, entirely absorbed in his own thoughts. It was only when I touched his arm that he roused himself with a violent start and stepped out of the carriage.

"Excuse me," said he, turning to Colonel Ross, who had looked at him in some surprise. "I was day-dreaming." There was a gleam in his eyes and a suppressed excitement in his manner which convinced me, used as I was to his ways, that his hand was upon a clue, though I could not imagine where he had found it.

"Perhaps you would prefer at once to go on to the scene of the crime, Mr Holmes?" said Gregory.

"I think that I should prefer to stay here a little and go into one or two questions of detail. Straker was brought back here, I presume?"

"Yes, he lies upstairs. The inquest is tomorrow."

"He has been in your service some years, Colonel Ross?"

"I have always found him an excellent servant."

"I presume that you made an inventory of what he had in his pockets at the time of his death, Inspector?"

"I have the things themselves in the sitting-room if you would care to see them."

"I should be very glad."

We all filed into the front room and sat round the central table, while the Inspector unlocked a square tin box and laid a small heap of things before us. There was a box of vesta matches, two inches of tallow candle, an A.D.P. briar-root pipe, a pouch of sealskin with half an ounce of long-cut Cavendish, a silver watch with a gold chain, five sovereigns in gold, an aluminium pencil-case, a few papers, and an ivory-handled knife with a very delicate inflexible blade marked Weiss and Co., London.

"This is a very singular knife," said Holmes, lifting it up and examining it minutely. "I presume, as I see bloodstains upon it, that it is the one which was found in the dead man's grasp. Watson, this knife is surely in your line."

"It is what we call a cataract knife," said I.

"I thought so. A very delicate blade devised for very delicate work. A strange thing for a man to carry with him upon a rough expedition, especially as it would not shut in his pocket."

"The tip was guarded by a disc of cork which we found beside his body," said the Inspector. "His wife tells us that the knife had lain for some days upon the dressing-table, and that he had picked it up as he left the room. It was a poor weapon, but perhaps the best that he could lay his hand on at the moment."

"Very possibly. How about these papers?"

"Three of them are receipted hay-dealers' accounts. One of them is a letter of instructions from Colonel Ross. This other is a milliner's account for thirty-seven pounds fifteen, made out by Madame Lesurier, of Bond Street, to William Derbyshire. Mrs Straker tells us that Derbyshire was a friend of her husband's, and that occasionally his letters were addressed here."

"Madame Derbyshire had somewhat expensive tastes," remarked Holmes, glancing down the account. "Twenty-two guineas is rather heavy for a single costume. However, there appears to be nothing more to learn, and we may now go down to the scene of the crime."

As we emerged from the sitting-room a woman who had been waiting in the passage took a step forward and laid her hand upon the Inspector's sleeve. Her face was haggard and thin and eager; stamped with the print of a recent horror.

"Have you got them? Have you found them?" she panted.

"No, Mrs Straker; but Mr Holmes, here, has come from London to help us, and we shall do all that is possible."

"Surely I met you in Plymouth at a garden party some little time ago, Mrs Straker," said Holmes.

"No, sir; you are mistaken."

"Dear me; why, I could have sworn to it. You wore a costume of dove-coloured silk with ostrich feather trimming."

"I never had such a dress, sir," answered the lady.

"Ah; that quite settles it," said Holmes; and, with an apology, he followed the Inspector outside. A short walk across the moor took us to the hollow in which the body had been found. At the brink of it was the furze bush upon which the coat had been hung.

"There was no wind that night, I understand," said Holmes.

"None; but very heavy rain."

"In that case the overcoat was not blown against the furze bushes, but placed there."

"Yes, it was laid across the bush."

"You fill me with interest. I perceive that the ground has been trampled up a good deal. No doubt many feet have been there since Monday night."

"A piece of matting has been laid here at the side, and we have all stood upon that."

"Excellent."

"In this bag I have one of the boots which Straker wore, one of Fitzroy Simpson's shoes, and a cast horseshoe of Silver Blaze."

"My dear Inspector, you surpass yourself!"

Holmes took the bag, and descending into the

hollow he pushed the matting into a more central position. Then stretching himself upon his face and leaning his chin upon his hands, he made a careful study of the trampled mud in front of him.

"Halloa!" said he suddenly, "What's this?"

It was a wax vesta, half burned, which was so coated with mud that it looked at first like a little chip of wood.

"I cannot think how I came to overlook it," said the Inspector, with an expression of annoyance.

"It was invisible, buried in the mud. I only saw it because I was looking for it."

"What! You expected to find it?"

"I thought it not unlikely." He took the boots from the bag and compared the impressions of each of them with marks upon the ground. Then he clambered up to the rim of the hollow and crawled about among the ferns and bushes.

"I am afraid that there are no more tracks," said the Inspector. "I have examined the ground very carefully for a hundred yards in each direction."

"Indeed!" said Holmes, rising. "I should not have the impertinence to do it again after what you say. But I should like to take a little walk over the moors before it grows dark, that I may know my ground tomorrow, and I think that I shall put this horseshoe into my pocket for luck."

Colonel Ross, who had shown some signs of impatience at my companion's quiet and systematic method of work, glanced at his watch.

"I wish you would come back with me, Inspector," said he. "There are several points on which I should like your advice, and especially as to whether we do not owe it to the public to remove our horse's name from the entries for the Cup."

"Certainly not," cried Holmes, with decision; "I should let the name stand."

The Colonel bowed. "I am very glad to have had your opinion, sir," said he. "You will find us at poor Straker's house when you have finished your walk, and we can drive together into Tavistock."

He turned back with the Inspector, while Holmes and I walked slowly across the moor. The sun was beginning to sink behind the stables of Capleton, and the long sloping plain in front of us was tinged with gold, deepening into rich, ruddy brown where the faded ferns and brambles caught the evening light. But the glories of the landscape were all wasted upon my companion, who was sunk in the deepest thought.

"It's this way, Watson," he said, at last. "We may leave the question of who killed John Straker for the instant, and confine ourselves to finding out what has become of the horse. Now, supposing that he broke away during or after the tragedy, where could he have gone to? The horse is a very gregarious creature. If left to himself his instincts would have been either to return to King's Pyland or go over to Capleton. Why should he run wild upon the moor? He would surely have been seen by now. And why should gipsies kidnap him? These people always clear out when they hear of trouble, for they do not wish to be pestered by the police. They could not hope to sell such a horse. They would run a great risk and gain nothing by taking him. Surely that is clear."

"Where is he, then?"

"I have already said that he must have gone to King's Pyland or to Capleton. He is not at King's Pyland, therefore he is at Capleton. Let us take that as a working hypothesis, and see what it leads us to. This part of the moor, as the Inspector remarked, is very hard and dry. But it falls away towards Capleton, and you can see from here that there is a long hollow over yonder, which must have been very wet on Monday night. If our supposition is correct, then the horse must have crossed that, and there is the point where we should look for his tracks."

We had been walking briskly during this conversation, and a few more minutes brought us to the hollow in question. At Holmes' request I walked down the bank to the right, and he to the left, but I had not taken fifty paces before I heard him give a shout, and saw him waving his hand to me. The track of a horse was plainly outlined in the soft earth in front of him, and the shoe which he took from his pocket exactly fitted the impression.

"See the value of imagination," said Holmes. "It is the one quality which Gregory lacks. We imagined what might have happened, acted upon the supposition, and find ourselves justified. Let us proceed."

We crossed the marshy bottom and passed over a quarter of a mile of dry, hard turf. Again the ground sloped and again we came on the tracks. Then we lost them for half a mile, but only to pick them up once more quite close to Capleton. It was Holmes who saw them first, and he stood pointing with a look of triumph upon his face. A man's track was visible beside the horse's.

"The horse was alone before," I cried.

"Quite so. It was alone before. Halloa! What is this?"

The double track turned sharp off and took the direction of King's Pyland. Holmes whistled, and we both followed along after it. His eyes were on the trail, but I happened to look a little to one side, and saw to my surprise the same tracks coming back again in the opposite direction.

"One for you, Watson," said Holmes, when I pointed it out. "You have saved us a long walk which would have brought us back on our own traces. Let us follow the return track."

We had not to go far. It ended at the paving of asphalt which led up to the gates of the Capleton stables. As we approached, a groom ran out from them.

"We don't want any loiterers about here," said he.

"I only wished to ask a question," said Holmes, with his finger and thumb in his waistcoat pocket. "Should I be too early to see your master, Mr Silas Brown, if I were to call at five o'clock tomorrow morning?"

"Bless you, sir, if anyone is about he will be, for he is always the first stirring. But here he is, sir, to answer your questions for himself. No, sir, no; it's as much as my place is worth to let him see me touch your money. Afterwards, if you like."

As Sherlock Holmes replaced the half-crown which he had drawn from his pocket, a fierce-looking elderly man strode out from the gate with a hunting-crop swinging in his hand.

"What's this, Dawson?" he cried. "No gossiping! Go

about your business! And you – what the devil do you want here?"

"Ten minutes' talk with you, my good sir," said Holmes, in the sweetest of voices.

"I've no time to talk to every gadabout. We want no strangers here. Be off, or you may find a dog at your heels."

Holmes leaned forward and whispered something in the trainer's ear. He started violently and flushed to the temples.

"It's a lie!" he shouted. "An infernal lie!"

"Very good! Shall we argue about it here in public, or talk it over in your parlour?"

"Oh, come in if you wish to."

Holmes smiled. "I shall not keep you more than a few minutes, Watson," he said. "Now, Mr Brown, I am quite at your disposal."

It was quite twenty minutes, and the reds had all faded into greys before Holmes and the trainer reappeared. Never have I seen such a change as had been brought about in Silas Brown in that short time. His face was ashy pale, beads of perspiration shone upon his brow, and his hands shook until the hunting-crop wagged like a branch in the wind. His bullying, overbearing manner was all gone too, and he cringed along at my companion's side like a dog with its master.

"Your instructions will be done. It shall be done," said he.

"There must be no mistake," said Holmes, looking round at him. The other winced as he read the menace in his eyes.

"Oh, no, there shall be no mistake. It shall be there. Should I change it first or not?"

Holmes thought a little and then burst out laughing. "No, don't," said he. "I shall write to you about it. No tricks now or—"

"Oh, you can trust me, you can trust me!"

"You must see to it on the day as if it were your own."

"You can rely upon me."

"Yes, I think I can. Well, you shall hear from me tomorrow." He turned upon his heel, disregarding the trembling hand which the other held out to him, and we set off for King's Pyland.

"A more perfect compound of the bully, coward and sneak than Master Silas Brown I have seldom met with," remarked Holmes, as we trudged along together.

"He has the horse, then?"

"He tried to bluster out of it, but I described to him so exactly what his actions had been upon that morning, that he is convinced that I was watching him. Of course, you observed the peculiarly square toes in the impressions, and that his own boots exactly corresponded to them. Again, of course, no subordinate would have dared to have done such a thing. I described to him how when, according to his custom, he was the first down, he perceived a strange horse wandering over the moor; how he went out to it, and his astonishment at recognizing from the white forehead which has given the favourite its name that chance had put in his power the only horse which could beat the one upon which he had put his money. Then I described how his first impulse had been to lead him back to King's Pyland, and how the devil had shown him how he could hide the horse until the race was over, and how he had led it back and concealed it at Capleton. When I told him every detail he gave it up, and thought only of saving his own skin."

"But his stables had been searched."

"Oh, an old horse-faker like him has many a dodge."

"But are you not afraid to leave the horse in his power now, since he has every interest in injuring it?"

"My dear fellow, he will guard it as the apple of his eye. He knows that his only hope of mercy is to produce it safe."

"Colonel Ross did not impress me as a man who would be likely to show much mercy in any case."

"The matter does not rest with Colonel Ross. I follow my own methods, and tell as much or as little as I choose. That is the advantage of being unofficial. I don't know whether you observed it, Watson, but the Colonel's manner has been just a trifle cavalier to me. I am inclined now to have a little amusement at his expense. Say nothing to him about the horse."

"Certainly not, without your permission."

"And, of course, this is all quite a minor case compared with the question of who killed John Straker."

"And you will devote yourself to that?"

"On the contrary, we both go back to London by the night train."

I was thunderstruck by my friend's words. We had only been a few hours in Devonshire, and that he should give up an investigation which he had begun so brilliantly was quite incomprehensible to me. Not a word more could I draw from him until we were back at the trainer's house. The Colonel and the Inspector were awaiting us in the parlour.

"My friend and I return to town by the midnight express," said Holmes. "We have had a charming little breath of your beautiful Dartmoor air."

The Inspector opened his eyes, and the Colonel's lips curled in a sneer.

"So you despair of arresting the murderer of poor Straker," said he.

Holmes shrugged his shoulders. "There are certainly grave difficulties in the way," said he. "I have every hope, however, that your horse will start upon Tuesday, and I beg that you will have your jockey in readiness. Might I ask for a photograph of Mr John Straker?"

The Inspector took one from an envelope in his pocket and handed it to him.

"My dear Gregory, you anticipate all my wants. If I might ask you to wait here for an instant, I have a question which I should like to put to the maid."

"I must say that I am rather disappointed in our London consultant," said Colonel Ross bluntly, as my friend left the room. "I do not see that we are any further than when he came."

"At least, you have his assurance that your horse will run," said I.

"Yes, I have his assurance," said the Colonel, with a shrug of his shoulders. "I should prefer to have the horse."

I was about to make some reply in defence of my friend, when he entered the room again.

"Now, gentlemen," said he, "I am quite ready for Tavistock."

As we stepped into the carriage one of the stable lads held the door open for us. A sudden idea seemed to occur to Holmes, for he leaned forward and touched the lad upon the sleeve.

"You have a few sheep in the paddock," he said. "Who attends to them?"

"I do, sir."

"Have you noticed anything amiss with them of late?"

"Well, sir, not of much account; but three of them have gone lame, sir."

I could see that Holmes was extremely pleased, for he chuckled and rubbed his hands together.

"A long shot, Watson; a very long shot!" said he, pinching my arm. "Gregory, let me recommend to your attention this singular epidemic among the sheep. Drive on, coachman!"

Colonel Ross still wore an expression which showed the poor opinion which he had formed of my companion's ability, but I saw by the Inspector's face that his attention had been keenly aroused.

"You consider that to be important?" he asked.

"Exceedingly so."

"Is there any other point to which you would wish to draw my attention?"

"To the curious incident of the dog in the night-time."

"The dog did nothing in the night-time."

"That was the curious incident," remarked Holmes.

Four days later Holmes and I were again in the train for Winchester, to see the race for the Wessex Cup. Colonel Ross met us, by appointment, outside the station, and we drove in his drag to the course beyond the town. His face was grave and his manner was cold in the extreme.

"I have seen nothing of my horse," said he.

"I suppose that you would know him when you saw him?" asked Holmes.

The Colonel was very angry. "I have been on the turf for twenty years, and never was asked such a question as that before," said he. "A child would know Silver Blaze with his white forehead and his mottled off foreleg."

"How is the betting?"

"Well, that is the curious part of it. You could have got fifteen to one yesterday, but the price has become shorter and shorter, until you can hardly get three to one now."

"Hum!" said Holmes. "Somebody knows something, that is clear!"

As the drag drew up in the enclosure near the grandstand, I glanced at the card to see the entries. It ran:

Wessex Plate. 50 sovs. each, h ft, with 1,000 sovs. added, for four- and five-year-olds. Second £300. Third £200. New course (one mile and five furlongs).

1. Mr Heath Newton's The Negro (red cap, cinnamon jacket).

2. Colonel Wardlaw's Pugilist (pink cap, blue and black jacket).

3. Lord Backwater's Desborough (yellow cap and sleeves).

4. Colonel Ross's Silver Blaze (black cap, red jacket).

5. Duke of Balmoral's Iris (yellow and black stripes).

6. Lord Singleford's Rasper (purple cap, black sleeves).

"We scratched our other one and put all hopes on your word," said the Colonel. "Why, what is that? Silver Blaze favourite?"

"Five to four against Silver Blaze!" roared the ring. "Five to four against Silver Blaze! Fifteen to five against Desborough! Five to four on the field!"

"There are the numbers up," I cried. "They are all six there."

"All six there! Then my horse is running," cried the Colonel, in great agitation. "But I don't see him. My colours have not passed."

"Only five have passed. This must be he."

As I spoke a powerful bay horse swept out from the weighing inclosure and cantered past us, bearing on its back the well-known black and red of the Colonel.

"That's not my horse," cried the owner. "That beast has not a white hair upon its body. What is this that you have done, Mr Holmes?"

"Well, well, let us see how he gets on," said my friend imperturbably. For a few minutes he gazed through my field-glass. "Capital! An excellent start!" he cried suddenly. "There they are, coming round the curve!"

From our drag we had a superb view as they came up the straight. The six horses were so close together that a carpet could have covered them, but half-way up, the yellow of the Capleton stable showed to the front. Before they reached us, however, Desborough's bolt was shot, and the Colonel's horse, coming away with a rush, passed the post a good six lengths before its rival, the Duke of Balmoral's Iris making a bad third.

"It's my race anyhow," gasped the Colonel, passing his hand over his eyes. "I confess that I can make neither head nor tail of it. Don't you think that you have kept up your mystery long enough, Mr Holmes?"

"Certainly, Colonel. You shall know everything. Let us all go round and have a look at the horse together. Here he is," he continued, as we made our way into the weighing inclosure where only owners and their friends find admittance. "You have only to wash his face and his leg in spirits of wine and you will find that he is the same old Silver Blaze as ever."

"You take my breath away!"

"I found him in the hands of a faker, and took the liberty of running him just as he was sent over."

"My dear sir, you have done wonders. The horse looks very fit and well. It never went better in its life. I owe you a thousand apologies for having doubted your ability. You have done me a great service by recovering my horse. You would do me a greater still if you could lay your hands on the murderer of John Straker."

"I have done so," said Holmes quietly.

The Colonel and I stared at him in amazement. "You have got him! Where is he, then?"

"He is here."

"Here! Where?"

"In my company at the present moment."

The Colonel flushed angrily. "I quite recognize that I am under obligations to you, Mr Holmes," said he, "but I must regard what you have just said as either a very bad joke or an insult."

Sherlock Holmes laughed. "I assure you that I have

not associated you with the crime, Colonel," said he. "The real murderer is standing immediately behind you!"

He stepped past and laid his hand upon the glossy neck of the thoroughbred.

"The horse!" cried both the Colonel and myself.

"Yes, the horse. And it may lessen his guilt if I say that it was done in self-defence, and that John Straker was a man who was entirely unworthy of your confidence. But there goes the bell; and as I stand to win a little on this next race, I shall defer a more lengthy explanation until a more fitting time."

We had the corner of a Pullman car to ourselves that evening as we whirled back to London, and I fancy that the journey was a short one to Colonel Ross as well as to myself, as we listened to our companion's narrative of the events which had occurred at the Dartmoor training stables upon that Monday night, and the means by which he had unravelled them.

"I confess," said he, "that any theories which I had formed from the newspaper reports were entirely erroneous. And yet there were indications there, had they not been overlaid by other details which concealed their true import. I went to Devonshire with the conviction that Fitzroy Simpson was the true culprit, although, of course, I saw that the evidence against him was by no means complete.

"It was while I was in the carriage, just as we reached the trainer's house, that the immense significance of the curried mutton occurred to me. You may remember that I was distrait, and remained sitting after you had all alighted. I was marvelling in my own mind how I could possibly have over-looked so obvious a clue."

"I confess," said the Colonel, "that even now I cannot see how it helps us."

"It was the first link in my chain of reasoning. Powdered opium is by no means tasteless. The flavour is not disagreeable, but it is perceptible. Were it mixed with any ordinary dish, the eater would undoubtedly detect it, and would probably eat no more. A curry was exactly the medium which would disguise this taste. By no possible supposition could this stranger, Fitzroy Simpson, have caused curry to be served in the trainer's family that night, and it is surely too monstrous a coincidence to suppose that he happened to come along with powdered opium upon the very night when a dish happened to be served which would disguise the flavour. That is unthinkable. Therefore Simpson becomes eliminated from the case, and our attention centres upon Straker and his wife, the only two people who could have chosen curried mutton for supper that night. The opium was added after the dish was set aside for the stable-boy, for the others had the same for supper with no ill effects. Which of them, then, had access to that dish without the maid seeing them?

"Before deciding that question I had grasped the significance of the silence of the dog, for one true inference invariably suggests others. The Simpson incident had shown me that a dog was kept in the stables, and yet, though someone had been in and had fetched out a horse, he had not barked enough to arouse the two lads in the loft. Obviously the midnight visitor was someone whom the dog knew well.

"I was already convinced, or almost convinced, that John Straker went down to the stables in the dead of the night and took out Silver Blaze. For what purpose? For a dishonest one, obviously, or why should he drug his own stable-boy? And yet I was at a loss to know why. There have been cases before now where trainers have made sure of great sums of money by laying against their own horses, through agents, and then prevented them from winning by fraud. Sometimes it is a pulling jockey. Sometimes it is some surer and subtler means. What was it here? I hoped that the contents of his pockets might help me to form a conclusion.

"And they did so. You cannot have forgotten the singular knife which was found in the dead man's hand, a knife which certainly no sane man would choose for a weapon. It was, as Dr Watson told us, a form of knife which is used for the most delicate operations known in surgery. And it was to be used for a delicate operation that night. You must know, with your wide experience of turf matters, Colonel Ross, that it is possible to make a slight nick upon the tendons of a horse's ham, and to do it subcutaneously so as to leave absolutely no trace. A horse so treated would develop a slight lameness which would be put down to a strain in exercise or a touch of rheumatism, but never to foul play."

"Villain! Scoundrel!" cried the Colonel.

"We have here the explanation of why John Straker wished to take the horse out on to the moor. So spirited a creature would have certainly roused the soundest of sleepers when it felt the prick of the knife. It was absolutely necessary to do it in the open air."

"I have been blind!" cried the Colonel. "Of course, that was why he needed the candle, and struck the match."

"Undoubtedly. But in examining his belongings, I was fortunate enough to discover not only the method of the crime, but even its motives. As a man of the world, Colonel, you know that men do not carry other people's bills about in their pockets. We have most of us quite enough to do to settle our own. I at once concluded that Straker was leading a double life, and keeping a second establishment. The nature of the bill showed that there was a lady in the case, and one who had expensive tastes. Liberal as you are with your servants, one hardly expects that they can buy twenty-guinea walking dresses for their women. I questioned Mrs Straker as to the dress without her knowing it, and having satisfied myself that it had never reached her, I made a note of the milliner's address, and felt that by calling there with Straker's photograph, I could easily dispose of the mythical Derbyshire.

"From that time on, all was plain. Straker had led out the horse to a hollow where his light would be invisible. Simpson, in his flight, had dropped his cravat, and Straker had picked it up with some idea, perhaps, that he might use it in securing the horse's leg. Once in the hollow he had got behind the horse, and had struck a light, but the creature, frightened at the sudden glare, and with the strange instinct of animals feeling that some mischief was intended, had lashed out, and the steel shoe had struck Straker full on the forehead. He had already, in spite of the rain, taken off his overcoat in order to do his delicate task, and so, as he fell, his knife gashed his thigh. Do I make it clear?"

"Wonderful!" cried the Colonel. "Wonderful! You might have been there."

"My final shot was, I confess, a very long one. It struck me that so astute a man as Straker would not undertake this delicate tendon-nicking without a little practice. What could he practise on? My eyes fell upon the sheep, and I asked a question which, rather to my surprise, showed that my surmise was correct."

"You have made it perfectly clear, Mr Holmes."

"When I returned to London I called upon the milliner, who at once recognized Straker as an excellent customer, of the name of Derbyshire, who had a very dashing wife with a strong partiality for expensive dresses. I have no doubt that this woman had plunged him over head and ears in debt, and so led him into this miserable plot."

"You have explained all but one thing," cried the Colonel. "Where was the horse?"

"Ah, it bolted and was cared for by one of your neighbours. We must have an amnesty in that direction, I think. This is Clapham Junction, if I am not mistaken, and we shall be in Victoria in less than ten minutes. If you care to smoke a cigar in our rooms, Colonel, I shall be happy to give you any other details which might interest you."

BLACK BEAUTY
ANNA SEWELL

Black Beauty is telling the story of his experiences in the household of Lord Westland. He has been renamed Black Auster.

I MUST NOW SAY a little about Reuben Smith, who was left in charge of the stables when York, the head groom, went to London. No one more thoroughly understood his business than he did, and when he was all right, there could not be a more faithful or valuable man. He was gentle and very clever in his management of horses, and could doctor them almost as well as a farrier, for he had lived two years with a veterinary surgeon. He was a first-rate driver; he could take a four-in-hand, or a tandem, as easily as a pair. He was a handsome man, a good scholar, and had very pleasant manners. I believe everybody liked him; certainly the horses did; the only wonder was that he should be in an under situation, and not in the place of a head coachman like York: but he had one great fault, and that was the love of drink. He was not like some men, always at it; he used to keep steady for weeks or months together; and then he would break out and have a "bout" of it, as York called it, and be a disgrace to himself, a terror to his wife, and a nuisance to all that had to do with him. He was, however, so useful, that two or three times York had hushed the matter up, and kept it from the Earl's knowledge; but one night, when Reuben had to drive a party home from a ball, he was so drunk that he could not hold the reins, and a gentleman of the party had to mount the box and drive the ladies home. Of course this could not be hidden, and Reuben was at once dismissed; his poor wife and little children had to turn out of the pretty cottage by the Park gate and go where they could. But shortly before Ginger and I came Smith had been taken back again. York had interceded for him with the Earl, who was very kindhearted, and the man had promised faithfully that he would never taste another drop as long as he lived there. He had kept this promise so well that York thought he might be safely trusted to fill his place whilst he was away, and he was so clever and honest that no one else seemed so well fitted for it.

It was now early in April, and the family was expected home some time in May. The light brougham was to be freshly done up, and as Colonel Blantyre was obliged to return to his regiment, it was arranged that Smith should drive him to the town in it, and ride back; for this purpose he took the saddle with him, and I was chosen for the journey. At the station the Colonel put some money into Smith's hand and bid him goodbye, saying, "Take care of your young mistress, Reuben, and don't let Black Auster be hacked about by any random young prig that wants to ride him – keep him for the lady."

We left the carriage at the maker's, and Smith rode

me to the White Lion, and ordered the ostler to feed me well and have me ready for him at four o'clock. A nail in one of my front shoes had started as I came along, but the ostler did not notice it till just about four o'clock. Smith did not come into the yard till five, and then he said he should not leave till six, as he had met with some old friends. The man then told him of the nail, and asked if he should have the shoe looked to.

"No," said Smith, "that will be all right till we get home."

He spoke in a very loud, off-hand way and I thought it very unlike him not to see about loose nails in our shoes. He did not come at six, nor seven, nor eight, and it was nearly nine o'clock before he called for me, and then it was in a loud rough voice. He seemed in a very bad temper, and abused the ostler, though I could not tell what for.

The landlord stood at the door and said, "Have a care, Mr Smith!" but he answered angrily with an oath; and almost before he was out of the town he began to gallop, frequently giving me a sharp cut with his whip, though I was going at full speed. The moon had not yet risen, and it was very dark. The roads were stony, having been recently mended; going over them at this pace my shoe became looser, and when we were near the turnpike gate it came off.

If Smith had been in his right senses, he would have been sensible of something wrong in my pace; but he was too madly drunk to notice anything.

Beyond the turnpike was a long piece of road, upon which fresh stones had just been laid; large sharp stones, over which no horse could be driven quickly without risk of danger. Over this road, with one shoe gone, I was forced to gallop at my utmost speed, my rider meanwhile cutting into me with his whip, and with wild curses urging me to go still faster. Of course my shoeless foot suffered dreadfully; the hoof was broken and split down to the very quick, and the inside was terribly cut by the sharpness of the stones.

This could not go on; no horse could keep his footing under such circumstances, the pain was too great. I stumbled, and fell with violence on both my knees. Smith was flung off by my fall and owing to the speed I was going at, he must have fallen with great force. I soon recovered my feet and limped to the side of the road, where it was free from stones. The moon had just risen above the hedge, and by its light I could see Smith lying a few yards beyond me. He did not rise, he made one slight effort to do so, and then there was a heavy groan. I could have groaned too, for I was suffering intense pain both from my foot and knees; but horses are used to bearing their pain in silence. I uttered no sound, but I stood there and listened. One more heavy groan from Smith; but though he now lay in the full moonlight, I could see no motion. I could do nothing for him nor myself, but, oh! how I listened for the sound of horse, or wheels, or footsteps. The road was not much frequented, and at this time of the night we might stay for hours before help came to us. I stood watching and listening. It was a calm, sweet, April night; there were no sounds but a few low notes of a nightingale, and nothing moved but the white clouds near the moon, and a brown owl that flitted over the hedge. It made me think of the summer nights long ago, when I used to lie beside my mother in the green pleasant meadow at Farmer Grey's.

It must have been nearly midnight when I heard at a great distance the sound of a horse's feet. Sometimes the sound died away, then it grew clearer again and nearer. The road to Earlshall led through plantations that belonged to the Earl: the sound came in that direction, and I hoped it might be someone coming in search of us. As the sound came nearer and nearer, I was almost sure I could distinguish Ginger's step; a little nearer still, and I could tell she was in the dog-cart. I neighed loudly, and was overjoyed to hear an answering neigh from Ginger and men's voices. They came slowly over the stones, and stopped at the dark figure that lay upon the ground.

One of the men jumped out, and stooped down over it. "It is Reuben!" he said, "and he does not stir."

The other man followed and bent over him. "He's dead," he said; "feel how cold his hands are."

They raised him up, but there was no life, and his hair was soaked with blood. They laid him down again, and came and looked at me. They soon saw my cut knees.

"Why, the horse has been down and thrown him! Who would have thought the black horse would have done that? Nobody thought he could fall. Reuben must have been lying here for hours! Odd, too, that the horse has not moved from the place."

Robert then attempted to lead me forward. I made a step, but almost fell again.

"Hallo! He's bad in his foot as well as his knees; look here – his hoof is cut all to pieces, he might well come down, poor fellow! I tell you what, Ned, I'm afraid it hasn't been all right with Reuben! Just think of him riding a horse over these stones without a shoe! Why, if he had been in his right senses, he would just as soon have tried to ride him over the moon. I'm afraid it has been the old thing over again. Poor Susan! She looked awfully pale when she came to my house to ask if he had not come home. She made believe she was not a bit anxious, and talked of a lot of things that might have kept him. But for all that she begged me to go and meet him – but what must we do? There's the horse to get home as well as the body – and that will be no easy matter."

Then followed a conversation between them, till it was agreed that Robert as the groom should lead me, and that Ned must take the body. It was a hard job to get it into the dog-cart, for there was no one to hold Ginger; but she knew as well as I did what was going on, and stood as still as a stone. I noticed that, because, if she had a fault, it was that she was impatient in standing.

Ned started off very slowly with his sad load, and Robert came and looked at my foot again; then he took his handkerchief and bound it closely round, and so he led me home. I shall never forget that night walk; it was more than three miles. Robert led me on very slowly, and I limped and hobbled on as well as I could with great pain. I am sure he was sorry for me, for he often patted and encouraged me, talking to me in a pleasant voice.

At last I reached my own box and had some corn, and after Robert had wrapped up my knees in wet cloths, he tied up my foot in a bran poultice to draw out the heat, and cleanse it before the horse doctor saw it in the morning, and I managed to get myself down on the straw, and slept in spite of the pain.

The next day, after the farrier had examined my wounds, he said he hoped the joint was not injured, and if so, I should not be spoiled for work, but I should never lose the blemish. I believe they did the best to make a good cure, but it was a long and painful one; proud flesh, as they called it, came up in my knees, and was burnt out with caustic, and when at last it was healed, they put a blistering fluid over the front of both knees to bring all the hair off: they had some reason for this, and I suppose it was all right.

As Smith's death had been so sudden, and no one was there to see it, there was an inquest held. The landlord and ostler at the White Lion, with several other people, gave evidence that he was intoxicated when he started from the inn. The keeper of the toll-gate said he rode at a hard gallop through the gate; and my shoe was picked up amongst the stones, so that the case was quite plain to them, and I was cleared of all blame.

Everybody pitied Susan; she was nearly out of her mind; she kept saying over and over again, "Oh! he was so good – so good! It was all that cursed drink; why will they sell that cursed drink? Oh, Reuben, Reuben!" So she went on till after he was buried, and then, as she had no home or relations, she, with her six little children, was obliged once more to leave the pleasant home by the tall oak trees, and go into that great gloomy Union House.

BELLEROPHON

L. S. HYDE

WHEN THE SUMMER suns had scorched the plains and dried the rivers of Greece till hardly any green thing was left, there were meadows, high on the snowy sides of Mount Helicon, that were bright with soft young grasses, and dotted with flowers of every colour.

In these meadows were the most glorious fountains. At certain times they sent their waters spouting far up into the blue sky, whence they came tumbling down again, to rise once more in a fine spray, in which could be seen a thousand rainbows.

The most beautiful fountain of all, and the one where the water was the sweetest and the coolest, was called the Fountain of Hippocrene. The waters of this fountain had a wonderful magic. There had been a time when no such fountain was to be seen on Mount Helicon. One bright moonlight night Pegasus, the winged horse, alighted in these meadows. He uttered a silvery neigh, and then struck the ground a sharp blow with his hoof. Immediately this Fountain of Hippocrene gushed forth. Pegasus drank of its sweet waters, and then flew away, far above the clouds. But he sometimes came back to drink of those waters again. There was no place on earth where a plain mortal would be more likely to see him.

The Muses, too, haunted these beautiful meadows of Helicon. They were nine sisters, with hair so black that it seemed violet in the moonlight. On nights when a full moon was in the sky, they used to come and dance around the Fountain of Hippocrene. Some people believed that Pegasus belonged to them.

Shepherds who fed their sheep at the foot of Mount Helicon, and watched all night long, lest some prowling wolf should attack the flock, sometimes caught a glimpse of Pegasus or the Muses; but very few people in the towns below even believed that either the winged horse or the nine sisters really existed at all.

Now it happened one day that a certain young hero, named Bellerophon, came to Mount Helicon to look for Pegasus. He had been sent by a king to slay the Chimaera, a kind of monstrous dragon with three heads, that was laying waste the country in a certain part of Asia. He thought that, with the help of the winged horse, he might win an easy victory over any earth-born monster.

So, night after night, Bellerophon came to the Fountain of Hippocrene and watched for Pegasus. For a long time he could not see so much as a feather of the horse's glorious wings; although, once or twice, when the moon was shining more brightly than usual, he did think that a shadow passed lightly over the grass, but when he looked up, there was nothing to be seen. Another time he heard a sudden rush of wings, and caught a glimpse of something white among the trees.

At last, it chanced one night that he found a lost child on the lower slopes of Mount Helicon, and knowing that it was in great danger of being devoured by wild beasts, he took it to one of the shepherds who were watching their sheep near by. Then he went on to the spring, where he arrived much later than usual.

That night he saw Pegasus careering gaily about the meadows. The horse's silvery wings were held high over his back, and his dainty pink hoofs scarcely touched the ground. His whinnying was like the tremulous music of a flute; but when he saw Bellerophon, he spread his great white wings, and soared away up into the depths of the sky.

Catch Pegasus! Bellerophon saw that it was of no use to try, and gave it up. Then he lay down and slept on the soft grass of the meadow.

But people who slept near the Fountain of Hippocrene were apt to dream. While Bellerophon slept, he dreamed that Minerva stood at his side with a golden bridle in her hand. In the dream she gave him the bridle, and then Pegasus came up to him, and bent his beautiful head to have it put on.

He woke in the morning with the first sunbeams shining in his face, and found the golden bridle of his dream in his hands. The head-piece was set with jewels, and the whole bridle was so gorgeous that it seemed fit, even for so wonderful a horse as Pegasus.

Bellerophon did not go down to the town that day, but stayed on Mount Helicon and lived on berries and sweet acorns. When night came, he again waited by the fountain for Pegasus.

With a light heart, he went to his usual place, where he was screened by the bushes. He had hardly seated himself before he saw a faint white speck in the sky, which grew larger and larger, and soon took the shape of a winged horse.

As the beautiful creature descended lower, he began to fly in great circles, as you have seen a hawk fly. But his shining white wings were more like the wings of an albatross than like those of any other bird we know. He came lower, and lower, till his feet touched the meadow; and then he cantered up to Bellerophon, and held down his head for the jewelled bridle, just as he had done in Bellerophon's dream. A moment more, and the bridle was over his head.

A more gentle horse than Pegasus never lived, nor one fonder of his rider. He seemed willing to take the owner of the bridle for his master, and was obedient to the slightest touch of the rein. It was wonderful when he tried his wings. Up above the clouds he soared, with Bellerophon on his back. Who need fear the Chimaera now?

This Chimaera was a frightful monster with three heads – the head of a lion, the head of a goat, and the head of a snake. Its body was something like the shaggy body of a goat in the middle, but ended in a dragon's tail. When the creature was roused, it could belch out fire and smoke from its three cavernous throats. Nearly the whole of the mountainous country it inhabited was a waste of ashes. The few people who had not lost their lives, nor left their homes and their flocks but still inhabited that region, lived in constant terror of this creature. So if one brave enough and strong enough could be found, there was need of a hero to slay the Chimaera.

When Bellerophon felt that he had perfect control

of Pegasus, he guided him straight towards the mountains of the Chimaera. Pegasus, with all his wonderful power of flight, sped through the air like an arrow, and in a very short time was hovering over the cruel monster, which lay sprawling in the midst of the waste it had caused.

Obedient to Bellerophon's wish, Pegasus swooped straight down to within striking distance of the Chimaera. Then, a flash from Bellerophon's lance, and the goat's head hung limp. What a roar followed from the lion's head! All the air became filled with the sickening odour, and it began to grow dark with smoke. But Bellerophon and Pegasus were safe, high above the earth.

They waited till the monster was quiet again, then made another quick dash, and off went the lion's head. There was no roaring this time, and not so much fire and smoke, although the angry writhing of the creature was terrible to see. But the Chimaera could not follow Pegasus into the pure upper air.

Once more horse and rider dashed down, and the snake's head was severed from the Chimaera's body. Then the terrible fires burned themselves out, and that was the end of the Chimaera.

The people of that country soon learned that the Chimaera was dead, and came back to their homes. Not long after, the hills, that had been so grey and desolate, were covered with vineyards and growing crops.

After this, Bellerophon, with the help of Pegasus, performed other wonderful feats, and became very famous. He married a king's daughter, and received half of her father's kingdom.

At last he felt as if, mounted on Pegasus, he was as strong as the gods themselves, and might ascend to Olympus. One day he was foolish enough to make the attempt. Then Jupiter caused Pegasus to throw him. Blinded by the near sight of Olympus, and lamed by the fall, he wandered about, for many years, an unhappy, helpless old man.

The time came when the gods took Pegasus up to Mount Olympus, and let us hope that Bellerophon, too, reached Olympus at last.

HORSE IN THE HOUSE
WILLIAM CORBIN

*Melanie has a burning ambition: to bring her horse, Orbit,
right into her house . . .*

IT WAS THE SAME way the next morning, and the
mornings after that. Always something to be done,
never time for a delicious moment. Mom's lists were
long, and while neither Melanie nor Katie could in
justice complain of overwork, they complained anyway.
It made their tasks easier.

Orbit's schooling for civilized house visiting, on the
other hand, really was hard work, but naturally Melanie
didn't complain about that. It was something that she
had no intention of postponing any longer than it took
to make sure Orbit was ready, and on Thursday she
decided he was ready.

She made the announcement at breakfast, feeling
rather portentous about it. "This," she told Katie, "is the
day!"

"Uh-huh," said Katie, who was of course reading at
the table now that Mom wasn't around to stop her.

"Katie! I said, this is the day! Today I'm going to
bring Orbit into the house!"

"Oh!" Katie said, rejoining the world with a start.

"Jolly good show! Shall I ring up the press?"

"Press? Oh, Conrad. No, we'll have him tomorrow. This is just the dress rehearsal."

"All right, I'll get dressed."

By three o'clock that afternoon everything was ready. Every detail that Melanie could think of had been taken care of and she stood in the middle of the living-room frowning in concentration. She had removed the treacherous rug from the front hall and replaced it with a strip of old carpet she found in the basement, fastening it securely to the floor with carpet tacks. A little wedge of wood held the front door open and back against the wall on the chance that it might slam shut behind Orbit and startle him. The telephone receiver was off its cradle so that it couldn't ring unexpectedly. All the alarm clocks that hadn't run down had been silenced. Vases, ash-trays and other breakable items were stowed away in the hall cupboard. Katie had been briefed to keep an eye on the front drive in order to intercept salesmen or anybody else who might feel an urge to ring the doorbell.

As for Orbit, he was as clean as the day he was born, thoroughly exercised but not weary, hungry but not too hungry, and completely unaware that he was about to be honoured in a manner which seldom in the history of the world had fallen to the lot of a member of his species.

In the kitchen Katie was slicing carrots, potatoes and apples into a dishpan. This was the teatime snack which would be laid before the guest of honour at the dining-room table, which now stood bare of everything but a layer of newspapers. She looked up as Melanie came into the kitchen. "How about a dollop of mayonnaise?" Katie said. "It seems a little inhospitable just plain."

Melanie greeted this suggestion with the silence it deserved. She took a very deep breath. Her frown vanished and she smiled. "Well," she said, "here I go."

But instead of going, she looked at Katie again, feeling oddly shy. "You know," she added, "all of a sudden it isn't just a stupid job I've got to do because I said I would. It's like it was the first time I thought of it, a long time ago. It's something I *want* to do, even if it's silly. I'm – I'm all excited."

Katie put down her paring knife and turned, giving Melanie a strange, intent look.

One of her jokes was coming, Melanie thought, just a shade unhappily. Somehow it didn't seem the time for jokes. A moment later she was fervently telling herself that never again would she underestimate her sister Kathleen. Katie said nothing at all, but took a sudden, unexpected step, put her arms around Melanie, squeezing hard, and kissed her on the cheek.

A second later she was back at the draining-board, a potato in her hand. "That," she said, looking firmly at the potato, "was for my old age."

Melanie could only stare at her.

"We're going to remember this," Katie went on, slicing away at the potato. "All our lives." The irrepressible glint came into her eyes. "We'll click our false teeth and cackle about it. Now go on and get your great big clumsy guest. I'll be dreaming up some party talk to entertain him with."

On her way out to the barn Melanie found herself in the grip of a strange exhilaration unlike anything she had ever known before. It held an odd mixture of sadness.

When she saw Orbit waiting patiently in his stall, there was a quick catch in her throat. He was so beautiful, and he had never belonged to anyone but her . . .

Forcing herself into a mould of brisk efficiency, she led him into the tack-room and got down her new green and gold plaid saddle blanket. Securing it to his back with a surcingle, she slipped his show bridle on – the soft black leather one tastefully decorated with little strips and studs of real silver. The guest of honour would be dressed up, even if the hostess wasn't.

The reins in her hand, she led him through the little door, up the lane past the house and into the front yard. Katie was waiting at the front steps, looking idiotic in a frilly white organdie party apron she had dug out of one of Mom's drawers. With her shorts and bare legs the apron looked like some sort of chorus-girl outfit.

When Melanie halted Orbit in front of her she held out her hand graciously and said, "Star-Wanderer! My, but it's nice to see you! Do come in!"

Orbit sniffed the proffered hand appreciatively. It smelled like carrots and potatoes. But he had to snort a little, too, because there was a lot more of Katie and *it* smelled like bubble bath.

Melanie made a quick hoof inspection, just in case he might have picked up a sharp bit of gravel on the drive. Then she took the reins and peered out towards the road, feeling furtive, like a robber about to enter a bank. It wouldn't do to be seen leading a horse into a house; the story would be all over the county in thirty minutes.

There was no one to be seen. "Well," she said, smiling nervously at Katie, "here we come. You go on in and sort of keep out of the way."

Katie disappeared, and Melanie reached up and scrubbed Orbit's forehead with her knuckles to put him in a pleasant mood, talking animatedly to prove that nobody was nervous, everything was lovely, and delightful things were about to happen. Then, after a brief pause, she uttered a low but sharp and distinct "Hup!", snapped the reins taut and stepped through the door as though she hadn't a doubt in the world that once she got inside she would still have a horse along with her.

It worked, as she had known it would. The habit of instant obedience was too much a part of Orbit for him to behave in any other way – unless, of course, something unexpected were to happen.

Something unexpected happened almost immediately.

Since her ears were all but turned backwards like a cat's and her entire mind was concentrated in them, Melanie knew exactly what each of his four feet was doing, though of course she couldn't see any of them. First his right hind hoof clicked on the concrete slab outside the door, then his right forefoot struck with a muffled sound the length of carpet just inside the door. Next the left hind clicked on the concrete and the left fore thumped on the rug. So it went, until all four were on the carpet, still moving obediently forward, and Melanie herself was already through the hall and several steps into the living-room.

That was the point at which the unexpected happened. What Melanie had not once thought of was that a floor with a basement underneath it is not the same thing at all as a floor made of planks laid on hard, unyielding ground. There is a spring to such a floor, though it goes unnoticed by even the biggest human being, and certainly by a ninety-five-pound girl. But when that floor takes the moving weight of nearly a thousand pounds of piano – or of horse – it has to give somewhere, and it has to crack and creak a little in the process. Furthermore, the farther the weight moves towards the centre of the room, away from the supporting walls or foundation, the more the floor sags and the louder it protests.

If Melanie's education had included piano moving, she would have been aware of these facts and prepared to deal with them. It hadn't, and when her straining ears caught the first faint ominous cracking sound from beneath her feet, her ears, body and voice all reacted with the instantaneous speed of an electric current suddenly switched on in a machine. In far less than a second, the floor cracked, her ear caught the sound and bounced it to her brain, which told her that an uncertain floor would frighten Orbit to an instant halt. Her brain then told her to halt him before he could halt himself, so that he wouldn't think it was his own idea, and at the same moment told her arm and her voice to do the halting.

"Ho!" she said sharply and gave a snap of the reins. Orbit stopped and looked round with an air of faint surprise. She patted his neck and put her brain to work at a less hair-trigger level. Now that she was aware of the problem, she knew instinctively that the farther Orbit went the shakier the floor would feel to him, and that meant trouble. The hardest thing she had ever done with him – the only battle she had come within a mere gasp of losing to him, was getting him to cross a tiny wooden bridge over a stream down by the river. It had taken more than an hour, worn them both out, and lathered them with sweat, but in the end Melanie had won. He had crossed the bridge. Not in his way, either, which would have been by means of a series of frantic, bone-jarring leaps, but in Melanie's way – a dignified and mannerly walk. He still feared and hated bridges, of course, and always would, but he would cross them if she told him to, and that was all that mattered.

This now was quite another matter. At the bridge there had been plenty of room for his skittish dancing from side to ride, his rearing and plunging and fighting the bit. Here there was no room at all. Any undisciplined behaviour would be disastrous.

She could of course back him out the way he had come, give up the whole insane idea. Instantly she rejected the thought. She couldn't give up, not when she had barely started. Melanie was an extremely determined girl, and though neither of them knew it, she had Orbit to thank – at least for a lot of it. But how to proceed from here?

"Great Caesar, but he looks big in here!" Melanie had to control a start as Katie spoke, having actually forgotten there was anybody around but herself and Orbit. Katie was leaning in the archway that connected the living- and dining-rooms, looking rather awed. "He makes me think," she went on, "of a puppet show I saw when I was little. At the end, the man who was working them jumped down on the stage. Scared me to death. I thought he was a giant."

"Katie," said Melanie suddenly. "Go get a couple of carrots." She had been thinking much too hard to pay attention to anything that was said to her, and was not conscious that she was ordering her sister around.

Katie moved to obey, then looked doubtfully from Melanie to Orbit and back. "Is there — anything wrong?"

"Not yet there isn't," Melanie replied, sounding gay and cheerful for Orbit's benefit. "It's the darn floor. It's going to make him spooky. I can tell."

Katie said, "Oh. And carrots will help. I'm on my way."

She was back in a moment, holding the carrots out towards Melanie. Orbit's ears pricked forward.

Melanie shook her head, "No, you keep them. I'll explain — and I'll sound like a nut while I'm doing it but don't pay any attention to that. I always talk sort of silly because he likes it and it keeps him nice and calm."

She chatted away in her high little-girl voice, explaining quickly about the floor and the bridge. She hadn't even finished when Katie's eyes lighted up. "I get it," she said. "And I've got an idea. Why don't you just keep him there while I drag the couch out in the middle. It's a monster for weight, and if I get on top of it maybe it'll sag the floor as far as it's going to sag. Then you can walk him around it."

"Gee!" Melanie said. "I never would have thought of that. My carrot idea was ten times as complicated." She hesitated, glancing at Orbit, who thus far was as relaxed as if he were in his stall, and added, "Of course, we may have to use both ideas."

Katie went into action. The couch was indeed a monster, custom-built to fit Pop when he was in a "stretching-out mood" on Sunday afternoons. Heaving and tugging at first one end and then the other, she gradually got it out into the middle of the room. In the process the floor cracked and groaned a time or two, prompting Katie to exclaim triumphantly, "It's sagging! I *told* you. Beautiful, beautiful sag!"

When the couch was in place, she toppled over backwards and lay flat on the seat, addressing the ceiling. "There! Me and this old couch, we probably weigh more than Orbit."

A horrible thought struck Melanie. "Gee!" she said. "With him and the couch both, do you think the floor will, you know, break through?"

The answer was a peal of laughter, and then, "You *are* in a state! Pop practically rebuilt this house. Elephants could play basketball in here!"

Reassured, Melanie took a new grip on the reins. "All right," she said. "We're on our way. Hup!"

Orbit moved forward readily and Melanie turned him to the right, heading for the space between the couch and the wall. There was no more sound from the floor, but with Orbit's first step she felt a faint trembling beneath her feet as the framework of the house adjusted itself to the moving weight. He felt it too. From the corner of her eye she saw his ears snap back in a sign of displeasure. This was something he definitely did not like.

Tightening her grip on the reins, Melanie kept going. There was nothing else to do. From somewhere in the house came a rattle of dishes, and Melanie started talking loudly, saying whatever came into her head.

She passed behind the couch, rounded the corner, and passed the archway to the dining-room. Katie's head appeared to be turning all the way round, like an owl's. On the wall beside the archway hung a mirror just above an antique occasional table that had belonged to Melanie's great-grandmother. The table, which ordinarily held a bowl of flowers and a pair of china figurines, was bare now, like every other surface in the room, and because of its bareness looked even more priceless and perishable than usual.

Probably because Melanie was already thinking ahead, considering what the next move would be, she made the second right turn without taking full account of the width of Orbit's hindquarters. As he came round to pass in front of the couch, his left hind leg gently brushed against the little table and it tipped to the right. Her eye caught sight of it a split second too late. It was going to crash to the floor. The crash would startle Orbit . . . She halted him instantly, her eyes riveted to the teetering antique in a kind of helpless horror.

Farther tipped the table. Farther still . . . then it paused and began to tip back the way it had come. Once its legs hit the floor it toppled the other way, then back and forth until it jiggled itself at last to its original motionless state. Melanie let her breath escape in an enormous sigh, and Katie said in a low, expressionless tone, "Mellie, how do I look with grey hair?"

Melanie laughed and was startled to find that the laughter came easily. For no very sound reason the tension was suddenly gone and she felt as completely relaxed as if she had Orbit in the middle of the pasture rather than in the middle of the living-room. What had she been so afraid of anyway? After all, she was Melanie and Orbit was Orbit, and she could handle him every bit as well in one place as another. Just to prove it, she hugged him hard, turned him round in a small, tight circle and walked him round the couch in the opposite direction, bringing him to a halt again with his head towards the dining-room.

Katie, who had lain down again, cradling her head on her folded arms while she watched the performance, said, "Now that I've got used to the idea, I sort of like it. A horse gives a certain chic to a house, don't you think?" Changing her voice to an overripe contralto that was supposed to sound like a society lady's, she went on, "I took tea with Mrs Webb today – Mrs Webb the aah–tist, donchu know? And I met the most chaahm–ing horse. He was telling me—"

"Hey!" Melanie interrupted. "You're supposed to be the hostess around here. The guest is hungry."

Katie rolled off the couch, landing on her feet. "Coming right up!" she said, and went out to the kitchen. Returning with the dishpan, she set it in the middle of the dining-table, pulled up a chair for herself and sat down.

Melanie hupped Orbit again and he started up, this time with his ears slanting eagerly forward, all thought of shaky doors and other trivial matters erased from his mind by the lovely raw-vegetable fragrances coming from the dishpan. Halting him with his nose above the table and his tail still in the living-room, Melanie dropped the reins and stood back a step, watching.

After a moment of this Katie asked, "What are you doing – waiting for him to ask for a fork?"

Melanie shook her head, then half turned, pretending not to watch him. He stood for at least a full minute without moving anything but his eyes and nostrils.

"I get it," Katie said. "Discipline." She paused, then added protestingly, "Gads, Mellie! The poor beast is dying of temptation."

About to relent, Melanie suddenly saw him begin to reach out his nose – slowly, cautiously. Still pretending not to notice, she let him reach almost to the pan. "Aaaaaaaaah!" The exclamation was a combination of warning, reproval and scorn, and Orbit's head snapped violently back to its proper position, the bridle jangling sharply. He managed to look guilty. "You know better than that," Melanie told him reprovingly. "You're in the house, and you've got to watch your manners! You didn't really think you'd get away with that, did you? Did you really think it would work?" The bridle jangled again and the trailing reins whipped in all directions as Orbit shook his head.

"All right, then." She let him wait a few moments longer, then reached up, unbuckled the bridle and slipped it off his head, holding it while he pushed the bit out with his tongue. Then she slapped his neck and he lost no time in helping himself to this unscheduled meal. Chewing loudly and placidly away at his first delicious mouthful, he raised his head and peered down at Katie with a sort of benevolent expression. Propping her chin in the heel of one hand, Katie peered back at him. "It's funny," she said, "but he makes me feel right at home, as if I ought to be passing the biscuits or something."

Katie had prepared an even more generous serving than her instructions called for, and soon Melanie got tired of standing. Pulling up another chair, she too sat down across from her sister and beside Orbit, resting both elbows on the table.

For a long time neither of them said anything. They merely sat, staring up at Orbit in a kind of trance induced by the leisurely rhythm of his crunching. After a while Melanie dropped her eyes and quite by accident encountered Katie's. They stared at each other, a little blankly at first, then Katie giggled. So did Melanie. A moment later the sound of Orbit's chewing was drowned out by their whoops and shrieks of laughter.

Orbit's ears twitched back, then forward again. His jaws stopped moving, he turned his head towards Melanie and peered at her, his big eyes looking mildly astonished and not altogether approving. This sent Katie into a new spasm of mirth, in which Melanie promptly joined her. They both tried to speak, and both failed utterly.

BANKS AND MOROCCO
RUTH MANNING-SANDERS

IN THE REIGN of Elizabeth the First, there lived in London a man named Banks, who had a little horse called Morocco. Morocco was a bay, with a long tail, a hog mane, and a flowing forelock. Banks taught him to perform, and showed him in the yard of an inn called La Belle Sauvage.

Morocco was very clever at his tricks; he could dance, walk on his hind legs, box with his master, standing up in manly fashion and hitting out right and left with his front feet; he could jump through a hoop, say yes and no by nodding or shaking his head, find anything you hid, however small, tell you the number of spots on a card or dice by scraping a forefoot so many times on the ground, do sums in the same manner, and point out any particular person in the audience, such as the man who had a green feather in his hat, or the woman who was carrying a basket, or the fattest person, or the thinnest person, or the one who was wearing a blue coat – he could even tell you the number of buttons on the coat!

People crowded into La Belle Sauvage yard to see Morocco go through his tricks; he became so famous that verses were written about him, and Shakespeare and other well-known writers made mention of him.

Indeed, so wonderful did it seem to the Elizabethan audiences that a mere horse could do such things, that some people even said that Banks must be a sorcerer, and that Morocco must be bewitched. For in those days everyone believed in sorcery and witchcraft.

Of course Morocco wasn't bewitched, neither was Banks a sorcerer; he trained Morocco as you would train your dog, with a lot of patience, a lot of praises, and a lot of rewards, such as carrots and sugar.

But, you might ask, how would that teach a horse to count, or to tell one person from another in the audience? It didn't teach him to count, nor did it teach him to tell one person from another. But what it did teach him was to watch his master with all his eyes, and listen with all his ears to the sounds his master made. When Morocco was telling his numbers and doing his sums by scraping the ground with his hoof, Banks would be clicking his finger and thumb together, making such a tiny little sound that no one but Morocco could hear it. As long as the clickings went on, Morocco scraped with his hoof, and when the clickings stopped, Morocco stopped scraping.

Then Banks would bow right and left, and say, "There you are, ladies and gentlemen, the number is nine! Correct?" And the people would gasp with astonishment, and applaud; and some of them would whisper, "That animal's no ordinary horse! He's the Devil in the shape of a horse, that's what he is!"

Banks carried a wand, too, and the little movements of the wand gave Morocco his clue for some of his other tricks, such as pointing out people, or standing up on his hind legs, or going down on his knees to bow . . .

After some years, Banks got tired of sticking about in the inn yard; he was something of a gipsy, he could speak several languages, and he loved to wander. So what did he do, but put Morocco on board ship, and take him over to France. He went to Paris, and made a lot of money there, and then he wandered on southward till he came to Orleans.

The French people were even more bewildered by Morocco's clever tricks than the English had been, and they, too, began to whisper to each other that "the horse was no ordinary horse". The whisperings grew to loud mutterings, and the loud mutterings grew to threats: Banks was a sorcerer, the horse "had a devil", no sorcerer could be allowed to live; there was only one thing to do with them.

"Burn the sorcerer and his horse with him!" they cried. "Tie them to two stakes, make a big fire round them, and burn them to ashes!"

What was Banks to do? Here he was in Orleans, with the whole town crying out against him, and the monks, especially, accusing him of sorcery. He couldn't get away, and it seemed that he and poor, innocent Morocco must suffer martyrdom.

But Banks wasn't a showman for nothing. He kept his wits about him, and demanded that he should be allowed to meet his accusers face to face and be given a fair trial. And the monks agreed.

So Banks and Morocco were brought into a large hall, with a clear space left for them in the middle of it. And sitting and standing all round them were the mayor and the town councillors and officials, and the abbot and the monks, and as many of the townsfolk as could squeeze themselves in. The place was packed, and there was a huge throng gathered outside the hall, too; for there was no room in the hall for all the people who were eagerly waiting to see Banks and Morocco led away to be burned at the stake.

If Banks was in a fright, he didn't show it. And, of course, Morocco didn't know but that this was quite an ordinary day . . . So he stood quietly, waiting to be told what to do. Such a handsome little animal with his glossy, shining coat, his neat little head, his long tail, and his dainty legs and feet – how could anyone be so cruel as to think of burning him alive?

Banks cleared his throat and began a little speech: "Your worship, the mayor," he said. "Your honours, the town councillors and officers, my lord abbot and very reverend monks, and you esteemed townsfolk of Orleans, we have been accused, my horse and I, of devilry and witchcraft. But I thank you all that we are not to be condemned without proof. I know, if you will give me your attention, that I can prove to you that we are not devils and sorcerers, but honest and God-fearing creatures, my horse and I."

"Prove it then, and be quick about it!" somebody shouted.

Banks held up his hand, and spoke loudly and slowly. "I am going to prove it. If I may have your attention, please!"

Now whilst Banks was making this little speech, he was turning from one to another in the audience. He was looking for something, and very soon his quick eye found it. In the front of the audience sat a dignified old fellow, wearing a cloak and a high-crowned hat; and fastened on the front of his hat was a crucifix.

"Now, Morocco," says Banks. "Attention! Look at me!"

Morocco lifted his beautiful head, and his big, intelligent eyes watched his master.

"Can you point out the gentleman in this gathering who is wearing a crucifix in his hat?"

The wand that Banks was swinging so carelessly in his right hand gave the tiniest little upward movement. Morocco nodded his head.

"You can? Then let these good people see you do it." The carelessly swinging wand was now making tiny circular movements. Morocco began moving round the ring of breathlessly watching people. When he came to the dignified old fellow he stopped, stretched out his nose, and very lightly touched the old fellow's knee.

The watching crowd gasped. How could they know that Banks' left hand, tucked into his belt in such a careless fashion, had clicked finger and thumb together.

"Very good!" says Banks. "Now, Morocco, kneel down before the Holy Cross."

Obediently Morocco knelt, for the point of the rod was resting on the ground.

"Very good!" said Banks again. He stepped back, flung out his arms and cried in a ringing voice, "And now, most worthy people, Morocco is going to prove to you all that he is not a devil, but is indeed a most good and Christian horse . . . Rise, Morocco. Rise and kiss the cross!"

Would Morocco understand? Would he do it? He had kissed his master often; and many a time he had picked out and kissed the prettiest girl in the yard of La

Belle Sauvage. But he had never kissed a crucifix, and now both their lives depended on it! The clue for "kiss" was the word itself, and the reward was sugar. But there was no clue for "crucifix". What if Morocco were merely to kiss the man, instead of the cross? Oh, if Banks could but sprinkle a little sugar on that crucifix! But he dared not move forward, dared make no visible sign!

He could feel the sweat pouring down his back. For what seemed to him an endless time, but was really scarcely the passing of a second, he held the image of the crucifix steadily in his mind, willing with all his might that the image might pass from his mind to Morocco's . . . Ah—h!

Morocco rose, stretched out his glossy neck, bent his head over the man in the high-crowned hat – and mumbled the crucifix with soft lips!

There was a moment's breathless silence in the hall. Then a tremendous roar broke out: they were all on their feet, shouting, clapping, waving hats and handkerchiefs, huzzaing.

"He has kissed the Cross! The horse has kissed the Cross! Long live the good Christian, Banks! Long life to the good Christian horse, Morocco! Now we know that he has not a devil, for no devil dare touch the Cross!"

In the centre of the applauding crowd, Banks and Morocco knelt together. Morocco was feeling very pleased with himself – he loved applause! But Banks was near to fainting. There was a mist before his eyes; he could scarcely see, scarcely hear. He had saved Morocco and himself from a dreadful death. But the strain had been appalling.

As quickly as he could, he got himself and Morocco out of the country. And he never ventured into France again.

THE GHOST IN THE TOP MEADOW

CHRISTINE PULLEIN-THOMPSON

WE HAD NOT LIVED at the Grange for long. It was an ideal place for us as it had six acres and stabling for eight horses. I was schooling in the top meadow when I first saw Philippa. I was attempting to ride a dressage test and everything was going wrong. Flicka simply would not walk, and every few minutes her quarters would swing outside the arena I had marked with stones. As the rally for which I was schooling was less than a week away, I was beginning to feel desperate.

I had just dismounted and was shouting, "Will you stand still, you idiot!" when a female suddenly appeared from the hedge and standing a bare three yards away said, "Calm down. It's your fault. You're holding your pony too tight. Your stirrups are at least six inches too short, and your curb chain is twisted."

My mouth fell open with surprise as I stared at this apparition who spoke with such authority. Walking towards me, she continued in the same authoritative voice, "Turn your curb chain in a clockwise direction; it should lie comfortably in the chin groove. That's better. Now get up and let down your stirrups – you ride longer for dressage. Sit deep into your saddle." And she touched me with a hand lighter than a feather.

"Use your back and seat. Don't just wiggle your bottom," she said. "My God, you're terrible. You're just like a sack of potatoes. Now then, walk on, on a loose rein. Let your poor pony drop her nose and relax. That's better."

When she was more than a few yards away, I could no longer see her; but I could still hear her voice and it had a strange tone to it, like a voice in a dream. Yet it was not a dream but completely and utterly real.

And, amazingly, her instructions worked. Straight away Flicka improved, so that quite soon I was trotting round my pathetic arena without any trouble.

Soon she moved into the middle and started to shout instructions and sometimes I could see her and sometimes I couldn't.

"Change the rein," she called. "Now sitting trot. Prepare to halt. Sit down. Don't tug. Halt. What's your name?"

"Mark," I answered, trying to get her into focus, but seeing only bits of her, the edges but not the centre.

"Halt, Mark. That was terrible. Do you call that straight?" she shouted, coming into focus again. "Try it once more."

I could feel myself improving. Flicka felt different too, more relaxed and supple, she dropped her nose, her hindlegs were engaged and she had impulsion.

"That's enough for today," said my instructor suddenly. "Do you want another lesson tomorrow? You haven't much time, have you?" and she patted Flicka with a transparent hand and she actually seemed to like it.

"Yes please, if it's not too much trouble," I answered.

"Fine. My name is Philippa. See you tomorrow then. Same time, same place. And come in a plain eggbutt snaffle. You'll get extra marks for a snaffle and your pony doesn't need a pelham. And clean your tack; it's as stiff as cardboard." And with that she vanished into the hedge again, leaving my mind in a turmoil.

Riding back to the stable, I decided I would tell no one. The whole incident was so fantastic that no one would believe me anyway. They will think I'm mad, or spoil it somehow, I thought, dismounting. But I had not reckoned with my little sister Clare. She was in Flicka's manger playing with the kittens born three weeks ago.

"Who on earth were you talking to? I looked but I couldn't see anyone. It wasn't Flicka, was it?" she asked.

"I was pretending I had an instructor," I lied, carrying my tack to the saddle room. "It helps me concentrate."

"I didn't know you could act so well! Perhaps you should be in the school play," suggested Clare. "I'll tell Mr Phipps."

"You dare," I shouted.

"Personally I think you're going bonkers," continued Clare, putting down the kittens. "Your eyes look funny, as though you've been seeing things. And you were talking like a woman."

"Just shut up, will you?" I shouted.

The next lesson went even better. When it finished, Philippa said, "There's an old tennis marker in the bean shed. Put some whitewash or ceiling white on it and use it to mark out a proper dressage arena. The right size will be on your dressage sheet. We'll start doing bits of the test tomorrow and perhaps some jumping. The day after, you'd better give Flicka a hack or she'll be getting stale. And remember to ride her up to the bridle whatever you're doing, and make her go straight."

I wanted to say, "Can I pay you?" or, "Come in for a drink," but I could not imagine her wanting either.

"Thank you very much," I said instead.

"Don't mention it. See you tomorrow, then." She patted Flicka and she looked pleased as though it was a very special sort of pat, and then she was gone.

This time Clare was leaning over the gate as I rode back to the stable. "Well, at it again. You even said thank you at the end. What's going on?" Her plaits were tight around her face and her voice was accusing.

"Nothing. Absolutely nothing," I said, riding past.

"I shall tell Mummy, or Daddy when he comes home from work. I shall tell them you are going bonkers," Clare called after me.

"You dare. You do and I'll kill you," I yelled and then, leaping off Flicka, I seized her plaits and twisted them round and round her head until she screamed.

"You dare," I repeated but without much conviction, because I knew I could not trust my little sister, that sooner or later she would tell someone and spoil everything.

I spent the afternoon marking out a dressage arena with the old tennis marker which Philippa had told me about. Mum was delighted that I had found something to do, that for once I was not loafing about getting on her nerves, or deafening her with my stereo system. Clare looked at me out of the corners of her small grey-green eyes, but remained silent.

I took my dressage test in my pocket for the next

lesson and read it out loud to Philippa.

"Ah, much like the old test," she commented. "We must concentrate on your transitions. You must not lose control as you change pace, one pace should glide naturally into the other."

"Are you pleased with the new arena?" I asked, looking past her to the hedge, behind which something was moving on all fours.

"Yes, it's wizard. Absolutely spot on," she answered, sounding gloriously old-fashioned. "Are you ready? Try to enter straight. And remember, a nice bow to the judge with your hat off."

Flicka went marvellously. I had never known her go so well before. Even Philippa was pleased. "When is the great day?" she asked me as we finished the test.

"The rally is in three days' time. I would like to get selected for the Horse Trials team, but I don't suppose I will," I answered.

"Do not despair. Hack tomorrow; then we can run through the test the day before. That should do the trick," Philippa told me, and for a moment I forgot that she was not quite real. "How about some jumping? There's the hedge and a nice little fence into the spinney," she suggested.

Years ago someone had made two jumping places in the long thorn hedge between the top meadow and the middle meadow and a little rail fence into the spinney. Flicka flew them, while Philippa called, "Steady. Keep her balanced. You're not going round the National. Well done," she said, as I stopped beside her. "Just remember to pull up your stirrups a couple of holes before you start jumping next time. You went round with a dressage seat. Goodbye." And she was gone again.

Clare met me by the field gate. There was a gleam in her eyes which I did not like. "I saw her over the hedge. I know your secret, Mark. I saw her with my own eyes. I want a lesson from your ghost, Mark. I need help, or I shall never pass C Test," she said, her eyes flashing, daring me to refuse.

"She's my instructor, not yours," I said.

"You can ask. You can't be that selfish," she whined. "And she's not your property, anyway, Mark."

"I'll think about it," I said, unsaddling.

If you knew my sister, her next remark would not surprise you: "If you don't, I'll tell Daddy, and that will put an end to it."

"Why not tell Mum as well," I said.

"I shall put an end to it," she repeated. "I don't know how, but I will."

And I knew she would. She's that kind of sister.

"All right. I'll see what I can do. But she's only a ghost and quite old, so she may not want to take you on as well," I said.

My last lesson before the rally was fantastic. Everything went marvellously. At the end I said, "I'm awfully sorry to bother you, Philippa, but I was wondering whether you might be able to help my little sister too. She's hoping to pass C Test this summer."

Philippa laughed and floated to the hedge and back before saying, "I know all about C Test. Is she a nice girl?"

(And what could I say – "awful"?)

"Sometimes."

"I'll have a go then," she said.

"I wish we could pay you something," I told her. "I don't like putting upon you in this way."

"I don't want money. It is the root of all evil," she cried in a shrill, excited voice. "I hate the stuff. And what would I do with it? I don't need it, thank God."

"Thank you," I said. We were quite near one another now, so that I could see her more clearly than ever before. She was wearing the same clothes as she had when we first met. She must have died in them, I thought.

Then she raised a transparent hand with fingers like glass, waved and was gone.

Flicka behaved marvellously at the rally. There were congratulations all round.

"What have you done to her? She's fantastic," said one of my rivals. "Where have you been?"

"I've found a new instructor," I said.

"Tell. Tell us who."

"Not likely," I answered quickly. "She's fully booked."

I was selected for the Horse Trials team. Our District Commissioner congratulated me in person saying, "Your progress is astounding. I wish you could get your instructor to come here. We would pay whoever it is to be our team trainer."

"She's not interested in money. And she doesn't want any more pupils. She's old and she does it as a favour. Sorry," I said.

"What a pity. Try to make her change her mind, Mark. If she can help you so much in a week, she could improve this branch out of all recognition," continued our District Commissioner. "We would be champions within a year."

★

Two days later I was saying, "Philippa, this is my little sister, Clare," and Clare was muttering, "I'm not little."

"Oh, the one who wants to pass C Test. How do you do," said Philippa holding out her hand.

Clare kept her hands tight on her reins. She had no intention of shaking hands with a ghost. She had never seen Philippa so close before and her complexion had turned a shade paler. "What's it like being a ghost?" she asked.

Philippa ignored the question. Looking at Clare's dark brown pony, Holly, she said, "He's a Dartmoor, isn't he?"

"That's right," agreed Clare nervously.

"Your saddle needs stuffing. It's nearly on his withers. Take it to Mr Bradbury. He's a wizard saddler and he'll only charge you a fiver."

"Mr Bradbury? He's not there any more. He hasn't been for years. It's Paxton and Co. now and it will cost forty pounds. I know, because Mum asked," replied Clare, who is utterly devoid of tact.

"Shut up," I muttered. "Just shut up."

The lesson was the best I have ever had. Flicka had a wonderful slow canter now, as slow as her walk, or almost, and yet full of impulsion. I only had to close my fingers on the reins when I wanted to stop, or to close my legs against her sides to increase pace. It was more like magic than reality.

"I am so grateful," I said at the end of the lesson. "I simply don't know how to thank you."

"Don't then," Philippa said, floating away. "I enjoy it. I was always happy in this field."

"Whew, I'm stiff. I can hardly move," moaned Clare. "Do you think we'll look like her when we are dead? I couldn't shake her hand, I just couldn't."

"So I noticed. I think you were most ill-mannered. Poor Philippa, she looked very hurt," I answered.

"But there's no expression on her face," complained Clare. "It's like a mask, a pale, terrifying mask. So how could she look hurt?"

It might have gone on like that forever. I might have competed in the Badminton Horse Trials or represented Britain at the Olympics if Clare could have kept a secret. But Clare was only eleven, with masses of friends. She also liked doing good deeds as long as they were not too much bother, and she liked giving presents if she could get someone else to pay for them. So it was not long before she was offering Philippa's instruction to all her friends. I tried to stop her. I ranted and raved and called her unrepeatable names, but to no effect.

"You must come," she told her nasty little friends. "She's a ghost and it's absolutely free." And of course they came in droves, for who could resist such an invitation – free instruction *and* a ghost?

I was furious, but Philippa seemed to enjoy it. "I love a big class," she said. "But not more than twelve, more than that is counter-productive."

Presently there was a waiting list, and I suppose it was inevitable that before long parents would start asking about such an amazing instructor.

No one knows who actually spilt the beans; but on a muzzy September day, when the top meadow was speckled with mushrooms and the hedges purple with blackberries, the end came.

Afterwards I blamed myself. I wept. I shook Clare until her teeth rattled and her face turned purple. I slammed doors and locked myself in my bedroom and tore my riding shirt to shreds. I could not eat. I wanted to die. For two terrible days I went berserk, but Philippa never returned.

There were twelve riders in the class that day, nearly all female, their eager faces pink with pleasure under their peaked riding caps, their ponies cleaner than they had been in years. They kept pushing inwards the better to see Philippa and at intervals they giggled shrilly, rather like delighted birds descending on an unexpected harvest of food.

I do not know exactly when someone's parents first appeared with a keen newspaperman in tow. No one had asked permission. I just became aware of spectators by the gate and felt the hair stand up along my spine. They could not see Philippa yet. The younger riders were practising the turn on the forehand with Philippa waving a transparent hand, her face lit by some unearthly inner light, so that it glowed visibly like a lantern.

"Well done!" she cried enthusiastically. "You get better every time. Just a little more impulsion as you halt."

Seeing the strangers, I was overcome by an appalling sense of doom. I wanted to shout, "Go away, what are you doing here?" but so great was the feeling that I was rendered speechless.

So they advanced chattering, insanely normal, like people going to a party, the newspaperman oozing eagerness like a terrier scenting a rabbit. *What a story!* shining all over his ruddy face.

When I found words, they were too late, for they had reached Philippa's orbit by then and the newspaperman was priming his camera, and then adjusting the filter with a hand shaking with excitement.

"Don't!" I shouted. "Please don't."

But too late, for at the same moment he pressed a switch and there was an enormous flash, and Philippa fell like a heap of clothes on a stick. There was nothing where she had stood but charred earth, and I knew with awful certainty that this was final, that now she was really dead for ever and ever, and that she would never come back again.

I leapt from Flicka like someone possessed, and seizing the camera flung it on the ground and jumped on it screaming, "You've killed her. Are you satisfied now? She's dead! She'll never come back!" Tears were streaming down my face.

And the silly children who had caused it all started to scream and cry and turn for home . . .

"Stop it, Mark, stop it," cried my mother who had appeared, alarmed by the noise, for now I had the newspaperman by the throat. "What's the matter? What's come over you?" she shrieked. Then someone led me to the house as though I was mentally ill, while another led Flicka to the stable, and I kept saying over and over again, "They've killed her! She was the best instructor I ever had and they killed her!"

It took me a long time to recover. For weeks I could not bear to enter the top meadow, for days Flicka remained bored and unridden, and I spoke not a word to Clare.

But time heals all and, odd to relate, some six weeks later when I was in the forge watching Flicka shod, I heard the story of Philippa. Flicka was having a hind shoe nailed on when a bent old man entered the forge and looking at me, said, "So you are the young man I keep hearing about. The one who's been having lessons from Miss Philippa, who's walking around with a broken 'eart, or so they're saying at the Coach and Horses."

"Yes. But she's dead now, and she won't come back," I replied mournfully.

He looked at me with a twinkle in his eye and said, "And you wouldn't be the first 'eart she's broken. What a girl she was! She an' 'er sisters had stables at your place, you know. They started with nothing, built it up from scratch, like. What girls they were; but she were the star, weren't she, Frank?" he asked, addressing the blacksmith who would never see fifty again.

"Yes, we always called her the boss; she ran it," he said.

"They had forty 'orses, you know. There was a lot more stabling then and they rented all the paddocks around. Oh, the village was different then, full of colour it was," the old man continued, his eyes brightening as he talked.

"The other two married, but Philippa stayed on. She could ride anything, you know, train it perfect, all done by kindness too. But it was an 'orse what killed her in the end. She couldn't stop working, you know, and she wasn't well at the time; she was just getting over pneumonia, wheezing terrible she was." The old man was sitting on a bench now, his gnarled hands clasped between his knees. "She took an 'orse no one could ride to the top meadow. She 'ad 'im on the lunge, see. No one knows what really happened but they found 'er with the rein tangled round 'er neck and the 'orse standing over 'er and they swore the 'orse was crying. 'E never gave any more trouble, but she was dead. You should 'ave seen the funeral. You couldn't get in the church for people. They came from miles away and the village 'as never been the same since. She was only forty, you know."

"Thank you for telling me," I said. "I knew she was the sort of person you meet only once in a lifetime. I miss her unbearably, and I only knew her for a short time."

"Perhaps she's at rest now," the blacksmith said, looking at my anguished face. "Perhaps it's better that way. No one should go on working when they're dead."

"But she loved it. She was so happy," I answered. And I had to look away and blink back my tears.

STRIDER: THE STORY OF A HORSE
LEO TOLSTOY

NESTER MOUNTED the gelding by the short stirrup, unwound his long whip, straightened his coat out from under his knee, seated himself in the manner peculiar to coachmen, huntsmen, and horsemen, and jerked the reins. The gelding lifted his head to show his readiness to go where ordered, but did not move. He knew that before starting there would be much shouting, and that Nester, from the seat on his back, would give many orders to Váska, the other groom, and to the horses. And Nester did shout: "Váska! Hullo, Váska! Have you let out the brood mares? Where are you going, you devil? Now then! Are you asleep . . . Open the gate! Let the brood mares get out first!" – and so on.

The gate creaked. Váska, cross and sleepy, stood at the gate-post holding his horse by the bridle and letting the other horses pass out. The horses followed one another and stepped carefully over the straw, smelling at it: fillies, yearling colts with their manes and tails cut, suckling foals, and mares in foal carrying their burden heedfully, passed one by one through the gateway. The fillies sometimes crowded together in twos and threes, throwing their heads across one another's backs and hitting their hoofs against the gate, for which they received a rebuke from the grooms every time. The foals sometimes darted under the legs of the wrong mares and neighed loudly in response to the short whinny of their own mothers.

Having driven the horses to the riverside where they were to graze, Nester dismounted and unsaddled. Meanwhile the herd had begun gradually to spread over the untrampled meadow, covered with dew and by the mist that rose from it and the encircling river.

When he had taken the bridle off the piebald gelding, Nester scratched him under the neck, in response to which the gelding expressed his gratitude and satisfaction by closing his eyes. "He likes it, the old dog!" muttered Nester. The gelding, however, did not really care for the scratching at all, and pretended that it was agreeable merely out of courtesy. He nodded his head in assent to Nester's words; but suddenly Nester quite unexpectedly and without any reason, perhaps imagining that too much familiarity might give the gelding a wrong idea of his importance, pushed the gelding's head away from himself without any warning and, swinging the bridle, struck him painfully with the buckle on his lean leg, and then without saying a word went up the hillock to a tree-stump beside which he generally seated himself.

Old age is sometimes majestic, sometimes ugly, and sometimes pathetic. But old age can be both ugly and majestic, and the gelding's old age was just of that kind.

He was tall, rather over 15 hands high. His spots were black, or rather they had been black, but had now turned a dirty brown. He had three spots, one on his head, starting from a crooked bald patch on the side of his nose and reaching half-way down his neck. His long mane, filled with burrs, was white in some places and brownish in others. Another spot extended down his off side to the middle of his belly, the third, on his croup, touched part of his tail and went half-way down his quarters. The rest of the tail was whitish and speckled. The big bony head, with deep hollows over the eyes and a black hanging lip that had been torn at some time, hung low and heavily on his neck, which was so lean that it looked as though it were carved of wood. The pendant lip revealed a blackish, bitten tongue and the yellow stumps of the worn lower teeth. The ears, one of which was slit, hung low on either side, and only occasionally moved lazily to drive away the pestering flies.

The expression on his face was one of stern patience, thoughtfulness, and suffering.

His forelegs were crooked to a bow at the knees; there were swellings over both hoofs, and on one leg, on which the piebald spot reached half-way down, there was a swelling at the knee as big as a fist. The hind legs were in better condition, but apparently long ago his haunches had been so rubbed that in places the hair would not grow again. The leanness of his body made all four legs look disproportionately long.

There was really something majestic in that horse's figure and in the terrible union in him of repulsive indications of decrepitude, emphasized by the motley colour of his hair, and his manner which expressed the self-confidence and calm assurance that go with beauty and strength. Like a living ruin he stood alone in the midst of the dewy meadow, while not far from him could be heard the tramping, snorting and youthful neighing and whinnying of the scattered herd.

That evening, as Nester drove the horses past the huts of the domestic serfs, he noticed a peasant horse and cart tethered to his porch: some friends had come to see him. When driving the horses in he was in such a hurry that he let the gelding in without unsaddling him and, shouting to Váska to do it, shut the gate and went to his friends. Whether because the gelding with his high saddle and without a rider presented a strangely fantastic spectacle to the horses, or for some other reason, at any rate something quite unusual occurred that night in the paddock. All the horses, young and old, ran after the gelding, showing their teeth and driving him all round the yard; one heard the sound of hoofs striking against his bare ribs, and his deep groaning. He could no longer endure this, nor could he avoid the blows. He stopped in the middle of the paddock, his face expressing first the repulsive, weak malevolence of helpless old age, and then despair: he dropped his ears, and then something happened that caused all the horses to quiet down. The oldest of the mares, Vyazapúrikha, went up to the gelding, sniffed at him and sighed. The gelding sighed too . . .

In the middle of the moonlit paddock stood the tall gaunt figure of the gelding, still wearing the high saddle with its prominent peak at the bow. The horses stood motionless and in deep silence around him as if they were learning something new and unexpected. And they had learnt something new and unexpected.

First Night

Yes, I am the son of Affable I and of Bába. My pedigree name is Muzhík, and I was nicknamed Strider by the crowd because of my long and sweeping strides, the like of which was nowhere to be found in all of Russia. There is no more thoroughbred horse in the world. I should never have told you this. What good would it have done? You would never have recognized me: even Vyazapúrikha, who was with me in Khrénovo, did not recognize me till now. You would not have believed me if Vyazapúrikha were not here to be my witness, and I should never have told you this. I don't need equine sympathy. But you wished it. Yes, I am that Strider whom connoisseurs are looking for and cannot find – that Strider whom the count himself knew and got rid of from his stud because I outran Swan, his favourite.

When I was born I did not know what piebald meant – I thought I was just a horse. I remember that the first remark we heard about my colour struck my mother and me deeply.

I suppose I was born in the night; by the morning, having been licked over by my mother, I already stood on my feet. I remember I kept wanting something, and that everything seemed very surprising and yet very simple. Our stalls opened into a long warm passage and had latticed doors through which everything could be seen.

My mother offered me her teats but I was still so innocent that I poked my nose now between her forelegs and now under her udder. Suddenly she glanced at the latticed door and, lifting her leg over me, stepped aside. The groom on duty was looking into our stall through the lattice.

"Why, Bába has foaled!" he said, and began to draw the bolt. He came in over the fresh bedding and put his arms round me. "Just look, Tarás!" he shouted, "What a piebald he is — a regular magpie!"

I darted away from him and fell on my knees.

"Look at him — the little devil!"

My mother became disquieted, but did not take my part. She only stepped a little to one side with a very deep sigh. Other grooms came to look at me, and one of them ran to tell the stud-groom.

Everybody laughed when they looked at my spots, and they gave me all kinds of strange names, but neither I nor my mother understood those words. Till then there had been no piebalds among all my relatives. We did not think there was anything bad in it. Everybody even then praised my strength and my form.

"See what a frisky fellow!" said the groom. "There's no holding him."

Before long the stud-groom came and began to express astonishment at my colour; he even seemed aggrieved.

"And who does the little monster take after?" he said. "The general won't keep him in the stud. Oh, Bába, you have played me a trick!" he addressed my mother. "You might at least have dropped one with just a star — but this one is all piebald!"

My mother did not reply, but as usual drew a sigh.

"And what devil does he take after — he's just like a peasant horse!" he continued. "He can't be left in the stud — he'd shame us. But he's well built — very well!"

said he, and so did everyone who saw me.

A few days later the general himself came and looked at me, and again everyone seemed horrified at something, and abused me and my mother for the colour of my hair. "But he's a fine colt – very fine!" said all who saw me.

Until spring we all lived separately in the brood mares' stable, each with our mother, and only occasionally when the snow on the stable roofs began to melt in the sun were we let out with our mothers into the large paddock strewn with fresh straw. There I first came to know all my near and my distant relations. Here I saw all the famous mares of the day coming out from different doors. They all gathered together with their foals, walking about in the sunshine, rolling on the fresh straw and sniffing at one another like ordinary horses. I have never forgotten the sight of that paddock full of the beauties of that day. It seems strange to you to think, and hard to believe, that I was ever young and frisky, but it was so. This same Vyazapúrikha was then a yearling filly whose mane had just been cut; a dear, merry, lively little thing, but – and I do not say it to offend her, although among you she is now considered a remarkable thoroughbred she was then among the poorest horses in the stud. She will herself confirm this.

My mottled appearance, which men so disliked, was very attractive to all the horses; they all came round me, admired me, and frisked about with me. I began to forget what men said about my mottled appearance, and felt happy. But I soon experienced the first sorrow of my life and the cause of it was my mother. When the thaw had set in, the sparrows twittered under the eaves, spring was felt more strongly in the air, and my mother's treatment of me changed.

Her whole disposition changed: she would frisk about without any reason to run round the yard, which did not at all accord with her dignified age; then she would consider and begin to neigh, and would bite and kick her sister mares, and then begin to sniff at me and snort discontentedly; then on going out into the sun she would lay her head across the shoulder of her cousin, Lady Merchant, dreamily rub her back and push me away from her teats.

One day the stud-groom came and had a halter put on her and she was led out of the stall. She neighed, and I answered and rushed after her, but she did not even look back at me. The strapper, Tarás, seized me in his arms while they were closing the door after my mother had been led out.

I bolted and upset the strapper on the straw, but the door was shut and I could only hear the receding sound of my mother's neighing; and that neigh did not sound like a call to me but had another expression. Her voice was answered from afar by a powerful voice – that of Dóbry I, as I learned later, who was being led by two grooms, one on each side, to meet my mother.

I don't remember how Tarás got out of my stall: I felt too sad, for I knew that I had lost my mother's love for ever. "And it's all because I am piebald!" I thought, remembering what people said about my colour, and such passionate anger overcame me that I began to beat my head and knees against the walls of the stall and continued till I was sweating all over and quite exhausted.

After a while my mother came back to me. I heard her run up the passage at a trot and with an unusual gait. They opened the door for her and I hardly knew her — she had grown so much younger and more beautiful. She sniffed at me, snorted, and began to whinny. Her whole demeanour showed that she no longer loved me.

She told me of Dóbry's beauty and her love of him. Those meetings continued, and the relations between my mother and me grew colder and colder.

Soon after that we were let out to pasture. I now discovered new joys which made up to me for the loss of my mother's love. I had friends and companions. Together we learnt to eat grass, to neigh like the grown ups, and to gallop round our mothers with lifted tails. That was a happy time. Everything was forgiven me, everybody loved me, admired me, and looked indulgently at anything I did. But that did not last long.

Soon afterwards something dreadful happened to me . . .

The gelding heaved a deep sigh and walked away.

The dawn had broken long before. The gates creaked. Nester came in, and the horses separated. The keeper straightened the saddle on the gelding's back and drove the horses out.

Second Night

In August they separated me from my mother and I did not feel particularly grieved. I saw that she was again heavy (with my brother, the famous Usán), and that I could no longer be to her what I had been. I was not jealous, but felt that I had become indifferent to her. Besides I knew that having left my mother I should be put in the general division of foals, where we were kept two or three together and were every day let out in a crowd into the open. I was in the same stall with Darling. Darling was a saddle-horse, who was subsequently ridden by the Emperor and portrayed in pictures and sculpture. At that time he was a mere foal, with soft, glossy coat, a swanlike neck, and straight, slender legs, taut as the strings of an instrument. He was always lively, good-tempered, and amiable, always ready to gambol, exchange licks, and play tricks on horse or man. Living together as we did we involuntarily made friends, and our friendship lasted the whole of our youth. He was merry and giddy. Even then he began to make love, courted the fillies, and laughed at my guilelessness. To my misfortune vanity led me to imitate him, and I was soon carried away and fell in love. And this early tendency of mine was the cause of the greatest change in my fate. It happened that I was carried away. . . Vyazapúrikha was a year older than I, and we were special friends, but towards the autumn I noticed that she began to be shy with me . . .

But I will not speak of that unfortunate period of my first love; she herself remembers my mad passion, which ended for me in the most important change of my life.

The strappers rushed to drive her away and to beat me. That evening I was shut up in a special stall where I neighed all night as if foreseeing what was to happen next.

In the morning the general, the stud-groom, the

stablemen and the strappers came into the passage where my stall was, and there was a terrible hubbub. The general shouted at the stud-groom, who tried to justify himself by saying that he had not told them to let me out but that the grooms had done it of their own accord. The general said that he would have everybody flogged, and that it would not do to keep young stallions. The stud-groom promised that he would have everything attended to. They grew quiet and went away. I did not understand anything, but could see that they were planning something concerning me.

The day after that I ceased neighing for ever. I became what I am now. The whole world was changed in my eyes. Nothing mattered any more; I became self-absorbed and began to brood. At first everything seemed repulsive to me. I even ceased to eat, drink, or walk, and there was no idea of playing. Now and then it occurred to me to give a kick, to gallop, or to start neighing, but immediately came the question: Why? What for? And all my energy died away . . .

Already before that I had shown a tendency towards gravity and thoughtfulness, but now a decided change came over me. My being piebald, which aroused such curious contempt in men, my terrible and unexpected misfortune, and also my peculiar position in the stud-farm, which I felt but was unable to explain, made me retire into myself. I pondered over the injustice of men, who blamed me for being piebald; I pondered on the inconstancy of mother-love and feminine love in general and on its dependence on physical condition; and above all I pondered on the characteristics of that strange race of animals with whom we are so closely connected, and whom we call men – those characteristics which were the source of my own peculiar position in the stud-farm, which I felt but could not understand.

The meaning of this peculiarity in people and the characteristic on which it is based was shown me later.

It was in winter at holiday time. I had not been fed or watered all day. As I learnt later this happened because the lad who fed us was drunk. That day the stud-groom came in, saw that I had no food, began to use bad language about the missing lad, and then went away.

Next day the lad came into our stable with another groom to give us hay. I noticed that he was particularly pale and sad, and that in the expression of his long back especially there was something significant which evoked compassion.

He threw the hay angrily over the grating. I made a move to put my head over his shoulder, but he struck me such a painful blow on the nose with his fist that I started back. Then he kicked me in the belly with his boot.

"If it hadn't been for this scurvy beast," he said, "nothing would have happened!"

"How's that?" inquired the other groom.

"You see, he doesn't go to look after the count's horses, but visits his own twice a day."

"What, have they given him the piebald?" asked the other.

"Given it, or sold it – the devil only knows! The count's horses might all starve – he wouldn't care – but just dare to leave his colt without food! 'Lie down!' he says, and they begin walloping me! No Christianity in it. He has more pity on a beast than on a man. He must be an infidel — he counted the strokes himself, the barbarian! The general never flogged like that! My whole back is covered with weals. There's no Christian soul in him!"

What they said about flogging and Christianity I understood well enough, but I was quite in the dark as to what they meant by the words "his colt", from which I perceived that people considered that there was some connection between me and the head groom. What that connection was I could not at all understand then. Only much later when they separated me from the other horses did I learn what it meant. At that time I could not at all understand what they meant by speaking of me as being a man's property. The words "my horse" applied to me, a live horse, seemed to me as strange as to say "my land", "my air", or "my water" . . .

I was thrice unfortunate: I was piebald, I was a gelding, and people considered that I did not belong to God and to myself, as is natural to all living creatures, but that I belonged to the stud-groom.

Their thinking this about me had many consequences. The first was that I was kept apart from the other horses, was better fed, oftener taken out on the line, and was broken in at an earlier age. I was first harnessed in my third year. I remember how the stud-groom, who imagined I was his, himself began to harness me with a crowd of other grooms, expecting me to prove unruly or to resist. They put ropes round me to lead me into the shafts; put a cross of broad straps on my back and fastened it to shafts so that I would not kick, while I was only awaiting an opportunity to show my readiness and love of work.

They were surprised that I started like an old horse. They began to break me and I began to practise trotting. Every day I made greater and greater progress, so that after three months the general himself and many others approved of my pace. But strange to say, just because they considered me not as their own, but as belonging to the head groom, they regarded my paces quite differently.

The stallions who were my brothers were raced, their records were kept, people went to look at them, drove them in gilt sulkies, and expensive horse-cloths were thrown over them. I was driven in a common sulky to Chesménka and other farms, on the head groom's business. All this was the result of my being piebald, and especially of my being in their opinion not the count's, but the head groom's property.

Tomorrow, if we are alive, I will tell you the chief consequence for me of this right of property the head groom considered himself to have.

All that day the horses treated Strider respectfully, but Nester's treatment of him was as rough as ever.

Third Night

For me the most surprising consequence of my not being the count's, nor God's, but the head groom's, was that the very thing that constitutes our chief merit – a fast pace – was the cause of my banishment. They were driving Swan round the track, and the head groom, returning from Chesménka, drove me up and stopped there. Swan went past. He went well, but all the same he was showing off and had not the exactitude I had developed in myself – so that directly one foot touched the ground another instantaneously lifted and not the slightest effort was lost but every atom of exertion carried me forward. Swan went by us. I pulled towards the ring and the head groom did not check me. "Here, shall I try my piebald?" he shouted, and when next Swan came abreast of us he let me go. Swan was already going fast, and so I was left behind during the first round, but in the second I began to gain on him, drew near to his sulky, drew level – and passed him. They tried us again – it was the same thing. I was the faster. And this dismayed everybody. The general asked that I should be sold at once to some distant place, so that nothing more should be heard of me: "Or else the count will get to know of it and there will be trouble!" So they sold me to a horse-dealer as a shafthorse. I did not remain with him long. An hussar who came to buy remounts bought me. All this was so unfair, so cruel, that I was glad when they took me away from Khrénovo and parted me for ever from all that had been familiar and dear to me. It was too painful for me among them. They had love, honour, freedom, before them; I had labour, humiliation, humiliation, labour, to the end of my life. And why? Because I was piebald, and because of that had to become somebody's horse . . .

Fourth Night

I have had opportunity to make many observations both of men and horses during the time I passed from hand to hand.

I stayed longest of all with two masters: a prince (an officer of hussars), and later with an old lady who lived near the church of St Nicholas the Wonder Worker.

The happiest years of my life I spent with the officer of hussars.

Though he was the cause of my ruin, and though he never loved anything or anyone, I loved and still love him for that very reason.

What I liked about him was that he was handsome, happy, rich, and therefore never loved anybody.

You understand that lofty equine feeling of ours. His coldness and my dependence on him gave special strength to my love for him. "Kill me, drive me till my wind is broken!" I used to think in our good days, "and I shall be all the happier."

He bought me from an agent to whom the head groom had sold me for eight hundred roubles, and he did so just because no one else had piebald horses. That was my best time. He had a mistress. I knew this because I took him to her every day and sometimes took them both out.

His mistress was a handsome woman, and he was handsome, and his coachman was handsome, and I loved them all because they were. Life was worth living then. This was how our time was spent: in the morning the groom came to rub me down – not the coachman himself but the groom. The groom was a lad from among the peasants. He would open the door, let out the steam from the horses, throw out the droppings, take off our rugs, and begin to fidget over our bodies with a brush, and lay whitish streaks of dandruff from a curry-comb on the boards of the floor that was dented by our rough horse-shoes. I would playfully nip his sleeve and paw the ground. Then we were led out one after another to the trough filled with cold water, and the lad would admire the smoothness of my spotted coat which he had polished, my foot with its broad hoof, my legs straight as an arrow, my glossy quarters, and my back wide enough to sleep on. Hay was piled onto the high racks, and the oak cribs were filled with oats. Then Feofán, the head coachman, would come in

Master and coachman resembled one another. Neither of them was afraid of anything or cared for anyone but himself, and for that reason everybody liked them. Feofán wore a red shirt, black velveteen knickerbockers, and a sleeveless coat. I liked it on a holiday when he would come into the stable, his hair pomaded, and wearing his sleeveless coat, and would shout:

"Now then, beastie, have you forgotten?" and push me with the handle of the stable fork, never so as to hurt me but just as a joke. I immediately knew that it was a joke, and laid back an ear, making my teeth click.

We had a black stallion, who drove in a pair. At night they used to put me in harness with him. That Polkán, as he was called, did not understand a joke but was simply vicious as the devil. I was in the stall next to his and sometimes we bit one another seriously. Feofán was not afraid of him. He would come up and give a shout: it looked as if Polkán would kill him, but no, he'd miss, and Feofán would put the harness on him.

Once he and I bolted down Smiths Bridge Street. Neither my master nor the coachman was frightened; they laughed, shouted at the people, checked us, and turned so that no one was run over.

In their service I lost my best qualities and half my life. They ruined me by watering me wrongly, and they foundered me . . . Still for all that it was the best time of my life. At twelve o'clock they would come to harness me, black my hoofs, moisten my forelock and mane, and put me in the shafts.

The sledge was of plaited cane, upholstered with velvet; the reins were of silk, the harness had silver buckles, sometimes there was a cover of silken fly-net, and altogether it was such that when all the traces and straps were fastened it was difficult to say where the harness ended and the horse began. We were harnessed at ease in the stable. Feofán would come, broader at his hips than at the shoulders, his red belt up under his arms: he would examine the harness, take his seat, wrap his coat round him, put his foot into the sledge stirrup, let off some joke, and for appearance's sake always hang a whip over his arm, though he hardly ever hit me, and would say "Let go!" and playfully stepping from foot to foot I would move out of the gate, and the cook who had come out to empty the slops would stop on the threshold and the peasant who had brought wood into the yard would open his eyes wide. We would come out, go a little way, and stop. Footmen would come out and other coachmen, and a chatter would begin. Everybody would wait: sometimes we had to stand for three hours at the entrance, moving a little way, turning back, and standing again.

At last there would be a stir in the hall: old Tíkhon with his paunch would rush out in his dress coat and cry "Drive up!" (In those days there was not that stupid way of saying "Forward!" as if one did not know that we moved forward and not back.) Feofán would cluck, drive up, and the prince would hurry out carelessly, as though there were nothing remarkable about the sledge, or the horse, or Feofán — who bent his back and stretched out his arms so that it seemed it would be impossible for him to keep them long in that position. The prince would have a shako on his head and wear a fur coat with a grey beaver collar hiding his rosy, black-browed, handsome face, that should never have been concealed. He would come out clattering his sabre, his spurs, and the brass backs of the heels of his overshoes, stepping over the carpet as if in a hurry and taking no notice of me or Feofán whom everybody but he looked at and admired. Feofán would cluck, I would tug at the reins, and respectably, at a foot pace, we would draw up to the entrance and stop. I would turn my eyes on the prince and jerk my thoroughbred head with its delicate forelock . . . The prince would be in good spirits and would sometimes jest with Feofán. Feofán would reply, half turning his handsome head, and without lowering his arms would make a scarcely perceptible movement with the reins which I understand: and then one, two, three . . . with ever wider and wider strides, every muscle quivering, and sending the muddy snow against the front of the sledge, I would go. In those days, too, there was none of the present day stupid habit of crying "Oh!" as if the coachman were in pain, instead of the sensible "Be off! Take care!" Feofán would shout "Be off! Look out there!" and the people would step aside and stand craning their necks to see the handsome gelding, the handsome coachman, and the handsome gentleman . . .

I was particularly fond of passing a trotter. When Feofán and I saw at a distance a turn-out worthy of the effort, we would fly like a whirlwind and gradually gain on it. Now, throwing the dirt right to the back of the sledge, I would draw level with the occupant of the vehicle and snort above his head: then I would reach the horse's harness and the arch of his troyka, and then would no longer see it but only hear its sounds in the distance behind. And the prince, Feofán and I, would all be silent, and pretend to be merely going on our own business and not even to notice those with slow horses whom we happened to meet on our way. I liked to pass another horse, but also liked to meet a good trotter. An instant, a sound, a glance, and we had passed each other and were flying in opposite directions.

The gate creaked and the voices of Nester and Váska were heard.

Fifth Night

The weather began to break up. It had been dull since morning and there was no dew, but it was warm and the mosquitoes were troublesome. As soon as the horses were driven in they collected round the piebald, and he finished his story as follows:

The happy period of my life was soon over. I lived in that way only two years. Towards the end of the second winter the happiest event of my life occurred, and following it came my greatest misfortune. It was during carnival week. I took the prince to the races. Glossy and Bull were running. I don't know what people were doing in the pavilion, but I know the prince came out and ordered Feofán to drive onto the track. I remember how they took me in and placed me beside Glossy. He was harnessed to a racing sulky and I, just as I was, to a town sledge. I outstripped him at the turn. Roars of laughter and howls of delight greeted me.

When I was led in, a crowd followed me and five or six people offered the prince thousands for me. He only laughed, showing his white teeth.

"No," he said, "this isn't a horse, but a friend. I wouldn't sell him for mountains of gold. Au revoir, gentlemen!"

He unfastened the sledge apron and got in.

"To Ostózhenka Street!"

That was where his mistress lived, and off we flew . . . That was our last happy day. We reached her home. He spoke of her as his, but she loved someone else and had run away with him. The prince learnt this at her lodgings. It was five o'clock, and without unharnessing me he started in pursuit of her. Then he did what had never been done to me before, struck me with the whip and made me gallop. For the first time I felt out of step and felt ashamed and wished to correct it, but suddenly I heard the prince shout in an unnatural voice: "Get on!" The whip whistled through the air and cut me, and I galloped, striking my foot against the iron front of the sledge. We overtook her after going sixteen miles. I got him there, but trembled all night long and could not eat anything. In the morning they gave me water. I drank it and after that was never again the horse that I had been. I was ill, and they tormented me and maimed me – doctoring me, as people call it. My hoofs came off, I had swellings, and my legs grew bent; my chest sank in and I became altogether limp and weak. I was sold to a horse-dealer who fed me on carrots and something else and made something of me quite unlike myself, though good enough to deceive one who did not know. My strength and my pace were gone.

When purchasers came the dealer also tormented me by coming into my stall and beating me with a heavy whip to frighten and madden me. Then he would rub down the stripes on my coat and lead me out.

An old woman bought me off him. She always drove to the Church of St Nicholas the Wonder Worker, and she used to have her coachman flogged. He used to weep in my stall and I learnt that tears have a pleasant, salty taste. Then the old woman died. Her steward took me to the country and sold me to a hawker. Then I over-ate myself with wheat and grew still worse. They sold me to a peasant. There I ploughed, had hardly anything to eat, my foot got cut by a ploughshare and I again became ill. Then a gipsy took me in exchange for something. He tormented me terribly and finally sold me to the steward here. And here I am.

All were silent. A sprinkling of rain began to fall.

A WAYSIDE ADVENTURE

C. S. LEWIS

Shasta, a fisherman's boy, and Bree, a Talking Horse, have run away together from the cruel country of Calormen and are heading for Narnia.

IT WAS NEARLY noon when Shasta was wakened by something warm and soft moving over his face. He opened his eyes and found himself staring into the long face of a horse; its nose and lips were almost touching his. He remembered the exciting events of the previous night and sat up. But as he did so he groaned.

"Ow, Bree," he gasped. "I'm so sore. All over. I can hardly move."

"Good morning, small one," said Bree. "I was afraid you might feel a bit stiff. It can't be the falls. You didn't have more than a dozen or so, and it was all lovely, soft, springy turf that must have been almost a pleasure to fall on. And the only one that might have been nasty was broken by that gorse bush. No: it's the riding itself that comes hard at first. What about breakfast? I've had mine."

"Oh bother breakfast. Bother everything," said Shasta. "I tell you I can't move." But the horse nuzzled at him with its nose and pawed him gently with a hoof till he had to get up. And then he looked about him and saw where they were. Behind them lay a little copse. Before them the turf, dotted with white flowers, sloped down to the brow of a cliff. Far below them, so that the sound of the breaking waves was very faint, lay the sea. Shasta had never seen it from such a height and never seen so much of it before, nor dreamed how many colours it had. On either hand the coast stretched away; headland after headland, and at the points you could see the white foam running up the rocks but making no noise because it was so far off. There were gulls flying overhead and the heat shivered on the ground; it was a blazing day. But what Shasta chiefly noticed was the air. He couldn't think what was missing, until at last he realized that there was no smell of fish in it. For of course, neither in the cottage nor among the nets, had he ever been away from that smell in his life. And this new air was so delicious and all his old life seemed so far away, that he forgot for a moment about his bruises and his aching muscles and said:

"I say, Bree, didn't you say something about breakfast?"

"Yes, I did," answered Bree. "I think you'll find something in the saddle-bags. They're over there on that tree where you hung them up last night – or early this morning, rather."

They investigated the saddle-bags and the results were cheering – a meat pasty, only slightly stale, a lump of dried figs and another lump of green cheese, a little flask of wine, and some money; about forty crescents in all, which was more than Shasta had ever seen.

While Shasta sat down – painfully and cautiously – with his back against a tree and started on the pasty,

Bree had a few more mouthfuls of grass to keep him company.

"Won't it be stealing to use the money?" asked Shasta.

"Oh," said the Horse, looking up with its mouth full of grass, "I never thought of that. A free horse and a talking horse mustn't steal, of course. But I think it's all right. We're prisoners and captives in enemy country. That money is booty, spoil. Besides, how are we to get any food for you without it? I suppose, like all humans, you won't eat natural food like grass and oats."

"I can't."

"Ever tried?"

"Yes, I have. I can't get it down at all. You couldn't either if you were me."

"You're rum little creatures, you humans," remarked Bree.

When Shasta had finished his breakfast (which was by far the nicest he had ever eaten), Bree said, "I think I'll have a nice roll before we put on that saddle again." And he proceeded to do so. "That's good. That's very good," he said, rubbing his back on the turf and waving all four legs in the air. "You ought to have one too, Shasta," he snorted. "It's most refreshing."

But Shasta burst out laughing and said, "You do look funny when you're on your back!"

"I look nothing of the sort," said Bree. But then suddenly he rolled round on his side, raised his head and looked hard at Shasta, blowing a little.

"Does it really look funny?" he asked in an anxious voice.

"Yes, it does," replied Shasta. "But what does it

matter?"

"You don't think, do you," said Bree, "that it might be a thing talking horses never do – a silly, clownish trick I've learned from the dumb ones? It would be dreadful to find, when I get back to Narnia, that I've picked up a lot of low, bad habits. What do you think, Shasta? Honestly, now. Don't spare my feelings. Should you think the real, free horses – the talking kind – do roll?"

"How should I know? Anyway I don't think I should bother about it if I were you. We've got to get there first. Do you know the way?"

"I know my way to Tashbaan. After that comes the desert. Oh, we'll manage the desert somehow, never fear. Why, we'll be in sight of the Northern mountains then. Think of it! To Narnia and the North! Nothing will stop us then. But I'd be glad to be past Tashbaan. You and I are safer away from cities."

"Can't we avoid it?"

"Not without going a long way inland, and that would take us into cultivated land and main roads; and I wouldn't know the way. No, we'll just have to creep along the coast. Up here on the downs we'll meet nothing but sheep and rabbits and gulls and a few shepherds. And by the way, what about starting?"

Shasta's legs ached terribly as he saddled Bree and climbed into the saddle, but the Horse was kindly to him and went at a soft pace all afternoon. When evening twilight came they dropped by steep tracks into a valley and found a village. Before they got into it Shasta dismounted and entered it on foot to buy a loaf and some onions and radishes. The Horse trotted round by the fields in the dusk and met Shasta at the far side. This became their regular plan every second night.

These were great days for Shasta, and every day better than the last as his muscles hardened and he fell less often. Even at the end of his training, Bree still said he sat like a bag of flour in the saddle. "And even if it was safe, young 'un, I'd be ashamed to be seen with you on the main road." But in spite of his rude words, Bree was a patient teacher. No one can teach riding so well as a horse. Shasta learned to trot, to canter, to jump, and to keep his seat even when Bree pulled up suddenly or swung unexpectedly to the left or the right – which, as Bree told him, was a thing you might have to do at any moment in a battle. And then of course Shasta begged to be told of the battles and wars in which Bree had carried the Tarkaan. And Bree would tell of forced marches and the fording of swift rivers, of charges and of fierce fights between cavalry and cavalry when the war horses fought as well as the men, being all fierce stallions, trained to bite and kick, and to rear at the right moment so that the horse's weight as well as the rider's would come down on an enemy's crest in the stroke of sword or battleaxe. But Bree did not want to talk about the wars as often as Shasta wanted to hear about them. "Don't speak of them, youngster," he would say. "They were only the Tisroc's wars and I fought in them as a slave and a dumb beast. Give me the Narnian wars where I shall fight as a free Horse among my own people! Those will be wars worth talking about. Narnia and the North! Bra-ha-ha! Broo hoo!"

Shasta soon learned, when he heard Bree talking like that, to prepare for a gallop. After they had travelled on for weeks and weeks past more bays and headlands and rivers and villages than Shasta could remember, there came a moonlit night when they started their journey at evening, having slept during the day. They had left the downs behind them and were crossing a wide plain with a forest about half a mile away on their left. The sea, hidden by low sandhills, was about the same distance on their right. They had jogged along for about an hour, sometimes trotting and sometimes walking, when Bree suddenly stopped.

"What's up?" said Shasta.

"S–s–ssh!" said Bree, craning his neck round and twitching his ears. "Did you hear something? Listen."

"It sounds like another horse – between us and the wood," said Shasta after he had listened for about a minute.

"It is another horse," said Bree. "And that's what I don't like."

"Isn't it probably just a farmer riding home late?" said Shasta with a yawn.

"Don't tell me!" said Bree. "That's not a farmer's riding. Nor a farmer's horse either. Can't you tell by the sound? That's quality, that horse is. And it's being ridden by a real horseman. I tell you what it is, Shasta. There's a Tarkaan under the edge of that wood. Not on his war horse – it's too light for that. On a fine blood mare, I should say."

"Well, it's stopped now, whatever it is," said Shasta.

"You're right," said Bree. "And why should he stop just when we do? Shasta, my boy, I do believe there's someone shadowing us at last."

"What shall we do?" said Shasta in a lower whisper

than before. "Do you think he can see us as well as hear us?"

"Not in this light so long as we stay quite still," answered Bree. "But look! There's a cloud coming up. I'll wait till that gets over the moon. Then we'll get off to our right as quietly as we can, down to the shore. We can hide among the sandhills if the worst comes to the worst."

They waited till the cloud covered the moon and then, first at a walking pace and afterwards at a gentle trot, made for the shore.

The cloud was bigger and thicker than it had looked at first and soon the night grew very dark. Just as Shasta was saying to himself, "We must be nearly at those sandhills by now," his heart leaped into his mouth because an appalling noise had suddenly risen up out of the darkness ahead; a long snarling roar, melancholy and utterly savage. Instantly Bree swerved round and began galloping inland again as fast as he could gallop.

"What is it?" gasped Shasta.

"Lions!" said Bree, without checking his pace or turning his head.

After that there was nothing but sheer galloping for some time. At last they splashed across a wide, shallow stream and Bree came to a stop on the far side. Shasta noticed that he was trembling and sweating all over.

"That water may have thrown the brute off our scent," panted Bree when he had partly got his breath again. "We can walk for a bit now."

As they walked Bree said, "Shasta, I'm ashamed of myself. I'm just as frightened as a common, dumb Calormene horse. I am really. I don't feel like a Talking

Horse at all. I don't mind swords and lances and arrows but I can't bear – those creatures. I think I'll trot for a bit."

About a minute later, however, he broke into a gallop again, and no wonder. For the roar broke out again, this time on their left from the direction of the forest.

"Two of them," moaned Bree.

When they had galloped for several minutes without any further noise from the lions, Shasta said, "I say! That other horse is galloping beside us now. Only a stone's throw away."

"All the b-better," panted Bree. "Tarkaan on it – will have a sword – protect us all."

"But, Bree!" said Shasta. "We might just as well be killed by lions as caught. Or I might. They'll hang me for horse-stealing."

He was feeling less frightened of lions than Bree because he had never met a lion; Bree had.

Bree only snorted in answer but he did sheer away to his right. Oddly enough the other horse seemed also to be sheering away to the left, so that in a few seconds the space between them had widened a good deal. But as soon as it did so there came two more lions' roars, immediately after one another, one on the right and the other on the left, and the horses began drawing nearer together. So, apparently, did the lions. The roaring of the brutes on each side was horribly close and they seemed to be keeping up with the galloping horses quite easily. Then the cloud rolled away.

The moonlight, astonishingly bright, showed up everything almost as if it were broad day. The two horses and the two riders were galloping neck to neck and knee to knee just as if they were in a race. Indeed Bree said (afterwards) that a finer race had never been seen in Calormen.

Shasta now gave himself up for lost and began to wonder whether lions killed you quickly or played with you as a cat plays with a mouse and how much it would hurt. At the same time (one sometimes does this at the most frightful moments) he noticed everything. He saw that the other rider was a very small, slender person, mail-clad (the moon shone on the mail) and riding magnificently. He had no beard.

Something flat and shining was spread out before them. Before Shasta had time even to guess what it was, there was a great splash and he found his mouth half full of salt water. The shining thing had been a long inlet of the sea. Both horses were swimming and the water was up to Shasta's knees. There was an angry roaring behind them and looking back Shasta saw a great, shaggy, and terrible shape crouched on the water's edge: but only one. "We must have shaken off the other lion," he thought.

The lion apparently did not think its prey worth a wetting; at any rate it made no attempt to take the water in pursuit.

The two horses, side by side, were now well out into the middle of the creek and the opposite shore could be clearly seen. The Tarkaan had not yet spoken a word. "But he will," thought Shasta. "As soon as we have landed. What am I to say? I must begin thinking out a story."

Then, suddenly, two voices spoke at his side.

"Oh, I am so tired," said the one.

"Hold your tongue, Hwin, and don't be a fool," said the other.

"I'm dreaming," thought Shasta. "I could have sworn that other horse spoke."

Soon the horses were no longer swimming but walking and soon with a great sound of water running off their sides and tails and with a great crunching of pebbles under eight hoofs, they came out on the farther beach of the inlet. The Tarkaan, to Shasta's surprise, showed no wish to ask questions. He did not even look at Shasta but seemed anxious to urge his horse straight on. Bree, however, at once shouldered himself in the other horse's way.

"Broo-hoo-hah!" he snorted. "Steady there! I heard you, I did. There's no good pretending, ma'am. I heard you. You're a Talking Horse, a Narnian horse just like me."

"What's it got to do with you if she is?" said the strange rider fiercely, laying hand on sword-hilt. But the voice in which the words were spoken had already told Shasta something.

"Why, it's only a girl!" he exclaimed.

"And what business is it of yours if I am *only* a girl?" snapped the stranger. "You're only a boy: a rude, common, little boy — a slave probably, who's stolen his master's horse."

"That's all you know," said Shasta.

"He's not a thief, little Tarkheena," said Bree. "At least if there's been any stealing, you might just as well say I stole him. And as for its not being my business, you wouldn't expect me to pass a lady of my own race in this strange country without speaking to her? It's only natural I should."

"I think it's very natural too," said the mare.

"I wish you'd held your tongue, Hwin," said the girl. "Look at the trouble you've got us into."

"I don't know about trouble," said Shasta. "You can clear off as soon as you like. We shan't keep you."

"No, you shan't," said the girl.

"What quarrelsome creatures these humans are," said Bree to the mare. "They're as bad as mules. Let's try to talk a little sense. I take it, ma'am, your story is the same as mine? Captured in early youth – years of slavery among the Calormenes?"

"Too true, sir," said the mare with a melancholy whinny.

"And now, perhaps – escape?"

"Tell him to mind his own business, Hwin," said the girl.

"No, I won't, Aravis," said the mare, putting her ears back. "This is my escape just as much as yours. And I'm sure a noble war horse like this is not going to betray us. We are trying to escape, to get to Narnia."

"And so, of course, are we," said Bree. "Of course you guessed that at once. A little boy in rags riding (or trying to ride) a war horse at dead of night couldn't mean anything but an escape of some sort. And, if I may say so, a high-born Tarkheena riding alone at night – dressed up in her brother's armour – and very anxious for everyone to mind their own business and ask her no questions – well, if that's not fishy, call me a cob!"

"All right then," said Aravis. "You've guessed it. Hwin and I are running away. We are trying to get to

Narnia. And now, what about it?"

"Why, in that case, what is to prevent us all going together?" said Bree. "I trust, Madam Hwin, you will accept such assistance and protection as I may be able to give you on the journey?"

"Why do you keep on talking to my horse instead of to me?" asked the girl.

"Excuse me, Tarkheena," said Bree (with just the slightest backward tilt of his ears), "but that's Calormene talk. We're free Narnians, Hwin and I, and I suppose, if you're running away to Narnia, you want to be one too. In that case Hwin isn't your horse any longer. One might just as well say you're her human."

The girl opened her mouth to speak and then stopped. Obviously she had not quite seen it in that light before.

"Still," she said after a moment's pause, "I don't know that there's so much point in all going together. Aren't we more likely to be noticed?"

"Less," said Bree; and the mare said, "Oh do let's. I should feel much more comfortable. We're not even certain of the way. I'm sure a great charger like this knows far more than we do."

"Oh come on, Bree," said Shasta, "and let them go their own way. Can't you see they don't want us?"

"We do," said Hwin.

"Look here," said the girl. "I don't mind going with you, Mr War Horse, but what about this boy? How do I know he's not a spy?"

"Why don't you say at once that you think I'm not good enough for you?" said Shasta.

"Be quiet, Shasta," said Bree. "The Tarkheena's

160

question is quite reasonable. I'll vouch for the boy, Tarkheena. He's been true to me and a good friend. And he's certainly either a Narnian or an Archenlander."

"All right, then. Let's go together." But she didn't say anything to Shasta and it was obvious that she wanted Bree, not him.

"Splendid!" said Bree. "And now that we've got the water between us and those dreadful animals, what about you two humans taking off our saddles and our all having a rest and hearing one another's stories."

Both the children unsaddled their horses and the horses had a little grass and Aravis produced rather nice things to eat from her saddle-bag. But Shasta sulked and said no thanks, and that he wasn't hungry. And he tried to put on what he thought very grand and stiff manners, but as a fisherman's hut is not usually a good place for learning grand manners, the result was dreadful. And he half knew that it wasn't a success and then became sulkier and more awkward than ever. Meanwhile the two horses were getting on splendidly. They remembered the very same places in Narnia – "the grasslands up above Beaversdam" and found that they were some sort of second cousins once removed.

This made things more and more uncomfortable for the humans until at last Bree said, "And now, Tarkheena, tell us your story. And don't hurry it – I'm feeling comfortable now."

Aravis immediately began, sitting quite still and using a rather different tone and style from her usual one. For in Calormen, story-telling (whether the stories are true or made up) is a thing you're taught, just as English boys and girls are taught essay-writing. The difference is that people want to hear the stories, whereas I never heard of anyone who wanted to read the essays.

RESCUE

WALTER FARLEY from The Black Stallion

*Alec and a black stallion, the Black, have been
shipwrecked on a remote island.*

ALEC'S EYES BLURRED; he couldn't see. He
stumbled and fell and then clambered to his feet. Again
he rushed forward. Then they had their arms around
him.

"For the love of St Patrick," the man called Pat
groaned. "He's just a boy!"

Words jumbled together and stuck in Alec's throat as
he looked into the five pairs of eyes staring at him.
Then he found his voice. "We're saved!" he yelled.
"We're saved, Black, we're saved!"

The sailors looked at him – he was a strange sight!
His red hair was long and dishevelled, his face and body
so brown that they would have taken him for a native
if it hadn't been for the torn remnants of his clothing
which hung loosely on him.

One of the men stepped forward. From his uniform
he was obviously the captain of the ship. "Everything is
going to be all right, son," he said as he placed an arm
around Alec and steadied him.

Slowly Alec gained control of himself. "I'm okay

now, sir," he said.

The sailors gathered around him. "Is there someone else with you on this island?" the captain asked.

"Only the Black, sir."

The men looked at one another, and then the captain spoke again. "Who's the Black, son?" he asked.

"He's a horse, sir," Alec answered.

And then he told them his story – of the storm and the shipwreck, the hours spent in the raging sea holding desperately to the rope tied to the stallion's neck, their fight against starvation on the island, his conquest of the Black, and the fire which that night had reduced his shelter to ashes. Sweat broke out upon his forehead, as in the vivid word pictures he once again lived the twenty days of hardships and suffering since the *Drake* had gone down.

When he finished there was a moment of silence, and then one of the men spoke. "This lad is imagining things, Captain. What he needs is some hot food and a good bed!"

Alec looked from one face to another and saw that they didn't believe him. Rage filled him. Why should they be so stupid? Was his story so fantastic? He'd prove it to them, then – he'd call the Black.

He raised his fingers to his lips and whistled. "Listen," he shouted. "Listen!" The men stood still. A minute passed, and then another – only the waves lapping on the beach could be heard in the terrifying stillness of the island.

Then the captain's voice came to him. "We have to go now, son. We're off our course and a way behind schedule."

Dazed, Alec's eyes turned from the island to the freighter lying at anchor, smoke belching from its two stacks. It was larger than the *Drake*.

The captain's voice again broke through his thoughts. "We're bound for South America – Rio de Janeiro is our first stop. We can take you there and wire your parents from the ship that you're alive!"

The captain and Pat had him by the arms; the others were in the boat ready to shove off. Desperately Alec tried to collect his thoughts. He was leaving the island. He was leaving the Black. The Black – who had saved his life! He jerked himself free, he was running up the beach.

Their mouths wide open, the sailors watched him as he stumbled up the hill. They saw him reach the top and raise his fingers to his lips. His whistle reached them – then there was silence.

Suddenly, an inhuman scream shattered the stillness – a wild, terrifying call! Stunned, they stood still and the hairs on the back of their necks seemed to curl. Then as if by magic, a giant black horse, his mane waving like flame, appeared beside the boy. The horse screamed again, his head raised high, his ears pricked forward. Even at this distance they could see that he was a tremendous horse – a wild stallion.

Alec flung his arms around the Black's neck and buried his head in the long mane. "We're leaving together, Black – together," he said. Soothingly he talked to the stallion, steadying him. After a few minutes he descended the hill and the horse hesitatingly followed. He reared as they approached the sailors, his legs pawing in the air. The men scrambled into the boat: only Pat and the captain stood their ground. Fearfully they watched the Black as he strode towards them. He drew back; his black eyes glanced nervously from Alec to the group of men. Alec patted him, coaxed him. His action was beautiful and every few steps he would jump swiftly to one side.

Approximately thirty yards away, Alec came to a halt.

"You just have to take us both, Captain! I can't leave him!" he yelled.

"He's too wild. We couldn't take him, we couldn't handle him!" came the answer.

"I can handle him. Look at him now!"

The Black was still, his head turned towards the freighter as if he understood what actually was going on. Alec's arm was around his neck. "He saved my life, Captain. I can't leave him!"

The captain turned, spoke with the men in the boat. Then he shouted, "There isn't any possible way of getting that devil on board, anyway!" He paused. "How're you going to get him out there?" The captain pointed to the ship.

"He can swim," answered Alec.

There was another discussion between captain and crew. When he turned, the captain's heavily-lined face was more grim than ever. He doffed his cap and ran a large hand through his grey hair. "OK, son," he said, "you win – but you'll have to get him out there!"

Alec's heart beat heavily and he gazed at the stallion. "Come on, Black," he said. He walked forward a few steps. The Black hesitated and then followed. Again Alec moved ahead. Slowly they approached the group.

Then the Black halted, his nostrils quivered and he reared.

"Get in the boat, Captain," Alec shouted. "Move up to the bow. I'm going to get in the stern when you get her in the water."

The captain ordered his men to shove off, and he and Pat climbed in; then they waited for Alec.

Alec turned to the Black. "This is our chance, Black," he said. "Don't let me down!" He could see the stallion was nervous; the horse had learned to trust him, but his natural instincts still warned him against the others. Soothingly Alec spoke to him. Slowly he backed away – the Black raised his head nervously, then followed. As the boy neared the boat, the stallion stopped. Alec kept backing up and climbed into the boat. "Row slowly," he said, without turning his eyes away from the horse.

As they moved away from the beach Alec called, "Come on, Black-boy!" The stallion pranced, his head and tail erect, his ears forward. He half-reared and then stepped into the water. Like a flash he was back on the beach, his foreleg pawing into the sand and sending it flying. His black eyes never left the boat as it moved slowly out into the water. He ran a short way down the beach, and then back again.

Alec realized the terrific fight that the stallion was waging with himself. He whistled. The Black stopped in his tracks and answered. Slowly the boat moved further away.

Suddenly the stallion rose high into the air on his hind legs, and then plunged into the water. "Come on, Black," shouted Alec. "Come on!"

The Black was in water up to his big chest now — then he was swimming and coming swiftly towards the boat.

"Row for the ship, Captain," yelled Alec.

The black head rose in the water behind them, the eyes fearfully following Alec as he half-hung out of the boat and called to the stallion. The large, black body slid through the water, his legs working like pistons.

Soon they reached the freighter. The captain and three men sprang up the ladder. Only Pat remained behind with Alec. "Keep him there for two minutes!" the captain yelled over his shoulder.

The Black reached the rowboat and Alec managed to get his hand on the stallion's head. "Good boy!" he murmured proudly. Then he heard the captain's hail from on top of the deck. He looked up and saw the cargo hoist being lowered; on the end was a belly band to go around the Black so that he could be lifted up. He had to get that band around the stallion's stomach!

Alec saw the Black's eyes leave him and gaze fearfully at the line descending over his head. Suddenly he swam away from the boat. Frantically Alec called to him.

As the band came within reach, Pat grabbed it — his fingers tore at the straps and buckles. "We've got to get this around him somehow!" he shouted to Alec. "It's the only way!"

Alec tried desperately to think. Certainly there must be some way! The stallion had turned and once again was looking in their direction. If he could only get close to him. "Let me have the band, Pat, and more line," he said.

Pat handed it to him and signalled above. "And what

are you going to do?" he asked.

But Alec didn't seem to hear his query. He gripped the straps of the band tightly. "We've come this far," he said to himself. He climbed over the side and lowered himself into the water, Pat was too astonished to speak. Alec swam a few yards towards the Black, the band stretched out behind him; then he stopped and trod water. He called softly and the stallion swam towards him.

He came within an arm's reach and Alec touched him, keeping his body far enough away to avoid the driving legs. How could he get the band around the stallion? Pat was yelling suggestions, but Alec could think of only one way that might be successful.

He sank lower in the water, his hand gradually sliding down the Black's neck; he held the straps of the belt tightly in the other. He took a deep breath and filled his lungs with air; then he dived sideways and felt the waters close over his head. Down he went, striving desperately to get enough depth to clear the stallion's legs. He swam directly beneath the Black's belly; the water churned white above his head and he caught a glimpse of striking hoofs. When he felt sure that he was on the other side, he started up, his fingers still tightly closed upon the straps and the band dragging behind.

When he reached the surface, he found the stallion in the same position, his eyes searching for him. Now the band was directly below the Black! He signalled for Pat to pull up the slack between the boat and the horse. All that he had to do now was to tighten the band around the stallion by getting these straps through the buckles on the other side! Alec moved closer to the

Black. He would have to take the chance of being kicked. He kept as close to the middle of the stallion as possible. Then he was beside him. He felt the waters swirling on both sides. The line was taut now, ascending in the air to the top of the hoist on the freighter.

The Black became uneasy. Alec reached over his back and desperately tried to pull the straps through the buckles. A searing pain went through his leg as one of the Black's hoofs struck him. His leg went limp. Minutes passed as his fingers worked frantically. Then he had the straps through and began pulling the band tighter. The stallion went wild with rage as he felt it tighten around him. Alec pulled harder. Once again he felt the Black's hoof strike his leg – but there was no pain. He had the straps through the buckles as far as they would go; he made sure they were securely fastened, and then wearily pushed himself away from the Black.

A safe distance away, Alec signalled the men on the freighter to hoist. He heard the starting of a motor and the chain line became more taut. Then the stallion was dragged through the water until he was beside the ship. His teeth were bared, his eyes were filled with hate! Then the hoist started lifting him up. Slowly the Black moved out of the water – up, up in the air he ascended, his legs pawing madly!

Alec swam towards the rowboat, his leg hanging limp behind him. When he reached it, Pat hung over the side and helped him up into the boat. "Good boy," he said.

The pain in his leg made Alec's head whirl. Blackness seemed to be settling down upon him – he shook his head. Then he felt Pat's big arm around his waist and he went limp.

When Alec regained consciousness, he found himself in bed. Beside him sat Pat – a large grin on his face, his blue eyes crinkling in the corners. "For the love of St Patrick," he exclaimed, "I thought you were going to sleep forever!"

"What time is it, Pat?" Alec asked. "Have I been sleeping long?"

Pat ran a large, gnarled hand through his black hair. "Well, not so long, son – you were pretty tired, y'know." He paused. "Let's see, we picked you up Tuesday morning and now it's Wednesday night."

"Whew!" said Alec, "that's some sleeping!"

"Well, we did wake you up a couple of times to give you some soup, but I guess you wouldn't be remembering now."

Alec moved slightly and felt a pain go through his leg. His eyes turned to Pat. "Did I get hurt bad?" he asked.

"The Doc says not – went to the bone, but it's healing nicely. You'll be all right in a few days."

"And the Black – what happened?"

"Lad, never in my life did I ever expect to see the like of him! What a fight he put up – he almost tore the boat apart!" Pat's blue eyes flashed. "Lord, what a devil! The moment his hoofs touched the deck he wanted to fight. If we hadn't still had the band around him, he would have killed us all! He plunged and struck his legs out like I've never seen before. He wouldn't stand still. You could have helped us, son. We hoisted him in the air again, off his feet. I thought he had gone crazy, his face was something terrible to see – and those screams, I'll hear them till my dying day!"

Pat stopped and moved uneasily in his seat. Then he continued, "It was when one of the boys got a little too close, and that black devil struck him in the side and he fell at our feet, that we decided there was nothing else to do but choke him! We got our lassoes around his neck and pulled until we had him pretty near gone. It was tough on him, but there was no other way. When he was almost unconscious, we let him down once again and somehow managed to lower him below.

"It was a job, lad, that I hope I'll never have to be in on again. We have some other horses and cattle in the hold, too, and they're all scared to death of him. It's a regular bedlam down there now, and I hate to think what might happen when that horse is himself again! We've got him in the strongest stall, but I'm wondering whether even that'll hold him!"

Pat rose from his chair and walked to the other side of the cabin.

Alec was silent, then he spoke slowly, "I'm sorry I've caused you all so much trouble. If only I'd been able to—"

"I didn't aim to make you feel like that, lad," Pat interrupted. "I guess we knew what we were doing, and from the looks of that animal he's worth it. Only we all realize now that he needs you to handle him – the Lord help anyone else that tries to!"

"Tell the captain I'll repay him and you fellows, too, Pat, somehow."

"Sure, lad, and now I have some work to do. You try and get some more sleep, and tomorrow or the next day you'll be on your feet again." He paused on his way to the door. "If you give me your address, we can wire your parents that you are safe, and tell them where we're bound for."

Alec smiled and wrote his address on the piece of paper Pat handed him. "Tell them I'll be with them — soon," he said as he finished.

THE ROCKING-HORSE WINNER

D. H. LAWRENCE

Paul's parents have money but it never seems to be enough.

AND SO THE HOUSE came to be haunted by the unspoken phrase: *There must be more money! There must be more money!* The children could hear it all the time, though nobody said it aloud. They heard it at Christmas, when the expensive and splendid toys filled the nursery. Behind the shining modern rocking-horse, behind the smart doll's house, a voice would start whispering: "There *must* be more money! There must be more money!" And the children would stop playing to listen for a moment. They would look into each other's eyes, to see if they had all heard. And each one saw in the eyes of the other two that they too had heard. "There must be more money! There must be more money!"

It came whispering from the springs of the still-swaying rocking-horse, and even the horse, bending his wooden, champing head, heard it. The big doll, sitting so pink and smirking in her new pram, could hear it quite plainly, and seemed to be smirking all the more self-consciously because of it. The foolish puppy, too, that took the place of the teddy-bear, he was looking so extraordinarily foolish for no other reason but that he heard the secret whisper all over the house: "There *must* be more money!"

Yet nobody ever said it aloud. The whisper was everywhere, and therefore no one spoke it. Just as no one ever says: "We are breathing!" in spite of the fact that breath is coming and going all the time.

"Mother," said the boy Paul one day, "why don't we keep a car of our own? Why do we always use Uncle's, or else a taxi!"

"Because we're the poor members of the family," said the mother.

"But why *are* we, Mother?"

"Well — I suppose," she said slowly and bitterly, "it's because your father had no luck."

The boy was silent for some time.

"Is luck money, Mother!" he asked, rather timidly.

"No, Paul. Not quite. It's what causes you to have money."

"Oh!" said Paul vaguely. "I thought that when Uncle Oscar said *filthy lucker*, it meant money."

"*Filthy lucre* does mean money," said the mother. "But it's lucre, not luck."

"Oh!" said the boy. "Then what is luck, Mother?"

"It's what causes you to have money. If you're lucky, you have money. That's why it's better to be born lucky than rich. If you're rich, you may lose your money. But if you're lucky, you will always get more money."

"Oh! Will you? And is father not lucky?"

"Very unlucky, I should say," she said bitterly.

The boy watched her with unsure eyes.

"Why?" he asked.

"I don't know. Nobody ever knows why one person is lucky and another unlucky."

"Don't they? Nobody at all? Does *nobody* know?"

"Perhaps God. But He never tells."

"He ought to then, and aren't you lucky either, Mother?"

"I can't be, if I married an unlucky husband."

"But by yourself, aren't you?"

"I used to think I was, before I married. Now I think I am very unlucky indeed."

"Why?"

"Well – never mind! Perhaps I'm not really," she said.

The child looked at her to see if she meant it. But he saw, by the lines of her mouth, that she was only trying to hide something from him.

"Well, anyhow," he said stoutly, "I'm a lucky person."

"Why?" said his mother, with a sudden laugh.

He stared at her. He didn't even know why he had said it.

"God told me," he asserted, brazening it out.

"I hope He did, dear!" she said, again with a laugh, but rather bitter.

"He did, Mother!"

"Excellent!" said the mother, using one of her husband's exclamations.

The boy saw she did not believe him; or rather, that she paid no attention to his assertion. This angered him somewhere, and made him want to compel her attention.

He went off by himself, vaguely, in a childish way,

seeking for the clue to "luck". Absorbed, taking no heed of other people, he went about with a sort of stealth, seeking inwardly for luck. He wanted luck, he wanted it, he wanted it. When the two girls were playing dolls in the nursery, he would sit on his big rocking-horse, charging madly into space, with a frenzy that made the little girls peer at him uneasily. Wildly the horse careered, the waving dark hair of the boy tossed, his eyes had a strange glare in them. The little girls dared not speak to him.

When he had ridden to the end of his mad little journey, he climbed down and stood in front of his rocking-horse, staring fixedly into its lowered face. Its red mouth was slightly open, its big eye was wide and glassy-bright.

"Now!" he would silently command the snorting steed.

"Now, take me to where there is luck! Now take me!"

And he would slash the horse on the neck with the little whip he had asked Uncle Oscar for. He *knew* the horse could take him to where there was luck, if only he forced it. So he would mount again and start on his furious ride, hoping at last to get there. He knew he could get there.

"You'll break your horse, Paul!" said the nurse.

"He's always riding like that! I wish he'd leave off!" said his elder sister Joan.

But he only glared down on them in silence. Nurse gave him up. She could make nothing of him. Anyhow, he was growing beyond her.

One day his mother and his Uncle Oscar came in.

when he was on one of his furious rides. He did not speak to them.

"Hallo, you young jockey! Riding a winner?" said his uncle.

"Aren't you growing too big for a rocking-horse? You're not a very little boy any longer, you know," said his mother.

But Paul only gave a blue glare from his big, rather close-set eyes. He would speak to nobody when he was in full tilt. His mother watched him with an anxious expression on her face.

At last he suddenly stopped forcing his horse into the mechanical gallop and slid down.

"Well, I got there!" he announced fiercely, his blue eyes still flaring, and his sturdy long legs straddling apart.

"Where did you get to?" asked his mother.

"Where I wanted to go," he flared back at her.

"That's right, Son!" said Uncle Oscar. "Don't you stop till you get there. What's the horse's name?"

"He doesn't have a name," said the boy.

"Gets on without all right?" asked the uncle.

"Well, he has different names. He was called Sansovino last week."

"Sansovino, eh? Won the Ascot. How did you know this name?"

"He always talks about horse-races with Bassett," said Joan.

The uncle was delighted to find that his small nephew was posted with all the racing news. Bassett, the young gardener, who had been wounded in the left foot in the war and had got his present job through

Oscar Cresswell, whose batman he had been, was a perfect blade of the "turf". He lived in the racing events, and the small boy lived with him.

Oscar Cresswell got it all from Bassett.

"Master Paul comes and asks me, so I can't do more than tell him, sir," said Bassett, his face terribly serious, as if he were speaking of religious matters.

"And does he ever put anything on a horse he fancies?"

"Well – I don't want to give him away – he's a young sport, a fine sport, sir. Would you mind asking him himself? He sort of takes a pleasure in it, and perhaps he'd feel I was giving him away, sir, if you don't mind."

Bassett was serious as a church.

The uncle went back to his nephew and took him off for a ride in the car.

"Say, Paul, old man, do you ever put anything on a horse?" the uncle asked.

The boy watched the handsome man closely.

"Why, do you think I oughtn't to?" he parried.

"Not a bit of it! I thought perhaps you might give me a tip for the Lincoln."

The car sped on into the country, going down to Uncle Oscar's place in Hampshire.

"Honour bright?" said the nephew.

"Honour bright, Son!" said the uncle.

"Well, then, Daffodil."

"Daffodil! I doubt it, sonny. What about Mirza?"

"I only know the winner," said the boy. "That's Daffodil."

"Daffodil, eh?"

There was a pause. Daffodil was an obscure horse comparatively.

"Uncle!"

"Yes, Son?"

"You won't let it go any further, will you? I promised Bassett."

"Bassett be damned, old man! What's he got to do with it?"

"We're partners. We've been partners from the first. Uncle, he lent me my first five shillings, which I lost. I promised him, honour bright, it was only between me and him; only you gave me that ten-shilling note I started winning with, so I thought you were lucky. You won't let it go any further, will you?"

The boy gazed at his uncle from those big, hot, blue eyes, set rather close together. The uncle stirred and laughed uneasily.

"Right you are, Son! I'll keep your tip private. Daffodil, eh? How much are you putting on him?"

"All except twenty pounds," said the boy. "I keep that in reserve."

The uncle thought it a good joke.

"You keep twenty pounds in reserve, do you, you young romancer? What are you betting, then?"

"I'm betting three hundred," said the boy gravely. "But it's between you and me, Uncle Oscar! Honour bright?"

The uncle burst into a roar of laughter.

"It's between you and me all right, you young Nat Gould," he said, laughing. "But where's your three hundred?"

"Bassett keeps it for me. We're partners."

"You are, are you! And what is Bassett putting on Daffodil?"

"He won't go quite as high I do, I expect. Perhaps he'll go a hundred and fifty."

"What, pennies?" laughed the uncle.

"Pounds," said the child, with a surprised look at his uncle. "Bassett keeps a bigger reserve than I do."

Between wonder and amusement Uncle Oscar was silent. He pursued the matter no further, but he determined to take his nephew with him to the Lincoln races.

"Now, Son," he said, "I'm putting twenty on Mirza, and I'll put five on for you on any horse you fancy. What's your pick?"

"Daffodil, Uncle."

"No, not the fiver on Daffodil!"

"I should if it was my own fiver," said the child.

"Good! Good! Right you are! A fiver for me and a fiver for you on Daffodil."

The child had never been to a race-meeting before, and his eyes were blue fire. He pursed his mouth tight and watched. A Frenchman just in front had put his money on Lancelot. Wild with excitement, he flayed his arms up and down, yelling "*Lancelot! Lancelot!*" in his French accent.

Daffodil came in first, Lancelot second, Mirza third. The child, flushed and with eyes blazing, was curiously serene. His uncle brought him four five-pound notes, four to one.

"What am I to do with these?" he cried, waving them before the boy's eyes.

"I suppose we'll talk to Bassett," said the boy. "I

expect I have fifteen hundred now; and twenty in reserve; and this twenty."

His uncle studied him for some moments.

"Look here, Son!" he said. "You're not serious about Bassett and that fifteen hundred, are you?"

"Yes, I am. But it's between you and me, Uncle. Honour bright?"

"Honour bright all right, Son! But I must talk to Bassett."

"If you'd like to be a partner, Uncle, with Bassett and me, we could all be partners. Only, you'd have to promise, honour bright, Uncle, not to let it go beyond us three. Bassett and I are lucky, and you must be lucky, because it was your ten shillings I started winning with . . ."

Uncle Oscar took both Bassett and Paul into Richmond Park for an afternoon, and there they talked.

"It's like this, you see, sir," Bassett said. "Master Paul would get me talking about racing events, spinning yarns, you know, sir. And he was always keen on knowing if I'd made or if I'd lost. It's about a year since, now, that I put five shillings on Blush of Dawn for him: and we lost. Then the luck turned, with that ten shillings he had from you: that we put on Singhalese. And since that time, it's been pretty steady, all things considering. What do you say, Master Paul?"

"We're all right when we're sure," said Paul. "It's when we're not quite sure that we go down."

"Oh, but we're careful then," said Bassett.

"But when are you sure?" smiled Uncle Oscar.

"It's Master Paul, sir," said Bassett in a secret,

religious voice. "It's as if he had it from heaven. Like Daffodil, now, for the Lincoln. That was as sure as eggs."

"Did you put anything on Daffodil?" asked Oscar Cresswell.

"Yes, sir, I made my bit."

"And my nephew?"

Bassett was obstinately silent, looking at Paul.

"I made twelve hundred, didn't I, Bassett? I told Uncle I was putting three hundred on Daffodil."

"That's right," said Bassett, nodding.

"But where's the money?" asked the uncle.

"I keep it safe locked up, sir. Master Paul, he can have it any minute he likes to ask for it."

"What, fifteen hundred pounds?"

"And twenty! And forty, that is, with the twenty he made on the course."

"It's amazing!" said the uncle.

"If Master Paul offers you to be partners, sir, I would, if I were you: if you'll excuse me," said Bassett.

Oscar Cresswell thought about it.

"I'll see the money," he said.

They drove home again, and, sure enough, Bassett came round to the garden-house with fifteen hundred pounds in notes. The twenty pounds reserve was left with Joe Glee, in the Turf Commission deposit.

"You see, it's all right, Uncle, when I'm *sure*! Then we go strong, for all we're worth. Don't we, Bassett?"

"We do that, Master Paul."

"And when are you *sure*?" said the uncle, laughing.

"Oh, well, sometimes I'm *absolutely* sure, like about Daffodil," said the boy; "and sometimes I have an idea; and sometimes I haven't even an idea, have I, Bassett?

Then we're careful, because we mostly go down."

"You do, do you! And when you're sure, like about Daffodil, what makes you sure, Sonny?"

"Oh, well, I don't know," said the boy uneasily. "I'm sure, you know, Uncle; that's all."

"It's as if he had it from heaven, sir," Bassett reiterated.

"I should say so!" said the uncle.

But he became a partner. And when the Ledger was coming on, Paul was "sure" about Lively Spark, which was a quite inconsiderable horse. The boy insisted on putting a thousand on the horse, Bassett went for five hundred, and Oscar Cresswell two hundred. Lively Spark came in first, and the betting had been ten to one against him. Paul made ten thousand.

"You see," he said, "I was absolutely sure of him."

Even Oscar Cresswell had cleared two thousand.

"Look here, Son," he said, "this sort of thing makes me nervous."

"It needn't, Uncle! Perhaps I shan't be sure again for a long time."

"But what are you going to do with your money?" asked the uncle.

"Of course," said the boy, "I started it for Mother. She said she had no luck, because father is unlucky, so I thought if I was lucky, it might stop whispering."

"What might stop whispering?"

"Our house. I *hate* our house for whispering."

"What does it whisper?"

"Why – why" – the boy fidgeted – "why, I don't know. But it's always short of money, you know, Uncle."

"I know it, my son, I know it."

"You know people send Mother writs, don't you, Uncle?"

"I'm afraid I do," said the uncle.

"And then the house whispers, like people laughing at you behind your back. It's awful, that is! I thought if I was lucky—"

"You might stop it," added the uncle.

The boy watched him with big blue eyes, that had a uncanny cold fire in them, and he said never a word.

"Well, then!" said the uncle. "What are we doing?"

"I shouldn't like Mother to know I was lucky," said the boy.

"Why not, Son?"

"She'd stop me."

"I don't think she would."

"Oh!" – and the boy writhed in an odd way – "I *don't* want her to know, Uncle."

"All right, Son! We'll manage it without her knowing."

They managed it very easily. Paul, at the other's suggestion, handed over five thousand pounds to his uncle, who deposited it with the family lawyer, who was then to inform Paul's mother that a relative had put five thousand pounds into his hands, which sum was to be paid out a thousand pounds at a time, on the mother's birthday, for the next five years.

"So she'll have a birthday present of a thousand pounds for five years," said Uncle Oscar. "I hope it won't make it all the harder for her later."

Paul's mother had her birthday in November. The house had been "whispering" worse than ever lately, and, even in spite of his luck, Paul could not bear up against it. He was very anxious to see the effect of the birthday letter, telling his mother about the thousand pounds.

There were no visitors, Paul now took his meals with his parents, as he was beyond the nursery control. His mother went into town nearly every day. She had discovered that she had an odd knack of sketching furs and dress materials, so she worked secretly in the studio of a friend who was the chief "artist" for the leading drapers. She drew the figures of ladies in furs and ladies in silk and sequins for the newspaper advertisements. This young woman artist earned several thousand pounds a year, but Paul's mother only made several hundreds, and she was again dissatisfied. She so wanted to be first in something, and she did not succeed, even in making sketches for drapery advertisements.

She was down to breakfast on the morning of her birthday. Paul watched her face as she read her letters. He knew the lawyer's letter. As his mother read it, her face hardened and became more expressionless. Then a cold, determined look came on her mouth. She hid the letter under a pile of others, and said not a word about it.

"Didn't you have anything nice in the post for your birthday, Mother?" said Paul.

"Quite moderately nice," she said, her voice cold and absent.

She went away to town without saying more.

But in the afternoon Uncle Oscar appeared. He said Paul's mother had had a long interview with the lawyer, asking if the whole five thousand could not be advanced at once, as she was in debt.

"What do you think, Uncle?" said the boy.

"I leave it to you, Son."

"Oh, let her have it, then! We can get some more with the other," said the boy.

"A bird in the hand is worth two in the bush, laddie!" said Uncle Oscar.

"But I'm sure to know for the Grand National; or the Lincolnshire; or else the Derby. I'm sure to know for one of them," said Paul.

So Uncle Oscar signed the agreement, and Paul's mother touched the whole five thousand. Then something very curious happened. The voices in the house suddenly went mad, like a chorus of frogs on a spring evening. There were certain new furnishings, and Paul had a tutor. He was *really* going to Eton, his father's school, in the following autumn. There were flowers in the winter, and a blossoming of the luxury Paul's mother had been used to. And yet the voices in the house, behind the sprays of mimosa and almond-blossom, and from under piles of iridescent cushions, simply trilled and screamed in a sort of ecstasy: "There *must* be more money! Oh-h-h; there *must* be more money. Oh, now, now-w! Now-w-w − there *must* be more money! − more than ever! More than ever!"

It frightened Paul terribly. He studied away at his Latin and Greek with his tutor. But his intense hours were spent with Bassett. The Grand National had gone by; he had not "known", and had lost a hundred pounds. Summer was at hand. He was in agony for the Lincoln. But even for the Lincoln he didn't "know", and he lost fifty pounds. He became wild-eyed and strange, as if something were going to explode in him.

"Let it alone, Son! Don't you bother about it!"

urged Uncle Oscar. But it was as if the boy couldn't really hear what his uncle was saying.

"I've got to know for the Derby! I've got to know for the Derby!" the child reiterated, his big blue eyes blazing with a sort of madness.

His mother noticed how overwrought he was.

"You'd better go to the seaside. Wouldn't you like to go now to the seaside, instead of waiting? I think you'd better," she said, looking down at him anxiously, her heart curiously heavy because of him.

But the child lifted his uncanny blue eyes.

"I couldn't possibly go before the Derby, Mother!" he said. "I couldn't possibly!"

"Why not?" she said, her voice becoming heavy when she was opposed. "Why not? You can still go from the seaside to see the Derby with your Uncle Oscar, if that's what you wish. No need for you to wait here. Besides, I think you care too much about these races. It's a bad sign. My family has been a gambling family, and you wouldn't know till you grow up how much damage it has done. But it has done damage. I shall have to send Bassett away, and ask Uncle Oscar not to talk racing to you, unless you promise to be reasonable about it: go away to the seaside and forget it. You're all nerves!"

"I'll do what you like, Mother, so long as you don't send me away till after the Derby," the boy said.

"Send you away from where? Just from this house?"

"Yes," he said, gazing at her.

"Why, you curious child, what makes you care about this house so much, suddenly? I never knew you loved it."

He gazed at her without speaking. He had a secret within a secret, something he had not divulged, even to Bassett or to his Uncle Oscar.

But his mother, after standing undecided and a little bit sullen for some moments, said:

"Very well, then! Don't go to the seaside till after the Derby, if you don't wish it. But promise me you won't let your nerves go to pieces. Promise you won't think so much about horse-racing, and *events*, as you call them!"

"Oh, no," said the boy casually. "I won't think much about them, Mother. You needn't worry. I wouldn't worry, Mother, if I were you."

"If you were me and I were you," said his mother, "I wonder what we *should* do!"

"But you know you needn't worry, Mother, don't you?" the boy repeated.

"I should be awfully glad to know it," she said wearily.

"Oh, well, you *can,* you know. I mean, you ought to know you needn't worry," he insisted.

"Ought I? Then I'll see about it," she said.

Paul's secret of secrets was his wooden horse, that which had no name. Since he was emancipated from a nurse and a nursery-governess, he had had his rocking-horse removed to his own bedroom at the top of the house.

"Surely you're too big for a rocking-horse!" his mother had remonstrated.

"Well, you see, Mother, till I can have a real horse, I like to have some sort of animal about," had been his quaint answer.

"Do you feel he keeps you company?" she laughed.

"Oh, yes! He's very good, he always keeps me company, when I'm there," said Paul.

So the horse, rather shabby, stood in an arrested prance in the boy's bedroom.

The Derby was drawing near, and the boy grew more and more tense. He hardly heard what was spoken to him, he was very frail, and his eyes were really uncanny. His mother had sudden strange seizures of uneasiness about him. Sometimes, for half an hour, she would feel a sudden anxiety about him that was almost anguish. She wanted to rush to him at once, and know he was safe.

Two nights before the Derby, she was at a big party in town, when one of her rushes of anxiety about her boy, her first-born, gripped her heart till she could hardly speak. She fought with the feeling, might and main, for she believed in common sense. But it was too strong. She had to leave the dance and go downstairs to telephone to the country. The children's nursery-governess was terribly surprised and startled at being rung up in the night.

"Are the children all right, Miss Wilmot?"

"Oh yes, they are quite all right."

"Master Paul? Is he all right?"

"He went to bed as right as a trivet. Shall I run up and look at him?"

"No," said Paul's mother reluctantly. "No! Don't trouble. It's all right. Don't sit up. We shall be home fairly soon." She did not want her son's privacy intruded upon.

"Very good," said the governess.

It was about one o'clock when Paul's mother and father drove up to their house. All was still. Paul's mother went to her room and slipped off her white fur cloak. She had told her maid not to wait up for her. She heard her husband downstairs, mixing a whisky and soda.

And then, because of the strange anxiety at her heart, she stole upstairs to her son's room. Noiselessly she went along the upper corridor. Was there a faint noise? What was it?

She stood, with arrested muscles, outside his door, listening. There was a strange, heavy, and yet not loud noise. Her heart stood still. It was a soundless noise, yet rushing and powerful. Something huge, in a violent, hushed motion. What was it? What in God's name was it? She ought to know. She felt that she knew the noise. She knew what it was.

Yet she could not place it. She couldn't say what it was. And on and on it went, like a madness.

Softly, frozen with anxiety and fear, she turned the door-handle.

The room was dark. Yet in the space near the window, she heard and saw something plunging to and fro. She gazed in fear and amazement.

Then suddenly she switched on the light, and saw her son, in his green pyjamas, madly surging on the rocking-horse. The blaze of light suddenly lit him up, as he urged the wooden horse, and lit her up, as she stood, blonde, in her dress of pale green and crystal, in the doorway.

"Paul!" she cried. "Whatever are you doing?"

"It's Malabar!" he screamed in a powerful, strange voice. "It's Malabar!"

His eyes blazed at her for one strange and senseless second, as he ceased urging his wooden horse. Then he fell with a crash to the ground, and she, all her tormented motherhood flooding upon her, rushed to gather him up.

But he was unconscious, and unconscious he remained, with some brain-fever. He talked and tossed, and his mother sat stonily by his side.

"Malabar! It's Malabar! Bassett, Bassett, I know! It's Malabar!"

So the child cried, trying to get up and urge the rocking-horse that gave him his inspiration.

"What does he mean by Malabar?" asked the heart-frozen mother.

"I don't know," said the father stonily.

"What does he mean by Malabar?" she asked her brother Oscar.

"It's one of the horses running in the Derby," was the answer.

And, in spite of himself, Oscar Cresswell spoke to Bassett, and himself put a thousand on Malabar: at fourteen to one.

The third day of the illness was critical: they were waiting for a change. The boy, with his rather long, curly hair, was tossing ceaselessly on the pillow. He neither slept nor regained consciousness, and his eyes were like blue stones. His mother sat, feeling her heart had gone, turned actually into stone.

In the evening, Oscar Cresswell did not come, but Bassett sent a message, saying could he come up for one moment, just one moment? Paul's mother was very angry at the intrusion, but on second thoughts she agreed. The boy was the same. Perhaps Bassett might bring him to consciousness.

The gardener, a shortish fellow with a little brown moustache and sharp little brown eyes, tiptoed into the room, touched his imaginary cap to Paul's mother, and stole to the bedside, staring with glittering, smallish eyes at the tossing, dying child.

"Master Paul!" he whispered. "Master Paul! Malabar came in first all right, a clean win. I did as you told me. You've made over seventy thousand pounds, you have; you've got over eighty thousand. Malabar came in all right, Master Paul."

"Malabar! Malabar! Did I say Malabar, Mother? Did I say Malabar? Do you think I'm lucky, Mother? I knew, Malabar, didn't I? Over eighty thousand pounds! I call that lucky, don't you, Mother? Over eighty thousand pounds! I knew, didn't I know I knew? Malabar came in all right. If I ride my horse till I'm sure, then I tell you, Bassett, you can go as high as you like. Did you go for all you were worth, Bassett?"

"I went a thousand on it, Master Paul."

"I never told you, Mother, that if I can ride my horse, and *get there*, then I'm absolutely sure – oh, absolutely! Mother, did I ever tell you? I *am* lucky!"

"No, you never did," said his mother.

But the boy died in the night.

And even as he lay dead, his mother heard her brother's voice saying to her: "My God, Hester, you're eighty-odd thousand to the good, and a poor devil of a son to the bad. But, poor devil, poor devil, he's best gone out of a life where he rides his rocking-horse to find a winner."

BEHOLD, THE PALIO!

MARGUERITE HENRY from Gaudenzia, Pride of the Palio

The Palio is one of the most dangerous horse races in the world, held every year in Siena, Italy. Giorgio, a young boy from the Maremma Marshes, is nursing Gaudenzia, who has been lamed in last year's Palio and is preparing her to take part in the next Palio. The "contradas" are the districts from which the "fantinos" (jockeys) and their horses are chosen to ride in the race. The "nerbos" are the whips they are allowed to use.

JUNE! THE HALLWAY into summer. The season for strong happenings, the season for living. Giorgio's mind was on tip-toe. Looking at his calendar one morning he thought, in a flash, of the ski slide on Mount Amiata, saw the skiers toiling up and up for one breathless whoosh into space. Now he knew how they felt. For months he and Gaudenzia had been toiling up and up for the wild two minutes of glory that was the Palio.

The days of June neither dragged nor flew. They were as alike as echoes. Walk Gaudenzia one kilometre, jog her three, gallop her three and a half. Bandage her hind legs, bandage her forelegs. Give her grain, a handful more each day. Cut down her hay and always, the inner command pounding through him: Don't let her reach the peak until July. Climb, climb, climb. Bring her right up *to* it.

In the last week of June, the long-awaited message from the Chief-of-the-Guards reached Giorgio. "Come to Siena! At once!" was all it said.

By cockcrow on the morning after, boy and mare were on their way, trotting along gay-spirited, as if the wheatfields spattered with wild red poppies, and the hills high-rising to the sky, and all the creatures in it were theirs. Gaudenzia wanted to race every moving thing − a rabbit skirting the edge of the road, a hound streaking for a bird − the bird too. Her friskiness, her eagerness to go filled him with a pride so strong he had to whistle to let the steam of his happiness escape. Nine months ago, with a bandage on her heel, she had made her way slow-footed over this same road. Now, like Mercury with wings, she was returning.

A solitary shepherd, hungry for human company, ran out on the road and invited Giorgio to share the meal he was preparing over an open fire. He pointed his crook at Gaudenzia.

"*Magnifico!*" he exclaimed, with a smile so wide it showed the dark hole where two of his teeth were missing.

"*Magnifica!*" Giorgio laughingly corrected him. "She is a mare!" He joined the herdsman in a meal of goat cheese and grilled eel. And while the mare grazed, her eyes ranging with the cloud of sheep, the lonely herder questioned Giorgio about his plans. Then he poured out his own heart. He too had a dream. He would teach a young boy to herd, teach him just where to rest the sheep, and which ones to watch in a storm. Then he would be free for a little while, and he would walk to Siena, and there, before he died, he would witness with his own eyes the manifestation of the Palio!

It was all Giorgio could do to break away from the man and his dream. With their final handshake the herder for the first time became mute. Wistfully, he watched Giorgio mount Gaudenzia and rein her out onto the road. When at last he found his voice, he cupped his hands and called out after them:

"Magnifica!"

In Siena, too, the mare created admiration, but it was thinned with doubts and forebodings. Entering the city through the Arch of Porta Romana in the early evening, Giorgio could feel at once the general air of agitation. The usual flow of promenaders had given way to excited knots of men choking the traffic. Bruco! Occa! Onda! Tartuca! The names of the contradas punctuated the talk. And town eyes were staring his way.

"What a beautiful beast goes there!" a voice said. And the same voice asked, "Boy, where did you get her? What are you going to do with her?"

Giorgio turned and saw a grizzle-headed old man, the centre of a group. "It's a long story, Signore," he answered. "She used to be Farfalla, but now she—"

The man did not let him finish. "Eh?" he exclaimed. "Can this be Farfalla returned from the dead?"

And another said, "A fine parade horse she would make. But for the race?" The shoulders owning the voice shrugged.

And then Giorgio overheard, "Would you wish to draw her for *your* contrada?"

A whole chorus answered, "No! No!" It was as if her

tortured limping in last year's Palio was a memory too fresh to be wiped out.

Giorgio himself flinched at the recollection. He touched his heels to Gaudenzia and hurried her through the crowd. "How they feel about you, I do not care," he told himself. "It is better so. Popular horses are nearly killed by too many sweets, too much petting and pulling of tail-hairs for souvenir. I believe, and the Chief believes!"

He found the Chief striding across Il Campo, heading for his home. They saw each other at the same moment.

"Giorgio!" the big man shouted, and his arms flung wide apart, as though he would clasp the boy and the mare both. "How are you? How is it with our *cavallina*? Tell me all about her! Don't keep me one minute more in this anxious waiting."

Giorgio suddenly felt shy. He answered with two little words. "All fine."

"That I can see!" the Chief laughed. "The mare, she is rekindled!" He stepped now in front of Gaudenzia, pulled off his white gloves, and with both hands felt her chest and forearms. "Not even sweating," he nodded in approval. "Come, let us walk to the stable, and while walking you will tell me how she goes in her work. Then, after she is bedded down, you will come to my home where we can engage in serious talk."

The stable was midway down a narrow alley with walls high-rising on either side. Giorgio's spirits plummeted at its darkness. It did have a window, but it was covered by a curtain of gunny sacking. There were two stalls divided by heavy planking. The one nearer the door was occupied by a bay gelding, and the other, deeply strawed, awaited Gaudenzia.

"To find stable room is very difficult," the Chief was explaining. "But Morello here is a good horse and the two will become friends and help each other to forget the Maremma. He, too, comes from your wilderness."

Across the partition Gaudenzia and Morello began at once to get acquainted – first in screams, then nips, and at last in low whinnies.

"How quick they make friends!" the Chief grinned. "Now then, the hay is piled here, the grain is in the sack yonder, and the medicines in the cabinet. Now you can take over."

Giorgio noted the racks already filled, the water buckets brimming. He would come back later to grain and groom Gaudenzia and to remove the gunny-sack curtain.

He followed the Chief to his home, which perched on a ledge of rock like an eagle's nest. The view was miniature compared to the world of the Maremma. Below was a tiny dim valley, and climbing the opposite hillside were busy little farm plots. But the same deep sky was overhead and the same stars beginning to punch holes in the blue.

The Chief's wife and daughter greeted Giorgio with politeness and relief. "The supper is ready," the Signora said with a hot-stove smile. "I would not want the chicken to cook a moment longer."

The meal was a feast such as Giorgio had not tasted since his days at the Ramallis'. First there was a piping hot broth of chicken with tiny pearls of dough swimming along the bottom. Then came a beautiful plate of antipasto — black olives, and mushrooms in oil, and little white onions, and small green peppers, and anchovies curved into tight nests, with a caper on each. Giorgio was encouraged to take something of everything. And still he had room for a drumstick and breast of chicken, and a baked tomato stuffed with ground beef.

All of this he sluiced down with a red Chianti wine which he thriftily diluted with water as though he were at home.

The Chief helped himself to the food sparingly, and in silence. He seemed preoccupied, brooding. But Giorgio ate heartily. The Signora beamed at him. "For a small man, as you are," she said, appreciatively, "you have *un bel appetito.*"

Giorgio felt his face flush and his ears redden at the half-and-half compliment.

With the dessert of fruit and cheeses on the table, the wife and daughter disappeared into the kitchen. The silence grew heavy. The Chief pushed back his plate without touching the food. At last the moment for talk had arrived.

But the words did not come. He ran his finger around the inside of his collar and cleared his throat. He got up and stood at the open door, looking out upon the night. He came back and sat down again. Then, gripping the edge of the table, he blurted out, "My boy, the Palio is not going to be as we dreamed it."

Giorgio swallowed whole the apricot in his mouth. It was as though an icy hand had gripped his throat.

"You see, the *people* want beautiful horses such as

199

Gaudenzia, but the judges, no!"

Giorgio's voice sank back so deep inside him it was scarcely audible. "But why?"

The Chief took a breath. For the boy's sake he wanted to sound matter-of-fact, to ease him gently into disappointment. "The news of Gaudenzia's win at Casole d'Elsa has spread to Siena. All at once she is known as the daughter of Sans Souci, a full-blood Arab. And the full-bloods are not wanted."

"But, Signore, she is only half-bred. Her dam was a farm horse."

"I know, I know," the Chief answered in irritation. "But because she is now too beautiful, too well-trained, the rejection may come."

Giorgio waited in numbness.

"High-mettled Arabians have caprices, the judges say. Besides, the turns of the course are too perilous and the layer of earth over the cobblestones too thin for a full-blood with the delicate toothpick legs."

There was a momentary pause as the Chief's daughter brought in two small cups of coffee.

"You see, Giorgio, we Sienese are like moles burrowing, always digging into our past. I have heard the judges say, as if only yesterday it happened, how in the year 1500 Cesare Borgio's big stallion reared on his hind legs and in coming back to earth hit the starting rope so hard he could not run in the Palio. And in 1885, the purebred La Gorgona cracked up in the last Prova, her legs brittle like eggshell. And you, Giorgio, you must remember Habana? You remember when she flew into the fence, and broke the boards to splinters!"

"But, Signore! It happens with the mixed blood,

too. Have they forgot Turbolento?"

"*He* fell, Giorgio. But the others? One might say they destroyed themselves."

Anger lit Giorgio's eyes. "Signore! This you should have told me before! Why did you send for Gaudenzia and me? Why did you let me nourish all the hopes to win?"

The Chief wiped his face tiredly. "I do not know, truly. Perhaps the hope is in me, too. Perhaps the hope is stronger than the reality. I fear, Giorgio," he said again, "the Palio is not going to be as we dreamed it."

"Signore! Shake yourself!" Giorgio's anger turned to wild appeal. His words tumbled out bravely, recklessly. "Something we can do! Something we *must* do! Think!" He took hold of the man's sleeve, actually shaking him in his eagerness.

The Chief closed his eyes thoughtfully. "What comes to mind," he said at last, "is a very simple plan. Maybe too simple."

"Tell me! Tell me!"

Something of the old vigour crept into the Chief's voice. "Listen well, my boy. In the trials when the horses are selected, you must make Gaudenzia appear mature, sensible; an average beast."

Giorgio nodded, listening with every fibre.

"And in her workouts she must appear tranquil."

"That is easy! Easy! What else?"

"Wherever you make talk, you must say how her dam was a poor old farm horse and how she herself was a cart horse for many years, and her colts were nothing at all, good only for the slaughterhouse."

"I will!"

"Margherita," the Chief called to his daughter, "our coffee is now cold." He turned back to Giorgio. "Only one thing is in our favour. You see . . ."

There was a pause as fresh coffee came and he liberally spooned sugar into both cups. "Because all the contradas think her nervous, unpredictable, none will ask for agreement from you to help another horse to win."

Giorgio sighed in deep relief. "Of that I am glad. When I am on Gaudenzia I am *simpatico* only to her. But why is it no one has ever come to me to make the secret agreement?"

The Chief could not help chuckling. "'The runt of Monticello,' they say, 'is young and green like a new spear of wheat. We do not make agreements with a boy so little he has to have double lining in his helmet to keep it on.'"

The man suddenly went silent. What if Giorgio were not asked to ride Gaudenzia in the Palio? He held his tongue. The boy had had enough worries for one night.

The day of the Palio

Seven o'clock. Time spinning itself out. Time throwing its shadows up and up the tower. Excitement mounting with the shadows. The knights and nobles, having completed the turn of the track, seat themselves on the benches in front of the Palazzo. The rich colours of their costumes make a dazzling design, like jewels in a crown – rubies and emeralds, sapphires and amethysts.

With the other fantinos Giorgio guides his charger into the big courtyard of the Palazzo. He takes a quick look back. The track is empty now except for the flag twirlers of all the contradas. His eyes are glued to them. They look like gnomes playing with sheets of fire, flinging their furled staffs thirty feet into the air until each one bursts in a blaze of crackling colour.

Before he has looked enough, the groom prods him along. "Come! Do you forget the race?"

Within the high-vaulted court all is disciplined order. Ten pages are leading the war chargers away. Ten grooms are tying their race horses to iron rings round the walls. Ten fantinos, with the help of their costumed boys, are changing clothes – from suede buskins to rubber-soled shoes, from velvet tunics to cotton jackets, from plumed headgear to steel helmets. Giorgio runs his finger inside the rim of his helmet. Yes! It has been padded to fit. He sees that his hands are trembling. He wipes their dampness on a rag which the groom tosses him. He casts sidelong glances at the other fantinos. Ivan-the-Terrible glares at him, carrying on the feud from last year.

The starter picks up his megaphone, barks out rules and warnings: "*Attenzione!* It is permissible to ward off your enemy with the nerbo, but never grasp the bridle of an enemy horse. The eyes of the world are upon you. Represent well the spirit of Siena, and of your contrada. Be brave!"

Only a few minutes to go. The barbaresco of Onda carries out his final duties – checks the bridle of Gaudenzia, her cheekstrap, her chinstrap, her reins; last of all her spennacchiera . . . is it anchored solidly in case her fantino should fall? He dips his hands in a basin of water and solemnly, as if he were performing a sacred rite, uses the flat of his hands to wet the mare's withers, her back, her barrel, her flanks.

"Giorgio—" His voice sounds winded, like a run-out dog. He tries again. "Giorgio, I have made her coat damp. It will help you stick on. Now, run the best race of your life." He unties her from the iron ring. "Here, she is yours. I have done all I can. *Now rules Fate, the Queen of the Palio.*"

Giorgio takes the reins and studies the mare from pricked ears to tail. Her neck is frosted with foam, her nostrils distended, her eyes darkly intent. He does not answer the groom. He has just himself to answer. "No! No! *Not Fate!*"

Only a few seconds to go.

A squad of guards marches in, surrounds the starter to escort him to his box beneath the judges' scaffold. The man walks out slowly, his face showing worry; he knows full well that if he releases the starting rope an instant too late, ten horses may fall, and his own life be threatened by angry throngs.

The Chief-of-the-Town-Guards takes his post at the entrance of the Palazzo. In one hand he holds a white flag, in the other, ten nerbos. He looks out into the square, watches the starter mount his box, watches the ragno, the little spider-man, climb up to his cage, ready to touch off the gunpowder. He turns his head to the courtyard. The horses and fantinos are ready.

Now! He lifts the white flag, waving it on high to alert the ragno. Bang! The air quivers as the bomb bursts in a deafening percussion. It is the signal for the fantinos to ride out. The roaring in the amphitheatre stops as if cut off by a sharp knife. The silence is full of mystery, almost of pain. Then sixty thousand throats cry out:

"*A cavallo! A cavallo!* To horse! To horse!"

As each jockey in turn rides out, the Chief presents him with the nerbo. Instinctively, the horses who have been in a Palio before shy in fright.

Giorgio's breath catches in his throat. His right hand, still tingling from gripping the lance, now accepts the nerbo from the firm hands of the Chief. "Will I have to use it?" he asks himself.

Out from the maw of the courtyard the cavalcade moves forward towards the starting rope. Through his legs and thighs he can feel the mare's heart pounding against him. He hears the starter call out the horses in order. He prays for first position – or last.

"Number one, Lupa, the Wolf!" A thunder of applause goes up, boos and cheers mingling.

"Number two, the Tower!

"Aquila, the Eagle, number three!

"Tartuca, the Turtle, four!"

As they are called, the horses prance up, take their positions between the ropes. Eagle and Wolf are jumpy, move about, change positions. The starter sternly sends all four horses back, recalls them again one by one, then goes on:

"Number five, Drago, the Dragon!

"Number six, Civetta, the Owl!

"Montone, the Ram, seven!"

The whistles and the shouts are strong. "Up with Montone! Up with Montone! Up with Ivan!"

"Istrice, the Porcupine, eight!

"Giraffa, nine!"

The nine wait tensely for the final call. Giorgio tries to conceal his joy. He will be number ten! He knows the rules, revels in them. The number ten horse starts behind the others.

With a rush she will come up to the rope and trigger the race.

The starter raises his megaphone. His voice shrills: "Number ten, Onda! Come on!"

Giorgio's heart beats with a wild gladness. Now it is! The time for action! He lifts Gaudenzia's head; she leaps forward. The rope drops at the split instant she touches it. It rolls free, coiling up on itself, almost onto her pasterns. As it falls to the track, ten horses are off like gunshot, Gaudenzia in the lead!

With Montone hot on her heels, she travels fast in spite of the sticky track. Landmarks spin by – the Fonte Gaia, the casino of the nobles, the palaces of Saracini and Sansedoni. Giorgio sucks in all the air his lungs can hold. Ahead lies the sharp right angle turn of San Martino, the waiting ambulance in plain sight.

From bleachers, from balconies, from all over the Piazza Gaudenzia's enemies are shrieking for blood. In full stride she goes up the incline. A moment of terror! She stumbles, breaks gait. Ivan, for Montone, tries to crowd her into the posts. But Giorgio grasps her mane, squeezes his right leg into her flanks. Squeezes tighter. It works! She recovers; she's safe!

"Bravo . . . Bravissimo!" The crowd is crazed with emotion.

Only the red jacket of Montone is anywhere near as Gaudenzia flies along the straight to the narrows of the Casato, and uphill for the strangles of that curve. Using her tail as a rudder, she veers round the curve, gallops down the stretch to pass the starter's box, still holding the lead.

The blood sings in Giorgio's ears. He clucks to Gaudenzia for the second lap, forgets he has a nerbo. The piston legs of Montone pound on relentlessly, press forward, gain on her at the fountain, gain going around San Martino. Almost to the Casato again, Giorgio tenses, deliberately cuts in front of Ivan. He has to, to get to the rail, to shorten the distance! This is battle! All in a split second Ivan's horse is forced to brake. In turn Lupa is blocked; she swerves, careens, hurtles to the ground, dragging the oncoming Giraffa and Tartuca with her. The track is a mad scramble of horses and riders! Gaudenzia for Onda is still streaking on.

"*Forza! Forza!*" the voices shriek. "Give it to us, Giorgio! Give us the Palio!"

And round for the third time she battles Montone, who is making one last desperate effort to catch up. But he is no match for Gaudenzia. Not weaving, not wobbling, moving at a terrific pace, she goes the whole lap. As she flashes by the flag of arrival, Giorgio wildly waves his nerbo in victory. He has not used it before!

With roars of triumph, the Onda victors spill out upon the track, hug their hero, lift him up, carry him on their shoulders. Angry losers close in, to pinch and pull and buffet him. A corps of howling, happy men of Onda try to force them back, but it is the Chief-of-the-Guards who succeeds. He makes himself a one-man shield and his voice bellows like a bull. "Lift him high! *Higher!*" he commands. "Before they murder him!" Then, eyes brimming in pride, he salutes Giorgio on both cheeks, and kisses his white mare full on the mouth.

The cart horse of Casalino has won the 536th running of the Palio.

A MAN JUSTLY POPULAR

R. D. BLACKMORE from Lorna Doone

IT HAPPENED UPON a November evening (when I was about fifteen years old, and out-growing my strength very rapidly, my sister Annie being turned thirteen, and a deal of rain having fallen, and all the troughs in the yard being flooded) that the ducks in the court made a terrible quacking, instead of marching off to their pen, one behind another. Thereupon Annie and I ran out to see what might be the sense of it, and when we got down to the foot of the courtyard where the two great ash-trees stand by the side of the little water, we found good reason for the urgence and melancholy of the duck-birds. Lo! the old white drake, the father of all, a bird of high manners and chivalry was now in a sad predicament, yet quacking very stoutly. For the brook was coming down in a great brown flood, as if the banks never belonged to it. The foaming of it, and the noise, and the cresting of the corners, and the up and down, like a wave of the sea, were enough to frighten any duck, though bred upon stormy waters, which our ducks never had been.

There is always a hurdle, nine feet long and four and a half in depth, swung by a chain at either end from an oak laid across the channel. But now this hurdle, which hung in the summer a foot above the trickle, would have been dipped more than two feet deep but for the power against it. For the torrent came down so vehemently that the chains at full stretch were creaking, and the hurdle buffeted almost flat. But saddest to see was between two bars, our venerable mallard jammed in by the joint of his shoulder, speaking aloud as he rose and fell, with his top-knot full of water, unable to comprehend it, with his tail washed far away from him, but often compelled to be silent, being ducked very harshly against his will by the choking fall-to of the hurdle.

Annie was crying, and wringing her hands, and I was about to rush into the water, although I liked not the look of it, but hoped to hold on by the hurdle, when a man on horseback came suddenly round the corner of the great ash-hedge on the other side of the stream, and his horse's feet were in the water.

"Ho, there," he cried. "Get thee back, boy. The flood will carry thee down like a straw. I will do it for thee, and no trouble."

With that he leaned forward, and spoke to his mare – she was just of the tint of a strawberry, a young thing, very beautiful – and she arched up her neck, as misliking the job; yet, trusting him, would attempt it. She entered the flood, with her dainty fore-legs sloped further and further in front of her, and her delicate ears pricked forward, and the size of her great eyes increasing; but he kept her straight in the turbid rush, by the pressure of his knee on her. Then she looked back, and wondered at him, as the force of the torrent grew stronger, but he bade her go on; and on she went, and it foamed up over her shoulders; and she tossed up her lip and scorned it, for now her courage was waking. Then as the rush of it swept her away, and she struck with her forefeet down the stream, he leaned from his saddle in a manner which I never could have thought possible, and caught up the old drake with his left hand, and set him between his holsters, and smiled at his faint quack of gratitude. In a moment all three were carried downstream, and the rider lay flat on his horse, and tossed the hurdle clear from him, and made for the bend of smooth water.

They landed, some thirty or forty yards lower, in the midst of our kitchen-garden, where the winter-cabbage was; but though Annie and I crept in through the hedge, and were full of our thanks and admiring him, he would answer us never a word, until he had spoken in full to the mare, as if explaining the whole to her. She answered him kindly with her soft eyes, and sniffed at him very lovingly, and they understood one another. Then he took from his waistcoat two peppercorns, and made the old drake swallow them, and tried him softly upon his legs, where the leading gap in the hedge was.

The gentleman turned round to us with a pleasant smile on his face, as if he were lightly amused with himself; and we came up and looked at him. He was rather short, but very strongly built and springy, as his gait at every step showed plainly, although his legs were bowed with much riding, and he looked as if he lived on horseback. To a boy like me he seemed very old, being over twenty, and well-found in beard; but he was not more than four-and-twenty, fresh and ruddy-looking, with a short nose, and keen blue eyes, and a merry waggish jerk about him, as if the world were not in earnest. Yet he had a sharp, stern way, like the crack of a pistol, if anything misliked him; and we knew (for children see such things) that it was safer to tickle than buffet him.

"Well, young uns, what be gaping at?" He gave pretty Annie a chuck on the chin, and took me all in without winking. "I am thy mother's cousin, boy, and am going up to house. Tom Faggus is my name, as everybody knows; and this is my young mare, Winnie."

What a fool I must have been not to know it at once! Tom Faggus, the great highwayman, and his young blood-mare, the strawberry! Already her fame was noised abroad, nearly as much as her master's, especially as there were rumours that she was not a mare after all, but a witch. However, she looked like a filly all over, and wonderfully beautiful, with her supple stride, and soft slope of shoulder, and glossy coat beaded with water, and prominent eyes full of docile fire.

Tom Faggus stopped to sup that night with us, and having changed his wet things first, he seemed to be in fair appetite, and praised Annie's cooking mightily, with a kind of noise like a smack of his lips, and a rubbing of his hands together, whenever he could spare them.

Tom Faggus was a jovial soul, if ever there has been one, not making bones of little things, nor caring to seek evil. There was about him such a love of genuine human nature, that if a traveller said a good thing, he would give him back his purse again. It is true that he took people's money more by force than fraud; and the law (being used to the inverse method) was bitterly moved against him, although he could quote precedent.

"Now let us go and see Winnie, Jack," he said to me after supper. "She must be grieving for me, and I never let her grieve long." I was too glad to go with him, and Annie came slyly after us. The filly was walking to and fro on the naked floor of the stable and without so much as a headstall on, for he would not have her fastened.

"Hit me, Jack, and see what she will do. I will not let her hurt thee." He was rubbing her ears all the time he spoke, and she was leaning against him. Then I made believe to strike him, and in a moment she caught me by the waistband, and lifted me clean from the ground, and was casting me down to trample upon me, when he stopped her suddenly.

"What think you of that, boy? Have you horse, or dog, that would do that for you? Ay, and more than that she will do. If I were to whistle, by and by, in the tone that tells my danger, she would break this stable-door down, and rush into the room to me. Nothing will keep her from me then, stone-wall, or church-tower. Ah, Winnie, Winnie, you little witch, we shall die together."

Now although Mr Faggus was so clever, and generous and celebrated, I know not whether, upon the whole, we were rather proud of him as a member of our family, or inclined to be ashamed of him. And sure, I should pity, as well as condemn him, though our ways in the world were so different, knowing as I do his story. Much cause he had to be harsh with the world;

and yet all acknowledged him very pleasant, when a man gave up his money. And often and often he paid the toll for the carriage coming after him, because he had emptied their pockets, and would not add inconvenience. By trade he had been a blacksmith, in the town of Northmolton, in Devonshire, a rough rude place at the end of Exmoor; so that many people marvelled if such a man was bred there. Not only could he read and write, but he had solid substance; a piece of land worth a hundred pounds, and right of common for two hundred sheep, and a score and a half of beasts, lifting up or lying down. And being left an orphan (with all these cares upon him) he began to work right early, and made such a fame at the shoeing of horses, that the farriers of Barum were like to lose their custom.

When his trade was growing upon him, and his sweetheart ready to marry him (for he loved a maid of Southmolton), suddenly, like a thunderbolt, a lawyer's writ fell upon him.

This was the beginning of a lawsuit with Sir Robert Bampfylde, a gentleman of the neighbourhood, who tried to oust him from his common, and drove his cattle and harassed them. And by that suit of law poor Tom was ruined altogether, for Sir Robert could pay for much swearing; and then all his goods and his farm were sold up, and even his smithery taken. But he saddled his horse, before they could catch him, and rode away to Southmolton, looking more like a madman than a good farrier, as the people said who saw him. But when he arrived there, instead of comfort, they showed him the face of the door alone and, a month after, his sweetheart married another.

All this was very sore upon Tom; and he took it to heart so grievously, that he said, as a better man might have said, being loose of mind and property, "The world hath preyed on me, like a wolf. God help me now to prey on the world."

And in sooth it did seem, for a while, as if Providence were with him; for he took rare toll on the highway, and his name was soon as good as gold anywhere this side of Bristowe. He studied his business by night and by day, with three horses all in hard work, until he had made a fine reputation.

One of his earliest meetings was with Sir Robert Bampfylde himself, who was riding along the Barum road, with only one serving-man after him. Tom Faggus put a pistol to his head, being then obliged to be violent, through want of reputation; while the serving-man pretended to be a long way round the corner. Then the baronet pulled out his purse, quite trembling in the hurry of his politeness. Tom took the purse, and his ring, and time-piece, and then handed them back with a very low bow, saying that it was against all usage for him to rob a robber. Then he turned to the unfaithful knave, and trounced him right well for his cowardice, and stripped him of all his property.

But now Mr Faggus kept only one horse, lest the Government should steal them; and that one was the young mare Winnie. When I have added that Faggus as yet had never been guilty of bloodshed (for his eyes, and the click of his pistol at first, and now his high reputation made all his wishes respected), and that he never robbed a poor man, neither insulted a woman, but was very good to the Church, and of hot patriotic opinions, and full of jest and jollity, I have said as much as is fair for him, and shown why he was so popular. All good people liked Mr Faggus – when he had not robbed them – and many a poor sick man or woman blessed him for other people's money; and all the hostlers, stable-boys, and tapsters entirely worshipped him.

FOLLYFOOT

MONICA DICKENS

ONE OF THE disastrous things that people did was to give their small children day-old chicks for Easter. Dear little fluffy yellow Easter chicks. You could buy them in cut-price stores.

Some of them fell out of the paper bags and were stepped on or run over in the crowded street. Some of them were crushed to death by hot little hands soon after they got home. Some died of cold. Some died of the wrong food. Some died of not bothering to live.

The few who survived were either given away when they grew into chickens, or kept in a cellar or a cupboard, or even the bath, until the people got sick of it and gave them away or killed them, or the chickens got sick of it and died. It was a total disaster for all concerned.

This Easter, a town family had staged an even bigger disaster.

Their little daughter was "mad about" horses, and so when she woke up on Easter morning, the car was standing in the road and there was a horse in the garage.

It was not much of a horse. The family had bought it quite cheaply at a sale. It had a big coffin head, lumps on its legs, a scrubby mane and a tail and large flat feet that had not seen a blacksmith for a long time.

"My horsie!" They had bought an old bridle with the horse, and they put it on back to front with the brow band where the throat latch should be and the reins crossed under its neck, and the little girl climbed on, rode away down the middle of the road and fell off before she got to the corner.

She hit her head and was in bed for two weeks, and the horse went back into the garage in disgrace.

Now and then when someone remembered, they fed it a soup can of oats, which it could not chew properly, because it had a long loose tooth hanging at the side of its mouth. It had no hay, because they thought that hay was only for the winter, and no bedding, because they did not know about bedding. There was a small patch of grass behind the garage, and the horse ate that bare, and then licked the ground.

When the little girl was better, she got on the horse again with her friend and the two of them rode round and round on a patch of waste land, clutching the mane and each other and shrieking with joy. Finally, the horse stumbled and fell down, and the children tumbled off, which seemed the easiest way to get down, and a great joke too.

The floor of the garage was concrete and the walls were concrete blocks, sweating a chill damp. When the horse lay down, which it did more often as it grew weaker, it rubbed sores on its elbows and hocks.

If it was lying down when she came home from school, the little girl would get it up by holding the soup can of oats a little way off. When it stood up, she would take the oats away and put on the bridle.

"Work before food, Rusty dear," she would tell it, and she and her friend would take Rusty to play circus on the piece of waste ground.

She was devoted to the horse. She sang to it. She made daisy chains to hang on its ear. She brushed it with her old hairbrush, but she could not get it very clean, because she did not like the smell of manure, and so she did not clean out the garage, although she told her father she did.

Her father hardly ever went to look at the horse, but he was very proud about it, and told everyone at work how his little girl thought the world of Rusty and it would do your heart good.

The mother did not look at the horse very much, because she was afraid of horses, and said she was allergic to them, which she thought was quite a grand thing to be, and she also did not like the smell that was accumulating in the garage.

But her little girl was happy, and she thought it was a lovely thing for a kiddie to have a faithful pet.

The faithful horse was willing enough to keep going somehow, although he was very thin and lumps of his hair fell out, and he was becoming dehydrated from only having small amounts of water, which the little girl brought him in a seaside toy bucket.

One day when she and her friend were riding him proudly down the road to the pillar box, slapping his ribs to keep him moving, he stopped and lay down in the road with his nose resting on the kerb. All the shrieks and the wails and kisses and smacks of the children and the shouts of some masons who were building a wall and the advice of housewives who came out of their houses and flapped their aprons could not get him up.

It happened that the Captain and Anna were taking a detour across the end of this road to avoid rush hour traffic. They saw the excitement, and turned the car up the street to see what it was.

The Captain walked through the small crowd and stood for a moment with his hands in his pockets, watching the little girls swarming round the horse like distressed bees, patting it and kissing it and begging it, *Rusty dear*, to get up. The Captain looked at the horse and the horse looked at the Captain, and a message passed between them like old friends.

When the Captain had got authority to take the horse, he telephoned for Paul to come with the horse box.

"But I don't understand." The mother had taken the little girl home and the father was back from work and standing nonplussed in the road, where street lamps were coming on and the masons had knocked off for the day and the housewives and the other children had gone indoors. "She loved that horse like her own brother. Thought the world of him, it would do your heart good."

"I'm sorry." The Captain was sitting on the kerb in his best suit with the horse's head in his lap. "But a small child can't be left alone to take care of a horse."

"But we didn't know!"

"Famous last words," the Captain muttered. "People who don't know anything about horses should stick to goldfish."

"That's a good idea." The man began to cheer up. He was glad he was going to be able to garage his car again, anyway. "I'll get her a bowl of nice fish tomorrow. Take her mind off it. They soon forget, the kiddies."

He went back to tell his wife and daughter the new idea. The Captain took off the jacket of his best suit and laid it over the rump of the horse, who lay like a heap of roadmenders' sand in the shadows between the street lamps.

At the farm, the Captain pulled out Rusty's loose tooth by rubbing the opposite gum to make that side more sensitive, and then quickly tapping out the tooth with a small hammer.

"Bran mashes now?" Paul let go the bluish tongue, which he had been holding out to the side to keep the horse's mouth open.

"Give him anything he'll eat, if he'll eat." The Captain got up from the straw where Rusty was lying. "He hasn't got much longer."

"Will he die?" From the doorway, Callie saw the horse through a glittery haze of tears.

The Captain nodded. That was the message that had passed between him and the horse in the road.

I am dying.

You shall die in peace.

"OH COBWEB, HOW COULD YOU?"

JOSEPHINE PULLEIN-THOMPSON

THE HAYFORD AND DISTRICT Annual Show was in full swing and almost everyone from the neighbouring villages was there; some had come to watch, but others were showing their onions, their hamsters or their homemade marmalade. There was a large entry in the competition for the dog with the waggiest tail and for the gymkhana, but the main crowd was gathered round the ring where the jumping events were being held.

The Scotts and the Eastwoods lived in Monksthistle, which was three miles from the showground, and, because they were almost the same age and the only people with ponies in the village, Philippa Scott and Fiona Eastwood were almost forced to be friends though they were quite different in character and didn't like each other very much.

Fiona, who had curly blonde hair and a plump, pink and white, rather discontented face, was an only child. She had proud parents who loved to show her off, and masses of pocket money, clothes and possessions. The only thing that Philippa really envied her was Cobweb, a lovely dapple grey mare, a 14.2 hands jumping pony, on whom Fiona competed in shows practically every

Saturday throughout the summer. Fiona had had several ponies since she started riding. She had won prizes on all of them, and every rosette and cup she had acquired since her leading rein days, was proudly displayed in a huge, glass-fronted cabinet in the Eastwood's sitting room.

Philippa, who was tall and thin, with long brown hair, and quite pretty, led a very different life. Her parents had divorced and her mother had married again, so she had a stepfather and a younger half brother and sister. Both her mother and stepfather worked, so, in the holidays, she looked after Charles and Minty. Her pony, Chocolate Soldier, Choccy for short, was a dark brown gelding, 12 hands high and brilliant at bending. He had been an eighth birthday present from her grandmother, but now Philippa's long thin legs dangled round his knees and it was nine-year-old Charlie who really fitted him. Her parents were always promising her a new pony, and her grandmother had offered to pay half, but somehow life at Orchard Cottage was always a rush, and there just didn't seem to be time to drive round the countryside trying the ponies that were advertised for sale.

Except for pony club gymkhanas, Hayford was the only show that the Scotts went to and it was a great day in their year. Despite the fact that Minty's hamster had been ignored by the judges and that Pip, their spaniel, had been seized by shyness and refused to wag his tail at all, the whole family were enjoying themselves tremendously. Minty and Choccy had come second in the leading-rein class and though Charlie had been hopeless in the egg and spoon, he had won the ten-and-under bending.

Philippa decided that she was really too large and heavy to ride Choccy in all the senior gymkhana events, so she had only entered for the bending and when, after three tough heats, Choccy was second by a nose, she tied him up in a shady spot and went to watch Fiona jumping.

Lately Cobweb hadn't been doing as well as usual, and the Eastwood parents' confidence in their daughter's ability to win had been shaken, so when Philippa joined them, just as Fiona cantered through the start, they both seemed very tense and anxious.

"She's *still* off form," said Mrs Eastwood, giving agonized gasps as Cobweb cleared the fences by only a fraction of an inch. "She's not the pony she used to be; the sparkle has quite gone out of her."

"I don't know what's the matter with the animal. We've tried everything," added Mr Eastwood angrily. "We've changed the bit, the bridle, the saddle. We've given her more oats, less oats, six different brands of pony nuts. We've given her a rest, we've exercised her hard and we've brought Fiona spurs, but there she is heaving herself over the jumps like any old crock at the pony club instead of a J.A. jumper."

As Fiona cantered out, the public address announced a clear round.

"Talk about stale, the pony looks half asleep," complained Mrs Eastwood. "Do for goodness' sake go and tell Fi to wake her up before the jump off," she told her husband. "She'd better give her a gallop and then put her over a really big practice fence just before she comes in." Mr Eastwood strode away muttering angrily.

The clear rounds were announced; there were only

six. As the stewards raised the course, Philippa watched Fiona's efforts to wake Cobweb up. Several sharp whacks and a gallop round the field did no good at all, you could see that it was only obedience to her rider that made Cobweb heave herself over the practice fence, all her spirit and energy had gone and she, who had won so often for Fiona in the past, no longer had any pleasure in jumping.

The jump-off course looked enormous and Philippa felt very sad for Cobweb; whatever was wrong it hardly seemed fair to force her round these fences.

The first four riders each had one down and Mr Eastwood began to look more cheerful. Mrs Eastwood was signalling to Fiona to keep the pony on her toes as she waited in the collecting ring.

"If *only* she can go clear," Mrs Eastwood murmured through gritted teeth as her daughter cantered in.

"Come *on,* you lazy lump," growled Mr Eastwood, as Cobweb heaved herself dutifully over the brush, the gate and the wall. "For God's sake give her a whack, Fi, you haven't the speed for the combination."

Fiona was riding as hard as she could, but Cobweb had no impulsion at all. Mr Eastwood groaned, Mrs Eastwood covered her eyes with a hand as the pony refused.

It was a huge treble. All three fences were wide, as well as high, and built solidly of countless heavy poles.

Fiona had turned and was trying to get up the speed she knew she needed, but Cobweb didn't respond. She cantered up slowly and stopped. Fiona took her back for a third try; the same thing happened. The bell rang.

"Oh, Cobweb, how *could* you," said Mrs Eastwood

with a choke in her voice, "to be eliminated *and* at a local show."

Mr Eastwood swore and Philippa followed them as they hurried through the collecting ring.

Fiona was scarlet in the face and struggling with tears.

"Beastly pony," she said as she flung herself off. "I'm never, ever going to jump her again. She just made up her mind she wouldn't jump; I whacked her as hard as I could and I spurred her like mad, but she didn't take any notice."

"You did everything you could; we could see that, Pet," Mrs Eastwood told her soothingly. "The pony's just packed up on us, goodness knows why, but we'll just have to cut our losses and buy a new one."

"Yes," agreed Mr Eastwood. "We ought to have done it before, we've hung about all summer waiting for her to come back on form and now she does this to us."

"It's simply not fair on Fi," Mrs Eastwood went on. "It's not good enough, after all you're only young once; the pony will have to go."

"Can we start looking for a new one tomorrow?" asked Fiona perking up.

Philippa had been stroking Cobweb's neck. She was such a lovely pony, so gentle and good and obliging, but now all the energy seemed to have gone out of her.

"Do you think she could be ill?" Philippa asked the Eastwoods.

"We had the vet to her a couple of months ago, when she started to go wrong," Mr Eastwood answered. "He couldn't find anything. And you can see for yourself, look at her eyes and her coat; that's not a sick pony."

"She's never been the same since last summer. She was turned out for three weeks when we went to the Costa Brava," Mrs Eastwood explained to Philippa. "We sent her to that very pricey stable near Foxley, where they're supposed to take great care of them, but it wouldn't surprise me if she had picked up something there, a virus or something."

"It might be her legs," said Philippa, crouching down. She looked for swellings, for bowed tendons, over-reaches and speedy cuts. Cobweb blew in her hair; the pony seemed to understand that she was trying to help.

"Who cares what's wrong with her; we've been going over and over it all summer," said Fiona in an exasperated voice. "She won't jump and that's all that matters. Let's get rid of her quickly, before she gets worse. And she'll have to go to a sale; it's no use people coming to try her when she won't jump."

"Yes, Fi's right. It looks like we've come to the end of the road," agreed Mr Eastwood.

"I wonder if my parents could afford to buy her," said Philippa diffidently. "She'd be lovely to hack with Charlie and Minty and I could gymkhana her."

The Eastwoods' faces brightened and their voices changed.

"What a brill idea!" Fiona sounded enthusiastic. "She'd be just the pony for you."

"Perfect," agreed Mrs Eastwood, "she's absolutely safe with small children; I've never seen her kick or bite. And it would be nice to know she'd gone to a good home."

"I'd better have a chat with your parents, hadn't I?"

suggested Mr Eastwood, looking round. "Are they still here?"

"Yes, they're looking after the stall in aid of the church tower," Philippa explained, "they promised to take it over for an hour so that the Baxters could have tea." She watched Mr Eastwood vanish into the crowd. Her heart seemed to be missing beats and her stomach was behaving oddly too. *Oh let them say yes*, she thought. She had always loved Cobweb but it had never entered her head that one day she might possibly possess her.

"I'm hot, I want an ice-cream, Mummy," said Fiona.

"All right, Pet, you shall have one. Would you like to ride the pony round, Philippa, dear?"

"No, I don't think I will. It may be just the heat that's affecting her, but she seems so tired," answered Philippa. "I'll look after her if you want to go for ice-creams."

Left alone with Cobweb, Philippa led her across to where Choccy was tied in the deep shade of a chestnut tree, and sitting on a log, she held the pony, who with head hanging and tail swishing lazily, drifted off into sleep.

Presently Mrs Eastwood and Fiona returned bringing Philippa an ice-cream.

"I really do think she would be the perfect pony for you Scotts," said Mrs Eastwood between bites. "I mean, you really don't jump at all, and Cobby's one hundred per cent in traffic and never any trouble to catch or shoe."

"Yes," agreed Philippa, freezing her face as she bolted the rest of her ice-cream, for she could see her mother and Mr Eastwood coming.

Mrs Eastwood immediately began to recite a catalogue of Cobweb's virtues.

"Yes, well, of course living so near we feel that we've known her for years," interrupted Mrs Scott, "but I just wanted to make sure that Philippa has thought this through and really doesn't mind having a pony that won't jump. I mean, if Fiona can't get Cobweb jumping, there isn't the smallest hope that we will." She looked hard at Philippa.

"I *would* like a jumping pony," Philippa admitted, "but they're terribly expensive; you're never going to afford one. Cobweb's perfect in every other way and it'll be lovely to go out for proper rides with Charlie."

"Well, if you're certain, Richard's agreed to our buying her provided she passes the vet. We'll ring Mr Smythe first thing on Monday," she told the Eastwoods, "and ask him to come over as soon as he can."

"Great," said Mr Eastwood shaking Mrs Scott's hand. "And I'm sure Philippa can't wait to have her new pony, so we'll turn her out in your orchard when we get home."

"And would you like to borrow our tack, just for a couple of days till you get your own?" suggested Mrs Eastwood, obviously delighted to have disposed of Cobweb so easily.

Philippa couldn't believe it. *Cobweb is mine! Cobweb is mine!* she told herself as she ran across the showground looking for Charlie and Minty. They were overjoyed too.

"She's the second nicest pony in the world," said Minty.

"She's the nicest *mare* in the world, and we'll be able to go for decent rides at last," added Charlie.

So long as she passes the vet, Philippa reminded herself.

The thought of Cobweb waiting in their orchard, and of Choccy's surprise when he found she had come to live with him, made Charlie and Minty quite willing to go home the moment the Open Jumping was over; there were no arguments about whether they should stay for the Scurry and Consolation classes.

The orchard was large with high overgrown hedges, a few very old apple trees and a hollow where Choccy liked to shelter from the winter winds. Cobweb was grazing, and she seemed very content with her new surroundings.

They stayed with the ponies while they ate their feeds and then they left them grazing side by side. Philippa decided to take Fiona's tack up to her bedroom; it was very new-looking, not a mend anywhere, and she didn't want anything awful to happen to it.

Her stepfather came home later. "Well, I've given the Eastwoods their cheque," he told her, "but don't get too starry-eyed, love, I had a beer with one of the judges and he thought there might be something wrong with Cobweb's heart, or that she could be starting ringbone, both of which would make her a useless buy, even for us."

"It's all right, I won't count on it," lied Philippa.

"Oh, I do hope she *is* OK," said Charlie anxiously, "because Choccy's looking over the moon now he's got a girl friend at last."

"We must keep our fingers crossed and hope," said Mrs Scott. "She really is the sweetest pony and I don't know how the Eastwoods could part with her so easily."

On Sunday morning Philippa woke early and with a great feeling of happiness. Then, suddenly, she remembered, Cobweb was hers. She jumped out of bed, dressed quickly, and ran down the garden to the orchard gate. Choccy was standing alone on the hump by the hollow. He looked strangely alert, with his head high and his ears pricked, as though he was on guard. He whinnied to Philippa, but he didn't move; there was no sign of Cobweb.

Suddenly afraid, Philippa ran towards him. "What's the matter? What's happened, Choccy?" she asked. They both looked down into the hollow where Cobweb, with a proud face and shining eyes, was nuzzling a small, dark-coated foal.

RED MORNING

JOANNA CANNAN

Jean and Judy are starting their own riding-school and are going to an auction to try and find a suitable show-jumper to add to their stables.

ON THE FOLLOWING Saturday, at noon, in Melchester cattle market, two figures might have been observed. One had neat red hair, the other had mouse-coloured hair, which was rather untidy and both were stamped with that indefinable something which marks the devotees of the noblest of all sports and the friends of that noble animal, the horse. The two figures were me and Judy, as I expect you have guessed.

At Melchester cattle market, which is the meeting place of Loamshire's large collection of farmers, stock-breeders, horse-dealers and other sporting and agricultural characters, the horses and ponies are sold in a large and dismal building quite separate from the buildings in which they sell the cows and the pigs and sheep and poultry and the sordid oddments, like bicycles and carpets and prams. The horses and ponies stand tethered to the walls until the moment comes for them to be sold; then, in turn, they are led up to one end of the building, where there is some tan on the ground, and they are made to show their paces, and people, who want them, bid for them.

I expect you know how to bid, but, in case you don't, I had better explain. You call out how much you will give for the horse, and, if another person wants it, *he* calls out a larger sum. Then, if you can afford it, you call out a larger sum still, and either he doesn't say anything and you get the horse, or else he bids higher still. There may be several people bidding, which makes it even more muddling, but actually it is not so muddling as it sounds. The auctioneer is the person who takes the bids and organises everything. Everyone who sells anything in the market pays him a small bit of what they are paid.

Of course the first thing Judy and I did when we arrived at the market was to get a catalogue of the horse-sale. The catalogue gives a brief description of all the horses to be sold, and each horse has a number, so it is quite easy to find. As we walked across the market, we read the catalogue. We both gave a shriek when we came to: *Number 26. 'Red Morning' Roan mare. 10 yrs. 14.2 hds. Would make a good show-jumper.*

"Exactly what we want," said Judy. "But you can't imagine her going for a hundred pounds," she added in despairing tones.

"She might have something wrong with her," I suggested.

"Then we don't want her," said Judy. "Dead pupils aren't a good advertisement for a riding-school, and we can't afford to keep a horse that's unsound."

We now entered the saleroom. The scene which met our eyes was a sad one. I am not sentimental, but it is not very nice to see that noble animal, the horse, tied up in a dismal draughty and rather dirty building, and waiting to be sold. There was quite a row of hunters all being sold "owing to the economic crisis". Several thin thoroughbreds that looked like cast-out racehorses which had failed in their second careers, there were also little old ponies, which were obviously being sold because they were unsound or slow. I talked to a very small dusty black one. He had harness galls and was resting a foreleg. I gave him a lump of sugar, but he had never *heard* of sugar and when I put it into his mouth he just let it fall to the ground. I said to Judy, "I wish we were rich and then could buy worn-out ponies and keep them in orchards for the rest of their lives."

Judy, who was talking to a dirty little grey pony with broken knees, said, "One day we shall be, and then we will, but in the meantime we'd better harden our hearts or we shall buy something we don't want at all. Come on. This one's number 24, and there's our mare."

We moved along the line of ponies and there in the corner stood the roan. As we went up to her, she turned her head and looked at us with a large soft and kindly eye. She had a nice little head and a long flexible neck and very high withers, and then she had a very, very long back, and at the end of it quite good quarters and a well-set-on-tail. She was a very peculiar colour; honestly, except for her head, which was brownish, and her tail and mane and legs, which were black, she was more mauve than roan. Her legs were clean and her hoofs, though on the smallish side, were nice and round.

Judy said, "What do you think of her?"

"Well," I said, "according to the books a good jumper should have a short back, and she's got the longest back I've ever seen."

"She's very ugly," said Judy, "except for her head."

As she spoke, the mare turned round again and nuzzled at the flap of Judy's pocket, and Judy added, "But she's sweet."

I said, "It's no use being sweet unless she can jump."

An old groomish-looking man had been standing nearby and now he came up to us. "If you young ladies are thinking of buying a pony, you can't do better than that mare. Nothing to look at, but I've seen 'er clear five foot."

Judy said, "She doesn't look like a jumper with that long back."

"Cor lummie!" said the old man. "You can't go by looks. No use showing 'er in the 'unter classes, but it isn't the ones what get the prizes there that comes into the ring when the jumping starts. Please yourselves. It's none of my business, but I tell you I've seen 'er jump."

"Who does she belong to?" I asked him.

"Young chap called Blackett over Marley way. Gone into the RAF 'e is. 'E didn't ride 'er though. Bought 'er for 'is girl friend, one of the Rectory girls, and then she jacked 'im up. That's 'ow 'twas."

I said, "Well, it wasn't the mare's fault that the Rectory girl was faithless, so I think it was jolly beastly of young Blackett just to send her down to the market to be sold."

"Perhaps his heart was broken," said Judy, who has a romantic mind, "so he didn't care. What do you think of her, Jean? If she can jump five feet . . ."

I said, "It's no use thinking. She'll go for much more than we can afford."

"Don't you be too sure, miss," said the old man. "There's a crisis on. Riding 'orses aren't wanted. Money's short, you see, and there were some real good ponies sold 'ere last month for a 'undred pounds. The big ones go for a lot more, the foreign butchers buy them for meat."

Judy said, "We can afford that much, but it doesn't seem possible," and the old man said, "Well, you 'ave a try, love," and he moved away.

I said, "Do you think it's true that she can jump five feet?" and Judy said rather crossly, "How can I tell?" She told me afterwards that she was cross because she was in an agony of indecision. Red Morning kept nuzzling in her pockets and Judy loved her, but there was her long, long back and the tiresome tradition that in horse-dealing you can't believe what anyone tells you.

For a few moments we stood in sulky silence and then I suddenly woke up to the fact that the cart-horses and some of the ponies had already been sold. I said, "Come on. We'd better get a place where we can bid, even if we don't want to," and we hurried across the building and joined in the throng which clustered round the auctioneer. The little, old black pony was sold for forty. The grey with broken knees went for thirty-five, and a thick-set bay for ninety. Then the auctioneer called out the number and description of Red Morning and she was walked and trotted up and down the tan. Even in a rope-halter her head-carriage was marvellous, but her trot was unbalanced, her back looked longer than ever and in the light from the open door she looked positively purple.

The auctioneer said, "Any bids for Red Morning? Come along, ladies and gentlemen. This mare will make a good show-jumper. Win you prizes anywhere."

The auctioneer said, "Come along, ladies and gentlemen. What am I bid for Red Morning?" and then, as nobody said anything, he said he would start the bidding at seventy. Somebody said, "Seventy-five."

I heard a funny swallowing sound beside me and Judy said, "Eighty," in loud firm tones.

The auctioneer looked round and Judy waved to him.

"The young lady bids eighty. Eighty I'm bid," said the auctioneer, and then the other tiresome voice said, "Eighty-five." Judy said, "Ninety," and the voice said, "Ninety-five." "One hundred," said Judy, and instead of the voice saying the fatal "one hundred and five", there was silence. "One hundred I'm bid," said the auctioneer. "The young lady bids one hundred. Any advance on one hundred pounds for this fine show-jumper, Red Morning?" He raised his hammer and said, "Going, going, gone!"

Judy gave a gasp like a fish out of water and the auctioneer's clerk leant over the desk and said, "Name, please?" Judy said, "Miss Leslie and Miss Charteris," and the clerk gave her a ticket. If you buy anything at the market you have to take the ticket to the office and pay for what you have bought before you can remove it. There is a policeman at the gate to see that you do.

Without saying anything to each other, Judy and I struggled out of the crowd and rushed to the office.

Except for the men in charge of it, it was empty, and Judy put her ticket on the table and said, "It's for a pony and can we take her now because we've a long way to go?" One of the men said, "Certainly, miss," and Judy turned to me and said, "You've got the cheque book." We paid and as we went out of the office, we remembered that we had forgotten to bring a halter, so we rushed to the fascinating stall where you can buy halters and rugs and stable implements, and we bought Red Morning a white one. There were some lovely coloured ones, but we were afraid they would clash with her mauve. Then we rushed back to the building and found her standing patiently in her corner – it must be awful to be sold and not to know who has bought you until they come to lead you away. We petted her for a bit and then we put on her new halter and Judy said, "Who's going to lead her?" and I said, "You'd better because she's really your Mickey and Minnie horse." Judy said, "Well, I'll lead her first and then you can have a turn," so started off and were soon out of the market, and I told Red Morning that, if she was a good pony, she would never return.

We went down Market Street and into the main road. Red Morning came along all right, but she goggled rather at prams and barrows of vegetables. As we passed under the railway bridge, she didn't turn into a herd of pink pigs, but just as we had got through, a train went rumbling over us and she shied and leapt about. Judy said, "I say, Jean, do you think she'll be quiet enough for the pupils? There was nothing in the catalogue about her being quiet and all the other ponies had *Has been ridden by a lady or Regularly ridden by children,* or *Quiet to ride and drive."*

"Gosh," I said, "I forgot all about the pupils. We might have asked the groomish man."

"Oh, he'd have *said* she was quiet," said Judy, "but that's no guarantee. We've no real guarantee that she can jump, either. I don't suppose she can. Look at her long back, And I think she's got rather straight shoulders. Won't it be awful if she turns out to be a bolter? The last book I read said that the only place for *them* was the knackers. Or perhaps she rears."

My heart had been sinking, but suddenly a ray of hope illumined the dark prospect. I said, "She must be fairly well-mannered, or young Bartlett over Marley way wouldn't have bought her for his girl."

Judy, as I said before, has a romantic mind. She said, "I don't agree. He may have got tired of his girl and wanted to murder her, so he bought her a confirmed rearer, but only succeeded in making the girl an invalid for life. Or perhaps he bought her innocently and she gave the girl an awful toss and she was annoyed and told young Bartlett that he was no judge of a horse, and they quarrelled and she came to the conclusion that he was bad tempered and 'jacked 'im up'."

I saw that Judy was determined to be gloomy, and I must say I felt rather nerve-racked myself. I expect you will think we were silly, but you must remember that we had spent our all, and our financial position would be far from satisfactory if it turned out that we had made a mistake. I said, "Oh, do shut up. You're like Jeremiah. When we get out of the traffic you can give me a leg up and I'll ride her and see."

We plodded on through the Melchester suburbs in sulky silence except for a few remarks about the awful houses, which were new ones trying to look old and had names like Dun-Roamin' and Wy-Wurrie and Chez Nous. At last we reached the big cross-roads and took the nice winding road to Hedger's Green. As soon as the hum of traffic had died away behind us, Judy gave me a leg up and I rode for about a mile. Red Morning went very quietly and passed the bus without playing up in a very narrow part of the road.

We took it in turns to walk and ride until we got home and then we couldn't resist doing something which, considering that Red Morning had just come six miles and had also gone into Melchester from Marley earlier, we ought not to have done. What we should have done, of course, was to water and feed her and leave her in the stable to rest and get over her trying experiences. I was haunted by remorse afterwards to think how awful we had been, but really neither of us could bear the suspense any longer – as I have already explained to you, we had risked our all. What we did was to fit Red Morning up with Cavalier's bridle and Black Auster's saddle and take her into the orchard to see if she could jump.

Cavalier and Charity were very inquisitive and as Judy rode Red Morning across the orchard they came cantering up, but I shooed them away. Judy said, "I'm only going to try one jump," and she cantered towards the bar, which, as Honor and Grace had been the last to jump it, was quite low. As she got near the bar, I saw Red Morning's ears go forward and her long mauve body gathered itself together and over she went with a gay whisk of her tail. Judy gave a whoop of joy and took the bush and turned Red Morning for the hurdles and the in-and-out and over she went, and over! Her style was marvellous and she jumped as though she absolutely loved it.

Judy said, "She's lovely. Do you want a try?" But I controlled myself and said, "No. She's had enough. I'll jump her tomorrow morning." Feeling frightfully pleased, we led our show-jumper down to the stable and now we did water and feed her and leave her to rest and get over her trying experiences.

WAR HORSE

MICHAEL MORPURGO

Joey is one of the many horses who saw active service during the First World War.

IT WAS ONLY WITH the greatest difficulty that I stayed standing on my three good legs in the veterinary wagon that carried me that morning away from the heroic little Welshman who had brought me in. A milling crowd of soldiers surrounded me to cheer me on my way. But out on the long rattling roads, I was very soon shaken off my balance and fell into an ungainly, uncomfortable heap on the floor of the wagon. My injured leg throbbed terribly as the wagon rocked from side to side on its slow journey away from the battle front. The wagon was drawn by two stocky, black horses, both well groomed out and immaculate in well-oiled harness. Weakened by long hours of pain and starvation I had not the strength even to get to my feet when I felt the wheels below me running at last on smooth cobblestones and the wagon came to a jerking standstill in the warm, pale autumn sunshine. My arrival was greeted by a chorus of excited neighing and I raised my head to look. I could just see over the sideboards a wide, cobbled courtyard with magnificent stables on either side and a great house with turrets beyond. Over every stable-door were the heads of inquisitive horses, ears pricked. There were men in khaki walking everywhere, and a few were running now towards me, one of them carrying a rope halter.

Unloading was painful, for I had little strength left and my legs had gone numb after the long journey. But they got me to my feet and walked me backwards gently down the ramp. I found myself the centre of anxious and admiring attention in the middle of the courtyard, surrounded by a cluster of soldiers who inspected minutely every part of me, feeling me all over.

"What in thunder do you think you're about, you lot?" came a booming voice echoing across the courtyard. "It's an 'orse. It's an 'orse just like the others." A huge man was striding towards us, his boots crisp on the cobbles. His heavy red face was half hidden by the shade of his peaked cap that almost touched his nose and by a ginger moustache that spread upwards from his lips to his ears. "It may be a famous 'orse. It may be the only thundering 'orse in the 'ole thundering war brought in alive from no-man's-land. But it is only an 'orse and a dirty 'orse at that. I've had some rough looking specimens brought in here in my time, but this is the scruffiest, dirtiest, muddiest 'orse I have ever seen. He's a thundering disgrace and you're all stood about looking at him." He wore three broad stripes on his arm and the creases in his immaculate khaki uniform were razor sharp. "Now there's a hundred or more sick 'orses 'ere in this 'ospital and there's just twelve of us to look after them. This 'ere young layabout was detailed to look after this one when he arrived, so the rest of you blighters can get back to your duties. Move it, you idle monkeys, move it!" And the men scattered in all directions, leaving me with a young soldier who began to lead me away towards a stable. "And you," came that booming voice again. "Major Martin will be down from the 'ouse in ten minutes to examine that 'orse. Make sure that 'orse is so thundering clean and thundering shiny so's you could use him as a shaving mirror, right?"

"Yes, Sergeant," came the reply. A reply that sent a sudden shiver of recognition through me. Quite where I had heard the voice before I did not know. I knew only that those two words sent a tremor of joy and hope and expectation through my body and warmed me from the inside out. He led me slowly across the cobbles, and I tried all the while to see his face better. But he kept just that much ahead of me so that all I could see was a neatly shaven neck and a pair of pink ears.

"How the divil did you get yourself stuck out there in no-man's-land, you old silly?" he said. "That's what everyone wants to know ever since the message came back that they'd be bringing you in here. And how the divil did you get yourself in such a state? I swear there's not an inch of you that isn't covered in mud or blood. Job to tell what you look like under all that mess. Still, we'll soon see. I'll tie you up here and get the worst of it off in the open air. Then I'll brush you up in the proper manner afore the officer gets here. Come on, you silly, you. Once I've got you cleaned up then the officer can see you and he'll tidy up the nasty cut of yours. Can't give you food, I'm sorry to say, nor any water, not till he says so. That's what the Sergeant told me. That's just in case they have to operate on you." And the way he whistled as he cleaned out the brushes was the whistle that went with the voice I knew. It confirmed my rising hopes and I knew then that I could not be mistaken. In my overwhelming delight I reared up on my back legs and cried out to him to recognize me. I wanted to make him see who I was. "Hey, careful there, you silly. Nearly had my hat off," he said gently, keeping a firm hold on the rope and smoothing my nose as he always had done whenever I was unhappy. "No need for that. You'll be all right. Lot of fuss about nothing. Knew a young horse once just like you, proper jumpy he was till I got to know him and he got to know me."

"You talking to them horses again, Albert?" came a voice from inside the next stable. "Gawd's strewth! What makes you think they understand a perishing word you say?"

"Some of them may not, David," said Albert. "But one day, one day one of them will. He'll come in here and he'll recognize my voice. He's bound to come in here. And then you'll see a horse that understands every word that's said to him."

"You're not on about your Joey again?" The head that came with the voice leant over the stable-door. "Won't you never give it up, Berty? I've told you before if I've told you a thousand times. They say there's near half a million ruddy horses out here and you joined the Veterinary Corps just on the off-chance you might come across him." I pawed the ground with my bad leg in an effort to make Albert look at me more closely, but he just patted my neck and set to work cleaning me up. "There's just one chance in half a million that your Joey walks in here. You got to be more realistic. He could be dead – a lot of them are. He could have gorn orf to ruddy Palestine with the Yeomanry. He could be anywhere along hundreds of miles of trenches. If you weren't so ruddy good with horses, and if you weren't the best friend I had, I'd think you'd gorn and gorn a bit screwy the way you do go on about your Joey."

"You'll understand why when you see him, David," Albert said crouching down to scrape the caked mud off my underside. "You'll see. There's no horse like him anywhere in the world. He's a bright red bay with a black mane and tail. He has a white cross on his forehead and four white socks that are all even to the last inch. He stands over sixteen hands and he's perfect from head to tail. I can tell you, I can tell you that when you see him you'll know him. I could pick him out of a crowd of a thousand horses. There's just something about him. Captain Nicholls, you know, him that's dead now, the one I told you about that bought Joey from my father, him that sent me Joey's picture; he knew it. He saw it the first time he set eyes on him. I'll find him, David. That's what I came all this way for and I'm going to find him. Either I'll find him, or he'll find me. I told you, I made him a promise and I'm going to keep it."

"You're round the ruddy twist, Berty," said his friend opening a stable-door and coming over to examine my leg. "Round the ruddy twist, that's all I can say." He picked up my hoof and lifted it gently. "This one's got

246

a white sock on his front legs anyway — that's as far as I can tell under all this blood and mud. I'll just sponge the wound away a bit, clean it up for you whilst I'm here. You'll never get this one cleaned up in time else. And I've finished mucking out my ruddy stables. Not a lot else to do and it looks as if you could do with a hand. Old Sergeant 'Thunder' won't mind, not if I've done all he told me, and I have."

The two men worked tirelessly on me, scraping and brushing and washing. I stood quite still trying only to muzzle Albert to make him turn and look at me. But he was busying at my tail and my hindquarters now.

"Three," said his friend, washing off another of my hoofs. "That's three white socks."

"Turn it up, David," said Albert. "I know what you think. I know everyone thinks I'll never find him. There's thousands of army horses with four white socks — I know that, but there's only one with a blaze in the shape of a cross on the forehead. And how many horses shine red like fire in the evening sun? I tell you there's not another like him, not in the whole wide world."

"Four," said David. "That's four legs and four white socks. Only the cross on the forehead now, and a splash of red paint on this muddy mess of a horse and you'll have your Joey standing 'ere."

"Don't tease," said Albert quietly. "Don't tease, David. You know how serious I am about Joey. It'll mean all the world to me to find him again. Only friend I ever had afore I came to the war. I told you. I grew up with him, I did. Only creature on this earth I felt any kinship for."

David was standing now by my head. He lifted my

mane and brushed gently at first then vigorously at my forehead, blowing the dust away from my eyes. He peered closely and then set to again brushing down towards the end of my nose and up again between my ears till I tossed my head with impatience.

"Berty," he said quietly, "I'm not teasing, honest I'm not. Not now. You said your Joey had four white socks, all even to the inch? Right?"

"Right," said Albert, still brushing away at my tail.

"And you said Joey had a white cross on his forehead?"

"Right." Albert was still completely disinterested.

"Now I have never ever seen a horse like that, Berty," said David, using his hand to smooth down the hair on my forehead. "Wouldn't have thought it possible."

"Well, it is, I tell you," said Albert sharply. "And he was red, flaming red in the sunlight, like I said."

"I wouldn't have thought it possible," his friend went on, keeping his voice in check, "not until now, that is."

"Oh, pack it in, David," Albert said, and there was a genuine irritation in his voice now. "I've told you, haven't I? I told you I'm serious about Joey."

"So am I, Berty. Dead serious. No messing. I'm serious. This horse has four white socks – all evenly marked like you said. This horse has a clear white cross on his head. This horse, as you can see for yourself, has a black mane and tail. This horse stands over 16 hands and when he's cleaned up he'll look pretty as a picture. And this horse is a red bay under all that mud, just like you said, Berty."

As David was speaking Albert suddenly dropped my tail and moved slowly around me, running his hand along my back. Then at last we stood facing one another. There was a rougher hue to his face I thought; he had more lines around his eyes and he was a broader, bigger man in his uniform than I remembered him. But he was my Albert, and there was no doubt about it, he was my Albert.

"Joey?" he said tentatively, looking into my eyes. "Joey?" I tossed up my head and called out to him in my happiness, so that the sound echoed around the yard and brought horses and men to the door of their stables. "It could be," said Albert quietly. "You're right, David, it could be him. It sounds like him even. But there's one way I know to be sure," and he untied my rope and pulled the halter off my head. Then he turned and walked away to the gateway before facing me, cupping his hands to his lips and whistling. It was his owl whistle, the same low, stuttering whistle he had used to call me when we were walking out together back at home on the farm all those long years before. Suddenly there was no longer any pain in my leg, and I trotted easily over towards him and buried my nose in his shoulder. "It's him, David," Albert said, putting his arms around my neck and hanging on to my mane. "It's my Joey. I've found him. He's come back to me just like I said he would."

"See?" said David wryly. "What did I tell you? See? Not often wrong, am I?"

"Not often," Albert said. "Not often, and not this time."

★

In the euphoric days that followed our reunion, the nightmare I had lived through seemed to fade into unreality, and the war itself was suddenly a million miles away and of no consequence. At last there were no guns to be heard, and the only vivid reminder that suffering and conflict was still going on were the regular arrivals of the veterinary wagons from the front.

Major Martin cleaned my wound and stitched it up; and though at first I could still put little weight on it, I felt in myself stronger with every day that passed. Albert was with me again, and that in itself was medicine enough; but properly fed once more with warm mash each morning and a never-ending supply of sweet-scented hay, my recovery seemed only a matter of time. Albert, like the other veterinary orderlies, had many other horses to care for, but he would spend every spare minute he could find fussing over me in the stable. To the other soldiers I was something of a celebrity, so I was scarcely ever left alone in my stable. There always seemed to be one or two faces looking admiringly over my door. Even old 'Thunder', as they called the Sergeant, would inspect me over-zealously, and when the others were not about he would fondle my ears and tickle me under my throat saying, "Quite a boy, aren't you? Thundering fine horse if ever I saw one. You get better now, d'you hear?"

But time passed and I did not get better. One morning I found myself quite unable to finish my mash and every sharp sound, like the kick of a bucket or the rattle of the bolt on the stable-door, seemed to set me on edge and made me suddenly tense from head to tail.

My forelegs in particular would not work as they should. They were stiff and tired, and I felt a great weight of pain all along my spine, creeping into my neck and even in my face.

Albert noticed something was wrong when he saw the mash I had left in my bucket. "What's the matter with you, Joey?" he said anxiously, and he reached out his hand to stroke me in the way he often did when he was concerned. Even the sight of his hand coming towards me, normally a welcome sign of affection, struck an alarm in me, and I backed away from him into the corner of the stable. As I did so I found that the stiffness in my front legs would hardly allow me to move. I stumbled backwards, falling against the brick wall at the back of the stable, and leaning there heavily. "I thought something was wrong yesterday," said Albert, standing still now in the middle of the stable. "Thought you were a bit off colour then. Your back's as stiff as a board and you're covered in sweat. What the divil have you been up to, you old silly?" He moved slowly now towards me and although his touch still sent an irrational tremor of fear through me, I stood my ground and allowed him to stroke me. "P'raps it was something you picked up on your travels. P'raps you ate something poisonous, is that it? But then that would have shown itself before now, surely? You'll be fine, Joey, but I'll go and fetch Major Martin just in case. He'll look you over and if there's anything wrong put you right 'quick as a twick', as my father used to say. Wonder what he would think now if he could see us together? He never believed I'd find you either, said I was a fool to go. Said it was a fool's errand and that I'd likely get myself killed in the process. But he was a different man, Joey, after you left. He knew he'd done wrong, and that seemed to take all the nastiness out of him. He seemed to live only to make up for what he'd done. He stopped his Tuesday drinking sessions, looked after Mother as he used to do when I was little, and he even began to treat me right – didn't treat me like a workhorse any more."

I knew from the soft tone of his voice that he was trying to calm me, as he had done all those long years ago when I was a wild and frightened colt. Then his words had soothed me, but now I could not stop myself from trembling. Every nerve in my body seemed to be taut and I was breathing heavily. Every fibre of me was consumed by a totally inexplicable sense of fear and dread. "I'll be back in a minute, Joey," he said. "Don't you worry. You'll be all right. Major Martin will fix you – he's a miracle with horses is that man." And he backed away from me and went out.

It was not long before he was back again with his friend, David, with Major Martin and Sergeant 'Thunder'; but only Major Martin came inside the stable to examine me. The others leaned over the stable-door and watched. He approached me cautiously, crouching down by my foreleg to examine my wound. Then he ran his hands all over me from my ears, down my back to my tail, before standing back to survey me from the other side of the stable. He was shaking his head ruefully as he turned to speak to the others.

"What do you think, Sergeant?" he asked.

"Same as you, from the look of 'im, sir," said

Sergeant 'Thunder'. "'E's standing there like a block of wood; tail stuck out, can't 'ardly move his head. Not much doubt about it, is there, sir?"

"None," said Major Martin. "None whatsoever. We've had a lot of it out here. If it isn't confounded rusty barbed wire, then it's shrapnel wounds. One little fragment left inside, one cut — that's all it takes. I've seen it time and again. I'm sorry, my lad," the Major said, putting his hand on Albert's shoulder to console him. "I know how much this horse means to you. But there's precious little we can do for him, not in his condition."

"What do you mean, sir?" Albert asked, a tremor in his voice. "How do you mean, sir? What's the matter with him, sir? Can't be a lot wrong, can there? He was right as rain yesterday, 'cept he wasn't finishing his feed. Little stiff p'raps but otherwise right as rain he was."

"It's tetanus, son," said Sergeant 'Thunder'. "Lockjaw they calls it. It's written all over 'im. That wound of 'is must have festered afore we got 'im 'ere. And once an 'orse 'as tetanus there's very little chance, very little indeed."

"Best to end it quickly," Major Martin said. "No point in an animal suffering. Better for him, and better for you."

"No, sir," Albert protested, still incredulous. "No you can't, sir. Not with Joey. We must try something. There must be something you can do. You can't just give up, sir. You can't. Not with Joey."

David spoke up now in support. "Begging your pardon, sir," he said. "But I remembers you telling us when we first come here that a horse's life is p'raps even more important than a man's, 'cos an horse hasn't got no evil in him 'cepting any that's put there by men. I remembers you saying that our job in the Veterinary Corps was to work night and day, twenty-six hours a day if need be to save and help every horse that we could, that every horse was valuable in hisself and valuable to the war effort. No horse, no guns. No horse, no ammunition. No horse, no cavalry. No horse, no ambulances. No horse, no water for the troops at the front. Lifeline of the whole army, you said, sir. We must never give up, you said, 'cos where there's life there's still hope. That's all what you said, sir, begging your pardon, sir."

"You watch your lip, son," said Sergeant 'Thunder' sharply. "That's no way to speak to an officer. If the Major 'ere thought there was a chance in a million of savin' this poor animal, 'e'd have a crack at it, wouldn't you, sir? Isn't that right, sir?"

Major Martin looked hard at Sergeant 'Thunder', taking his meaning, and then nodded slowly. "All right, Sergeant. You made your point. Of course there's a chance," he said carefully. "But if once we start with a case of tetanus, then it's a full-time job for one man for a month or more, and even then the horse has hardly more than one chance in a thousand, if that."

"Please, sir," Albert pleaded. "Please, sir. I'll do it all, sir, and I'll fit in my other horses too, sir. Honest I would, sir."

"And I'll help him, sir," David said. "All the lads will. I know they will. You see, sir, that Joey's a bit special for everyone here, what with his being Berty's own horse back home an' all."

"That's the spirit, son," said Sergeant 'Thunder'. "And it's true, sir, there is something a bit special about this one, you know, after all he's been through. With your permission, sir, I think we ought to give 'im that chance. You 'ave my personal guarantee, sir, that no other 'orse will be neglected. Stables will be run shipshape and Bristol fashion, like always."

Major Martin put his hands on the stable-door. "Right, Sergeant," he said. "You're on. I like a challenge as well as the next man. I want a sling rigged up in here. This horse must not be allowed to get off his legs. Once he's down he'll never get up again. I want a note added to Standing Orders, Sergeant, that no one's to talk in anything but a whisper in this yard. He won't like any noise, not with tetanus. I want a bed of short, clean straw – and fresh every day. I want the windows covered over so that he's kept always in the dark. He's not to be fed any hay – he could choke on it – just milk and oatmeal gruel. And it's going to get worse before it gets better – if it does. You'll find his mouth will tighten as the days go by, but he must go on feeding and he must drink. If he doesn't then he'll die. I want a twenty-four-hour watch on this horse – that means a man posted in here all day and every day. Clear?"

"Yes, sir," said Sergeant 'Thunder', smiling broadly under his moustache. "And if I may say so, sir, I think you've made a very wise decision. I'll see to it, sir. Now, look lively, you two layabouts. You heard what the officer said."

That same day a sling was strung up around me and my weight supported from the beams above. Major Martin opened up my wound again, cleaned and cauterized it. He returned every few hours after that to examine me. It was Albert of course who stayed with me most of the time, holding up the bucket to my mouth so that I could suck in the warm milk or gruel. At nights David and he slept side by side in the corner of the stable, taking turns to watch me.

As I had come to expect, and as I needed, Albert talked to me all he could to comfort me, until sheer fatigue drove him back into his corner to sleep. He talked much of his father and mother and about the farm. He talked of a girl he had been seeing up in the village for a few months before he left for France. She didn't know anything about horses, he said, but that was her only fault.

The days passed slowly and painfully for me. The stiffness in my front legs spread to my back and intensified; my appetite was becoming more limited each day and I could scarcely summon the energy or enthusiasm to suck in the food I knew I needed to stay alive. In the darkest days of my illness, when I felt sure each day might be my last, only Albert's constant presence kept alive in me the will to live. His devotion, his unwavering faith that I would indeed recover, gave me the heart to go on. All around me I had friends, David and all the veterinary orderlies, Sergeant 'Thunder' and Major Martin – they were all a source of great encouragement to me. I knew how desperately they were willing me to live; although I often wondered whether they wanted it for me or for Albert for I knew they held him in such high esteem. But on reflection I think perhaps they cared for both of us as if we were their brothers.

Then one winter's night after long painful weeks in the sling, I felt a sudden looseness in my throat and neck, so much so that I could call out, albeit softly, for the first time. Albert was sitting in the corner of the stable as usual with his back against the wall, his knees drawn up and his elbows resting on his knees. His eyes were closed, so I nickered again softly, but it was loud enough to wake him. "Was that you, Joey?" he asked, pulling himself to his feet. "Was that you, you old silly? Do it again, Joey. I might have been dreaming. Do it again." So I did and in so doing I lifted my head for the first time in weeks and shook it. David heard it too and was on his feet and shouting over the stable-door for everyone to come. Within minutes the stable was full of excited soldiers. Sergeant 'Thunder' pushed his way through and stood before me. "Standing Orders says whisper," he said. "And that was no thundering whisper I heard. What's up? What's all the 'ullabaloo?"

"He moved, Sarge," Albert said. "His head moved easily and he neighed."

"Course 'e did, son," said Sergeant 'Thunder'. "Course 'e did. 'E's going to make it. Like I said 'e would. I always told you 'e would, didn't I? And 'ave any of you layabouts ever known me to be wrong? Well, 'ave you?"

"Never, Sarge," said Albert, grinning from ear to ear. "He is getting better, isn't he, Sarge? I'm not just imagining it, am I?"

"No, son," said Sergeant 'Thunder'. "Your Joey is going to be all right by the looks of 'im, long as we keeps 'im quiet and so long as we don't rush 'im. I just 'opes that if I'm ever poorly I 'ave nurses around me that looks after me like you lot 'ave this 'orse. One thing, though, looking at you, I'd like them to be an 'ole lot prettier!"

Shortly after, I found my legs again and then the stiffness left my back for ever. They took me out of the sling and walked me one spring morning out into the sunshine of the cobbled yard. It was a triumphant parade, with Albert leading me carefully, walking backwards and talking to me all the while. "You've done it, Joey. You've done it. Everyone says the war's going to be over quite soon – I know we've been saying that for a long time, but I feel it in my bones this time. It'll be finished before long and then we'll both be going home, back to the farm. I can't wait to see the look on Father's face when I bring you back up the lane. I just can't wait."

THE BROGUE

SAKI

THE HUNTING SEASON had come to an end, and the Mullets had not succeeded in selling the Brogue. There had been a kind of tradition in the family for the past three or four years, a sort of fatalistic hope, that the Brogue would find a purchaser before the hunting was over; but seasons came and went without anything happening to justify such ill-founded optimism. The animal had been named Berserker in the earlier stages of its career; it had been rechristened the Brogue later on, in recognition of the fact that, once acquired, it was extremely difficult to get rid of. The unkinder wits of the neighbourhood had been known to suggest that the first letter of its name was superfluous. The Brogue had been variously described in sale catalogues as a light-weight hunter, a lady's hack, and, more simply, but still with a touch of imagination, as a useful brown gelding, standing 15.1 hands. Toby Mullet had ridden him for four seasons with the West Wessex; you can ride almost any sort of horse with the West Wessex as long as it is an animal that knows the country. The Brogue knew the country intimately, having personally created most of the gaps that were to be met with in banks and hedges for many miles round. His manners and characteristics were not ideal in the hunting field, but he was probably rather safer to ride to hounds than he was as a hack on country roads. According to the Mullet family, he was not really road-shy, but there were one or two objects of dislike that brought on sudden attacks of what Toby called swerving sickness. Motors and cycles he treated with tolerant disregard, but pigs, wheelbarrows, piles of stones by the roadside, perambulators in a village street, gates painted too aggressively white, and sometimes, but not always, the newer kind of beehives, turned him aside from his tracks in vivid imitation of the zigzag course of forked lightning. If a pheasant rose noisily from the other side of the hedgerow the Brogue would spring into the air at the same moment, but this may have been due to a desire to be companionable. The Mullet family contradicted the widely prevalent report that the horse was a confirmed crib-biter.

It was about the third week in May that Mrs Mullet, relict of the late Sylvester Mullet, and mother of Toby and a bunch of daughters, assailed Clovis Sangrail on the outskirts of the village with a breathless catalogue of local happenings.

"You know our new neighbour, Mr Penricarde?" she vociferated; "awfully rich, owns tin mines in Cornwall, middle-aged and rather quiet. He's taken the Red House on a long lease and spent a lot of money on alterations and improvements. Well, Toby's sold him the Brogue!"

Clovis spent a moment or two in assimilating the astonishing news; then he broke out into unstinted congratulation. If he had belonged to a more emotional race he would probably have kissed Mrs Mullet.

"How wonderful lucky to have pulled it off at last! Now you can buy a decent animal. I've always said that Toby was clever. Ever so many congratulations."

"Don't congratulate me. It's the most unfortunate thing that could have happened!" said Mrs Mullet dramatically.

Clovis stared at her in amazement.

"Mr Penricarde," said Mrs Mullet, sinking her voice to what she imagined to be an impressive whisper, though it rather resembled a hoarse, excited squeak, "Mr Penricarde has just begun to pay attentions to Jessie. Slight at first, but now unmistakable. I was a fool not to have seen it sooner. Yesterday, at the Rectory garden party, he asked her what her favourite flowers were, and she told him carnations, and today a whole stack of carnations has arrived, clove and malmaison and lovely dark red ones, regular exhibition blooms, and a box of chocolates that he must have got on purpose from London. And he's asked her to go round the links with him tomorrow. And now, just at this critical moment, Toby has sold him that animal. It's a calamity!"

"But you've been trying to get the horse off your hands for years," said Clovis.

"I've got a houseful of daughters," said Mrs Mullet, "and I've been trying – well, not to get them off my hands, of course, but a husband or two wouldn't be amiss among the lot of them; there are six of them, you know."

"I don't know," said Clovis. "I've never counted, but I expect you're right as to the number; mothers generally know these things."

"And now," continued Mrs Mullet, in her tragic whisper, "when there's a rich husband-in-prospect imminent on the horizon, Toby goes and sells him that miserable animal. It will probably kill him if he tries to ride it; anyway it will kill any affection he might have felt towards any member of our family. What is to be done? We can't very well ask to have the horse back; you see, we praised it up like anything when we thought there was a chance of his buying it, and said it was just the animal to suit him."

"Couldn't you steal it out of his stable and send it to grass at some farm miles away?" suggested Clovis. "Write 'Votes for Women' on the stable-door, and the thing would pass for a Suffragette outrage. No one who knew the horse could possibly suspect you of wanting to get it back again."

"Every newspaper in the country would ring with the affair," said Mrs Mullet; "can't you imagine the headline, 'Valuable Hunter Stolen by Suffragettes'? The police would scour the countryside till they found the animal."

"Well, Jessie must try and get it back from Penricarde on the plea that it's an old favourite. She can say it was only sold because the stable had to be pulled down under the terms of an old repairing lease, and that now it has been arranged that the stable is to stand for a couple of years longer."

"It sounds a queer proceeding to ask for a horse back when you've just sold him," said Mrs Mullet, "but something must be done, and done at once. The man is not used to horses, and I believe I told him it was as quiet as a lamb. After all, lambs go kicking and twisting about as if they were demented, don't they?"

"The lamb has an entirely unmerited character for sedateness," agreed Clovis.

Jessie came back from the golf links next day in a state of mingled elation and concern.

"It's all right about the proposal," she announced, "he came out with it at the sixth hole. I said I must have time to think it over. I accepted him at the seventh."

"My dear," said her mother, "I think a little more maidenly reserve and hesitation would have been advisable, as you've known him so short a time. You might have waited until the ninth hole."

"The seventh is a very long hole," said Jessie; "besides, the tension was putting us both off our game. By the time we'd got to the ninth hole we'd settled lots of things. The honeymoon is to be spent in Corsica, with perhaps a flying visit to Naples if we feel like it, and a week in London to wind up with. Two of his nieces are to be asked to be bridesmaids, so with our lot there will be seven, which is rather a lucky number. You're to wear your pearl grey, with any amount of Honiton lace jabbed into it. By the way, he's coming over this evening to ask your consent to the whole affair. So far all's well, but about the Brogue it's a different matter. I told him the legend about the stable, and how keen we were about buying the horse back, but he seems equally keen on keeping it. He said he must have horse exercise now that he's living in the country, and he's going to start riding tomorrow. He's ridden a few times in the Row on an animal that was accustomed to carry octogenarians and people undergoing rest cures, and that's about all his experience in the saddle – oh, and he rode a pony once in Norfolk, when he was fifteen and the pony twenty-four; and tomorrow he's going to ride the Brogue! I shall be a widow before I'm married, and I do so want to see what Corsica's like; it looks so silly on the map."

Clovis was sent for in haste, and the developments of the situation put before him.

"Nobody can ride that animal with any safety," said Mrs Mullet, "except Toby, and he knows by long experience what it is going to shy at, and manages to swerve at the same time."

"I did hint to Mr Penricarde – to Vincent, I should say – that the Brogue didn't like white gates," said Jessie.

"White gates!" exclaimed Mrs Mullet; "did you mention what effect a pig has on him! He'll have to go past Lockyer's farm to get to the high road, and there's sure to be a pig or two grunting about in the lane."

"He's taken rather a dislike to turkeys lately," said Toby.

"It's obvious that Penricarde mustn't be allowed to go out on that animal," said Clovis, "at least not till Jessie has married him, and tired of him. I tell you what: ask him to a picnic tomorrow, starting at an early hour; he's not the sort to go out for a ride before breakfast. The day after I'll get the rector to drive him over to Crowleigh before lunch, to see the new cottage hospital they're building there. The Brogue will be standing idle in the stable and Toby can offer to exercise it; then it can pick up a stone or something of the sort and go conveniently lame. If you hurry on the wedding a bit the lameness fiction can be kept up till the ceremony is safely over."

Mrs Mullet belonged to an emotional race, and she kissed Clovis.

It was nobody's fault that the rain came down in torrents the next morning, making a picnic a fantastic impossibility. It was also nobody's fault, but sheer ill-luck, that the weather cleared up sufficiently in the afternoon to tempt Mr Penricarde to make his first essay with the Brogue. They did not get as far as the pigs at Lockyer's farm; the rectory gate was painted a dull unobtrusive green, but it had been white a year or two ago, and the Brogue never forgot that he had been in the habit of making a violent curtsey, a back-pedal and a swerve at this particular point of the road. Subsequently, there being apparently no further call on his services, he broke his way into the rectory orchard, where he found a hen turkey in a coop; later visitors to the orchard found the coop almost intact, but very little left of the turkey.

Mr Penricarde, a little stunned and shaken, and suffering from a bruised knee and some minor damages, good-naturedly ascribed the accident to his own inexperience with horses and country roads, and allowed Jessie to nurse him back into complete recovery and golf-fitness within something less than a week.

In the list of wedding presents which the local newspapers published a fortnight or so later appeared the following item:

"Brown saddle-horse, 'The Brogue,' bridegroom's

gift to bride."

"Which shows," said Toby Mullet, "that he knew nothing."

"Or else," said Clovis, "that he had a very pleasing wit."

ACKNOWLEDGEMENTS

For permission to reproduce copyright material, acknowledgement and thanks are due to the following:

Laurence Pollinger Ltd for the extract from *My Friend Flicka* © the Estate of Mary O'Hara 1943; The author for the extract from *The Wild Heart* by Helen Griffiths © 1963; Aitken & Stone Ltd for the extract from *Breed of Giants* by Joyce Stranger © 1966; Harrap Ltd for "Bellerophon" from *Favourite Greek Myths* by L. S. Hyde, first published by George G. Harrap 1905 © All rights reserved; Curtis Brown Ltd for the extract from *Horse in the House* by William Corbin © 1964 William McGraw; David Higham Associates Ltd for "Banks and Morocco" from *Animal Stories* (OUP) by Ruth Manning-Sanders © 1961; Jennifer Luithlen for "The Ghost in the Top Meadow" by Christine Pullein-Thompson, "Oh Cobweb, How Could You?" by Josephine Pullein-Thompson and "Red Morning" from *More Ponies for Jean* (Collins) by Joanna Cannan © 1943; HarperCollins Publishers for "A Wayside Adventure" from *The Horse and His Boy* © the Estate of C. S. Lewis 1954, published in Lions, an imprint of HarperCollins Publishers Ltd; Hodder & Stoughton Ltd for "Rescue" from *The Black Stallion* by Walter Farley © 1941; Octopus Children's Books for the extract from *War Horse* (Heinemann) by Michael Morpurgo © 1982; Patricia Robertson for the extract from *Follyfoot* © the Estate of Monica Dickens 1971.